(Not) Your Basic Love Story

LINDSAY MAPLE

RISING ACTION

Cover illustration © Ashley Santoro Designs ashleysantoro.com

Proofread by Marthese Fenech

978-1-990253-20-1

978-1-990253-19-5

FIC027250**FICTION** / Romance / Romantic Comedy

FIC027020**FICTION** / Romance / Contemporary

FIC027230**FICTION** / Romance / Multicultural and

Interracial

For Doug

A Special Thanks

As a white writer, I tried to be very careful with my portrayal of Punjabi and Sikh people while writing this book. Hours were spent reading novels by Indian-Canadian and Indian-American women, watching YouTube videos, and scouring the internet to ensure that my representation was respectful and accurate. There were also many people who helped me along the way! I'd like to thank Jag and Dal Rai for introducing me to your culture and religion, and Dal for emailing me back and forth to get all my information correct. Thank you to Alisha Sapach for chatting with me for hours on the phone. Thank you to Bharat Krishnan for sending me your awesome books to read, and sensitivity reading mine. Thank you to Ravinder Haley for answering all my random text messages, for reaching out to your extended family for me, and for introducing me to Indian-Canadian weddings and all the customs that come along with them. Thank you to Maria Marianayagam for beta reading and ensuring the various plot points were accurate. Thank you to Gurleen Maan for sensitivity reading my novel and for your encouragement. Thank you to Subaj Rakar for being my sole male sensitivity reader, and for your perspective and assistance.

I'm ashamed to admit, I had several early sensitivity readers that I've lost contact with, who were *immensely* helpful. There was a point with this novel where I thought nothing was going to come of it, and I'd completely given up hope. I deleted all my emails and documents pertaining to the book and shelved it ... and then I received an email that changed everything. So, if you remember reading this novel in its earliest form, with its original title, please reach out to me through Rising Action Publishing Co. and I'll send you a special thank-you gift!

I hope you enjoy reading this novel as much as I enjoyed writing it!

Lindsay Maple

If you enjoy this book, try...

Farah Heron's *Accidentally Engaged*
  Annika Sharma's *Love, Chai, and Other Four Letter Words*
  Sara Desai's *The Singles Table*
  Sonya Lalli's *Jaya and Rasa*
  Sandhya Menon's *When Dimple Met Rishi*
  Samira Ahmed's *Love, Hate, and Other Filters*

(Not) Your Basic Love Story

One

I ALWAYS HAVE A PLAN. *Always.* The empty seat next to me was definitely not in the plan. Even worse, it served as a painful reminder of the loneliness I was about to face for the entirety of my weekend in Mexico.

Not that it was a vacation. If it were possible to cancel, I would have.

I fidgeted with my unclasped seatbelt. I'm usually more relaxed by the time I've boarded. I did, after all, get to the airport an hour early and have a beer (or two) in the lounge. My anxiety remained high because of the unknown factor: who would be sitting in the row with me. Knowing my luck, I'd be stuck sitting next to the chattiest person in British Columbia.

If only I had the window seat. It's easy to ignore people from the window, watching the landscape fly by. Unfortunately, I was stuck in the aisle as people stuffed their winter coats into the overhead compartments and jostled their luggage past.

Now began my tradition of guessing who would be sitting next to me.

An old lady approached with her ancient carpetbag, sun hat already on her head, fake pastel flowers along the brim matching her blouse. She smiled at me, and for a moment, I resigned myself to having to talk about all ten of her cats for the entire five-and-a-half-hour flight ahead. She checked her printed ticket, squinted at the numbers above her head, and kept moving.

Next was a young mother travelling alone with a rambunctious little boy, who was already whining and fighting against her. As much as I love kids, I don't love being confined in a tiny space with them for hours at a time. Sitting next to a toddler would also make my empty seat barrier moot; there would be zero defence against the screams of pain from tiny ears popping or the smell of dirty diapers. I released a relieved sigh as the mom worked her way past. I hoped whoever she sat next to would be helpful.

Oh no. Worst case scenario. An older man approached, coughing into his hands and sniffling through his red, runny nose. Too early in the season for allergies. Just my luck to leave on vacation and return home with the flu. There wasn't enough sanitizer in the world to help me here. Luckily, he and his germs also kept moving.

My breath caught in my throat at the next passenger. Tall. Dark. Handsome. All the clichés. His black hair shined, perfectly combed atop his head, and his beard was trimmed along his jawline and faded into his sideburns, emphasizing his angular features.

Time slowed as he checked his phone and then looked up at me. His gorgeous, deep brown eyes were pools of hot, sweaty summers and mysterious backstory. The quirk of his gentle smile hinted at various talents other than containing his perfectly straight teeth, their pristine whiteness a stark contrast against the warm colour of his skin. I couldn't help but smile back, warmth flushing my cheeks.

He said words. "Hmm?"

He pointed past me. "That's my seat." "Oh!"

I stood, shuffling by him awkwardly as he ducked and slid into his spot. His chest brushed up against mine momentarily, accompanied by the gentle, welcoming aroma of his tasteful cologne and perhaps a hint of tequila.

I sat back down and buckled in as he situated himself. My pulse quickened. Did I really get to sit next to Mr. Sexypants for the whole flight? *Oh, shit*. That meant I had to figure out how to string words into sentences without conveying how awkward I am, which was difficult to do even under normal circumstances.

He put his immaculately cared-for iPhone on airplane mode before tucking it into his canvas and leather messenger bag and went to shove it under the seat in front of him, but I interjected.

"You can put it under the middle seat. I mean, if you want. More legroom for you." I offered a polite smile, trying to avoid direct eye contact.

He looked up at me, and caught my gaze. Again, I was lost in those intense eyes of his. I tried not to blush. I failed.

"Nobody's sitting here?" he asked, eyebrows raised and brow slightly furrowed.

I shook my head. "It's just the two of us."

"Thanks." He smiled and took me up on my offer. As he slid his bag under the seat, I noted the absence of any rings on his fingers.

I forced my eyes forward. *Get it together*. He's a perfect

stranger. He's not interested. Your bed is barely cold, and here you are, fantasizing about a stranger on a plane. Miranda was right. I should have spent the last two weeks swiping right instead of eating ice cream and watching *The Bachelor*. But Tinder, ugh. I wasn't ready for that dumpster fire yet.

"First time going to Mexico?" he asked, rolling up the sleeves of his black dress shirt, perhaps a bit too formal for travel, to reveal thick forearms with a spattering of dark hair.

Relax, girl. It's only a forearm. Although, it's one of the top five sexiest parts of a man's body. Maybe he *is* interested. A little flirting never hurt anyone, right?

"No, I've been a few times. You?"

He shook his head. "Never to Mexico. I haven't been on a plane since I was a kid, and I barely remember it."

I smiled. "Well, if you need anything, I'm a veteran flier."

"Thanks. I'm a little nervous. I wish I wasn't by the window." As he turned to look out, his jaw tightened.

"The window is the best part! Take-off and landing are usually a little bumpy, but other than that it's quite boring. You won't see too much once we're up there, just clouds. Once we get closer to Mexico and start our descent you'll see the ocean." I was babbling. Luckily, the pre-flight checklists forced me to stop before I could embarrass myself any further.

Silence grew between us as the plane taxied to the runway. The flight attendant gave out safety instructions in both English and French while everyone ignored her. I glanced over at my seatmate to see him studying the laminated emergency response instruction card.

He looked up, catching my amused smile. "I had to see if the people in the pictures were as calm as that movie said."

I thought for a moment, racking my brain for the refer-ence. "*Fight Club*?" I guessed.

A surprised smile lit up his face. "You know it?"

I grinned. "Do I? I practically have it memorized."

"So if this is *Fight Club*," he said, leaning closer, "are you Tyler Durden, or am I?"

"We'd both be Tyler Durden, obviously. But I'd be Brad Pitt."

"No way. If anyone's Brad Pitt here, it's me."

I chuckled. "Not that there's anything wrong with Edward Norton. I mean, he's a babe."

He smiled at me for a long moment, his eyes twinkling. Then, he slid the instructions back into the seat pocket and reached his hand across the empty seat between us. I took it, his large hand enveloping my comparatively dainty one; his grip was confident but gentle, nails trimmed with care.

"Dev," he offered.

"Rebecca," I replied.

He held onto my hand for exactly three heartbeats before letting go. I forced my eyes forward, biting the inside of my cheek to keep from smiling.

The plane increased its throttle, rumbling and shaking as we darted down the runway, engines roaring. Dev inhaled sharply through his teeth and gripped the armrests. I took note of the tendons and veins as they rippled beneath the skin of his hands. His eyes were shut tight, a light sweat forming on his brow. My stomach dropped a bit as we gained elevation, but soon we were at a steady incline, and everything was normal.

"You okay, Dev?" I asked, enjoying the taste of his name on my tongue.

He opened his eyes and nodded once.

"The worst part's over. Want something to drink? My treat."

A curious smile played upon his face. "I don't think a lady has ever offered to buy me a drink."

"Well, I'm a feminist," I said with a smirk.

He laughed. "Sure, yeah, I can't turn that down."

"So, what takes you to Mexico?" I asked, small talk coming easily for once as I waited for the attendants to begin their service.

"Winter break, final year of college. Next semester is my last one. It was kind of a last-minute decision. A bunch of my cousins are going down. They're up there, near the front somewhere. They talked me into it. It's been a while since I've travelled, and I thought it would be fun to get out of the rain and have some sunshine for once."

"Ooh, what's your major?" I twisted in my seat to face him.

"Business administration. Are you a graduate?" I nodded. "Engineering."

"Wow, that's impressive. You must have a really cool job."

My job was ... meh. It wasn't what I'd imagined myself doing as a little girl when I dreamed of becoming an engineer. Everything was different than I'd imagined ... I changed the subject.

"Are you from Vancouver?"

"No, Surrey."

Surrey was just east of the Greater Vancouver Area. It would be an hour from my place to his, at least, and I'd have to get off the Skytrain. Probably take a couple of busses.

Wait, what? Why was I even thinking that? Geez, Rebecca. You've known him for like five minutes, and here you are—

"How about you?" he asked.

His question caught me off guard; I'd been in my head again instead of paying attention to the conversation. "I live in Vancouver."

He smiled. "No, what brings you to Mexico?"

"Oh!" I laughed it off. "My best friend Miranda is getting married. I'm one of her bridesmaids."

"Sounds like fun," he said, wiping a light sheen of sweat from his brow.

The attendant addressed us in his chipper voice. "Anything to drink?"

"Yeah, um, I'll have tequila and orange juice. Dev?" I looked over at him.

He nodded. "Sure, sounds good."

I silently praised myself for guessing his drink; the slight whiff of tequila I'd gleaned from him was accurate. I paid with a tap of my card as the attendant handed me the cups with ice and orange juice, as well as two tiny bottles of Cuervo. I poured them out, a little heavier on the tequila than I'd intended with a bump of turbulence. Cup in one hand, I offered the other to Dev.

He sniffed it. "Whew, that's a strong drink!"

"Sorry, but I mean, we're going to Mexico. It's only getting started."

We raised our little plastic cups, tapped them together, said cheers, and took a drink. It was awful. I'm not one for tequila at the best of times, and semi-warm orange juice didn't do it any favours.

I glanced at Dev. "How long are you—"

A panicked expression appeared on his face. He dropped the cup and fumbled through the seat pocket in front of him. My stomach clenched, but nothing could prepare me for what happened next.

Dev puked all over himself.

By the smell of it, he'd ingested quite a bit of tequila

already, along with what may have been a greasy burger and fries. I looked away as fast as possible, fighting my gag reflex.

"Oh teri," he cursed.

Moans of disgust erupted from the other seats. The attendant reappeared with napkins and plastic bags. I quickly excused myself down the aisle to the bathroom, thankful there wasn't a line-up.

After splashing some cold water on my face, I glanced up at myself in the tiny mirror. My skin was somehow even more pale than usual. My mousy brown hair was damp around the frame of my face and at the back of my neck from sweat. I glanced down at my clothes. *Ugh*! *Was that* ..? Gross. I wiped at my grey tank top and faded jeans with some paper towel, getting most of the vomit off.

I took a steadying breath as the plane shook again and prepared to return to my seat. When I was sure my stomach would hold, I exited the tiny room and nearly ran into Dev. Slime covered his trousers and once-nice shirt, an embarrassed grimace on his face.

Stomach, don't betray me now! I inched past him and made my way back to my seat. Though the attendants had done a good job cleaning everything up, nothing could be done about the acrid smell I was now stuck with for *five. More. Hours.*

Just when I'd thought my luck was getting better, it had, in fact, not turned around at all. If only my seatmate was the old lady with the cats, or the mom with the toddler, or even the guy with the germs. Nope. I was stuck sitting next to the guy with motion sickness because of course I was.

I grabbed my iPhone from my purse and quickly put in my ear pods, turning on RuPaul's Drag Race, thankful I'd saved several episodes ahead of time.

When Dev made his way back he looked defeated. I felt bad

for him. I moved my knees and he shuffled into his seat. He said more words.

I pulled one of my pods out, just an inch.

"'Scuse me?"

"I said, I'm sorry. About that."

"It's fine." I smiled, teeth still clenched, the awful smell stronger with him there. Didn't he have a spare change of clothes in his carry-on? I shoved my pod back in and looked at my phone, hoping he would take the hint and leave me alone, my fun and flirtatious five-hour flight ruined.

ONCE WE LANDED, I bee-lined it off the plane, eager to get to the hotel and shower the smell of tequila-barf off of me. I didn't say goodbye to Dev, since I couldn't even look at him without triggering my gag reflex—which was too bad; we'd gotten off on such a great start. I breathed a little easier with each step closer to the exit, glad to put the memory of my queasy companion behind me and move on with my trip.

Mexico's humidity hit me like I'd just walked into a wall, the balmy climate so different than the stuffy airplane or cold, rainy winter season in Vancouver. My shoes clicked on the laminate flooring as I made my way to the baggage carousel, absentmindedly going through the schedule of plans for Miranda's wedding over the next few days.

Tonight was a meet-and-greet cocktail hour at some fancy restaurant by the beach. Tomorrow the rehearsal dinner. The next day Miranda had been secretive about, probably some sort of adventure she had planned, knowing her. Then, the wedding. Next day, flying home.

It couldn't be over fast enough.

Not that I didn't love Miranda. We'd been friends since high school, and now, at twenty-nine, she was really the only friend I had left from those days. I'd been with her all her ups and downs, so now, seeing her settling down, I couldn't be happier for her. Derek was a great guy. He'd make a great dad someday. It was doing it all alone that I wasn't excited about. The whole trip, right down to the romantic ocean-view suite with the jacuzzi tub I'd paid extra for, was going to be a reminder of what a failure I was at love.

Thankfully, I didn't have long to dwell upon those thoughts. My luggage, an unmistakable bright pink plastic case with lime-green palm fronds on it, was one of the first to come down the chute. I'd had to splurge on new luggage when *he* took mine two and a half weeks ago.

I booked it out of there, eyes focused on the floor in front of me, lest I accidentally see Dev again and have to smile at him awkwardly, or worse, actually talk to him. I jumped into a cab, eager for a shower and some fresh clothes.

I texted Miranda. *Landed! OMG u wouldn't believe what happened on the plane.*

She replied a minute later. *Yaaaaay! Meet us at the bar when ur ready! Winky kiss emoji. Champagne emoji. Sunshine emoji. Three heart emojis.* She was drunk, already.

LOL will do, bae. Kiss emoji. Three heart emojis. Dancing emoji.

I definitely needed a drink. But NOT tequila. Anything but more tequila. Tequila might be permanently ruined for me, and I'd only been in Mexico for about ten minutes.

Two

THE ALL-INCLUSIVE RESORT was in the famous Cancun hotel zone. Miranda had spared no expense—rather, Derek's parents had spared no expense—and we were staying at a super luxurious one. It had four bars, not including the swim-up pool bar, five restaurants, and a wide, private beach.

The palm-lined road was familiar, given I had stayed at a different resort several years ago on a girls' trip. I didn't remember much else. The only souvenir I had from that escapade was a questionable lower-back tattoo: an infinity symbol with a heart and some dandelion tufts.

Blinking in the sunshine, I took in the gorgeous setting while the driver unloaded my bags. The architecture was incredible and reminded me of my backpacking trip through Europe. So much glass and concrete with pyramidal shapes, reminiscent of the Louvre. Or, you know, the actual pyramids. Not that I'd been to Egypt. Yet.

The lobby was equally impressive, with cool marble on the floors and walls and suspended greenery descending like the hanging gardens of Babylon. Perhaps they'd built this place with that idea in mind. Regardless of their inspiration, I was totally out of place here amongst all the well-dressed, very tanned upper-class people inhabiting the resort.

I checked in. A few minutes later, after my credit card was swiped and the key handed over, I was on my way. The bellboy took my bags and led me to my ocean-view suite. I tipped him, making a mental note of having to exchange more of my Canadian dollars into American (their currency of choice), and then closed the door, eager to be by myself after the bustle of travel.

The suite was exquisite. Giant floor-to-ceiling windows met with a sliding glass door, which opened to my balcony and granted an uninhibited view of clear, blue ocean and an equally stunning sky. A massive king-sized bed with a soft white duvet sat along one wall. My eyes settled on the red rose petals sprinkled suggestively overtop, two towels folded into the shape of kissing swans.

Nope.

I swept the petals off the bed and onto the floor, then shook out the swans.

Keep it together, Rebecca. It's been two and a half weeks. You can do this. All you need is a shower—a shower and a drink.

I helped myself to a Corona from the mini-bar and made my way to the bathroom.

Much like the rest of the suite, the bathroom was incredible, decked out in cool white marble with grey veins. A huge jacuzzi tub took up one wall next to a rain-head shower and double sink. I looked in the mirror; my hair was frazzled from the humidity, my makeup needed a do-over, and my clothes were rumpled and smelled nasty. I stripped naked and stepped into the shower with my beer.

A shower beer can fix many problems.

Alone, hot water pouring down my body, drink in hand, my mind wandered back to how I'd imagined it when I booked the room several weeks ago. How I'd imagined it with *him*. Pushing into the doorway, kissing and giggling, jumping onto the bed. Romantic evenings walking barefoot along the beach. Hot, sticky nights fuelled by champagne. Perhaps a proposal, which I'd keep secret from Miranda for a few days until the magic of her wedding had worn off.

Had I been out of line, imagining a proposal? We'd been together for over a year and a half. That was a reasonable amount of time to date before becoming engaged, right? But he had to go and ruin it.

How could someone throw it all away, weeks before a destination wedding he knew was so important to me? It was like he wanted to punish me, to force me to attend those dinner parties and cocktail receptions alone, answering, "Oh, where's your boyfriend?" with "Oh, we broke up." Followed by the requisite, "Aw, too bad!"

Yeah, no shit, Sherlock. It is too bad.

The timing wasn't his fault, I guess. Everything else was, though.

I chugged my beer, then went through the process of cleaning the airport (and Dev's lunch) off me.

Despite everything, it was impossible to look out those giant windows at the incredible, cloudless blue sky and be in a bad mood. One towel wrapped around my torso, another twisted on top of my head, I unzipped my suitcase as I hummed an old Katy Perry song that had no business being hummed by anyone anymore, and—

What the ...?

This wasn't my bag! Instead of pumps and cocktail dresses,

there were men's shirts and shorts and a very expensive-looking pair of brown leather sandals, size eleven.

Of course, I would fuck up and grab the wrong bag. I hadn't even considered for the slightest moment that two people would have the same ridiculous luggage. This was not my day.

I texted Miranda. *FML babe. Gonna be late. Grabbed wrong luggage!*

She didn't reply. Probably busy. That was fine. Everything was fine.

I called the concierge, hoping this wasn't the first time something like this had happened. Sure enough, the person on the other end of the line assured me that this happened from time to time and that they'd take care of it. I gave them my own name as well as the name of the unlucky person who—

Oh shit! They had my bag!

I hung up the phone and sat on the edge of my bed with my head in my hands. Not only were all my clothes in there, but I'd grabbed my vibrator and thrown it right on top of everything else because, let's be honest, I was going to need it.

Several minutes of pacing later, the phone rang. It was the concierge. They found the person who had my bag, and they were staying at another resort in the area. All I had to do was bring the incorrect bag to the front desk, make the swap, and then I could move on with my day.

I looked down at the floor where my dirty clothes were piled in a heap. The absolute last thing I wanted to do was put them back on. Thankfully, I found a fuzzy white robe in the closet and donned it. Hair still up in my towel, improper luggage zipped and rolling, I walked back to the front desk. This was the last thing I needed. I hated being late. I'm always the friend who shows up fifteen minutes early for everything. I hugged myself in my robe and shifted from foot to foot while I waited, doing my best to remain calm, hoping I wouldn't bump into anyone from Miranda's wedding while I was half-naked.

Thankfully, I didn't have to wait long.

In walked none other than Dev, wheeling a gaudy bright pink plastic luggage case with lime-green palm fronds behind him.

Oh God...

He took one look at me and stopped dead in his tracks, eyes wide in shock.

"Hi," I mumbled, feeling naked in my robe and silly with the towel on my head.

He pushed my suitcase towards me, and we fumbled to grab the opposite handles without dropping anything or touching one another.

"Hey," he said. He had on a flamboyant shirt with 'Cancun' on the front and hideous shorts which were far too big, obviously purchased from a tourist shop to get out of his nasty airplane clothes. Despite his hilarious attire and everything that had happened, his smile was still completely disarming.

"You didn't... open this, did you?" I asked, finding my voice, unsure if my face could get any hotter.

"Um, no! No, I didn't. I saw the name, and I didn't open it or see anything."

He was lying. I was thankful for that.

"Okay, well, thank you. I have to go get ready..."

I turned and began to walk away, eager to put this all behind me and have about ten more beers.

"Wait," he called.

I looked over my shoulder as he took three steps with his long legs to catch up to me.

"Let me make it up to you," he said. "Please."

I waved a hand dismissively. The last thing I wanted was to be asked out right now, half-naked in a robe with a towel on my head while late for my BFF's party. "I took your luggage, not the other way around. Trust me, it's fine."

"No, I mean, for the airplane. I'd already been drinking quite a bit with my cousins."

"I could tell."

"And I'd like the opportunity to make it up to you. Maybe dinner later? I could pick you up here at seven."

I hardened my facial expression to make it obvious this was a polite, yet firm, no. He persisted, staring at me with those giant brown eyes and ridiculously long eyelashes. He was going to make me say it, wasn't he? "Sorry, I have plans tonight. Honestly, it's fine. You barely got any on me and—"

"I got some on you?" He hid his face in his hands and then peeked out at me between his fingers. A bit immature. I was growing tired of this.

"It's fine, don't worry." I tried to assure him.

"Let me at least pay for the dry cleaning."

I hesitated. "Fine. Yes, that would be nice."

He grinned. "Thank you. And I'm sorry. I'll go talk to the front desk. You have a lovely night, Rebecca."

I turned and walked away, wheeling my luggage behind me, eager to get into my room and crack another beer and put this whole strange exchange in the past.

Back in my suite, Miranda had texted me. *Not ur luck, babe! Hurry up, I can't wait to see you!!!* Another string of emojis. I was going to need to catch up.

I unzipped my suitcase to see nothing out of place, my vibrator right on top exactly as I had left it, which was a stupid mistake. Even though female masturbation is nothing to be ashamed of, my cheeks reddened, knowing Dev had likely seen my purple rabbit. I tucked it into the drawer next to the bed, you know, for convenience later.

～

HAIR CURLED, dress donned, and makeup applied, I checked the itinerary and headed out.

The resort was massive. It took me three wrong turns and asking for directions before I found the right place. A hoard of well-dressed, tipsy people had already gathered in the huge reception area, a drink in one hand and a plate of appetizers in the other. I weaved my way around the crowd and, with a sigh of relief, finally spotted Miranda.

Everything about her seemed effortless, from the way she walked to her wide, confident smile. Her bright lipstick complemented her ivory skin tone and popped against her white cocktail dress. A silver necklace matched the bangles along her wrists but did not distract from the giant diamond on her finger. Princess cut. So fitting.

Though she looked like a flawless, elegant woman now, every time I looked at her, I still saw the dorky teenager I'd first met so many years ago, all braces and pimples and *Eragon* fanfiction. I nearly cried, so overwhelmed with love and relief that I was finally here, finally with my best friend in the whole wide world, whom I so desperately needed.

"Becky!" she squealed, spotting me in the distance. She offered a polite excuse to the people she was chatting with and walked over to me. We embraced in a tight hug. She smelled like Chanel and chardonnay. When she released me, she smooched me right on the lips, not unusual for her, and then held me at arm's length, admiring my sunflower-print cocktail dress.

"You look stunning, Becky!" she gushed.

"Aww! So do you, babe!"

"How was your flight?"

"Awful. You wouldn't believe—"

I was cut off when an old couple entered the room and stole Miranda's attention.

"Oh, you *have* to meet Derek's parents!" She waved to get their attention. "Mom! Dad! This is my best friend, Becky!" She grabbed my hand and dragged me over to them, then around the room, introducing me to Mr. and Mrs. So-and-So, related to these people over here, and then some other people who were important because of reasons, on and on and on. I was able to snatch a glass of wine from a tray and a mouthful of crab cake, which was delicious, in between greeting these people whose names I made no effort to remember.

Finally, we found the other bridesmaids sitting on a couch near one of the balconies. The salty ocean breeze was a welcome change from the stuffy, crowded room.

"Becky, you remember Nicole. This is Hannah, from work. My cousin, Charlotte. And, obviously— " Miranda was interrupted when a younger, shorter, and much more curvaceous version of herself jumped up and gave me a giant hug, nearly knocking the wine out of my glass.

"Becky!" her sister Angelina cried, squeezing me far too tight.

"Hey, Angel!" I said. "Wow, it's been so long since I've seen you! You must have graduated by now, right?"

"Yeah, now I'm just figuring out what I want to do next."

"Any plans so far?"

Miranda touched my shoulder. "I have to go, Derek's calling me over."

I turned to see her fiancé standing a short distance away. I waved. He waved back. He was generally considered handsome. While we were polite with one another, we never had much to talk about. I wasn't offended he didn't come over to talk; I didn't feel like trying to talk to him, either.

Watching the two of them walk away triggered a yearning from deep within my core. Miranda and Derek's love story was like a Nicholas Sparks movie. I mean, before it got all depressing. Three winters ago, she spent the winter working as an RN at the ski resort in Whistler and dealt with a lot of injuries. One such injured person had been Derek. I guess you could say they fell in love right away and went out on a date as soon as it wasn't inappropriate given the obvious problems of dating your patient.

Derek's family came from wealth, and he managed his family's charity which helped with sanitation in third world countries.

I envied the way they met. It all sounded so perfect. I'll never forget the excitement in her voice over the phone that day when she relayed every moment. I've been on the sidelines, witnessing every step since then leading up to this point.

My turn would come. Eventually.

I hoped.

I realized with a start that Angelina had been talking this whole time. I blinked back to the present as she told me about her plans for after High School since her year off was coming to a close. She was considering becoming a dental hygienist. Nice.

I sat down on the couch and made cordial small talk. I met

her cousin, Charlotte, when we were teenagers. She worked as an accountant and had three young kids, a hero in her own right. Her husband hovered close by, obviously glad to be rid of the kids for the weekend and have his wife to himself. Hannah worked with Miranda at the hospital, both of them RNs. Her husband was at home with their toddler. This was her weekend away, and by the looks of the empty glasses next to her she was going to take full advantage. They both seemed nice; people I could get along with easily.

Then there was Nicole. Now, Nicole, I didn't like. I didn't like her from the moment she became roommates with Miranda all those years ago in college. Everything about her was fake. Not only her fake eyelashes and fake nails and giant, fake boobs. I mean, whatever. You do you, girl. It was her *presence*. She'd always been over-the-top nice to me, like one of those girls in high school who would pretend to be your friend to get dirt on you and then laugh at you behind your back. Not only that, but she was the *college* bestie, and I was merely the *high school* bestie.

They had become friends as adults, whereas Miranda and I had become friends as teenagers. It could be argued either way which relationship was more important. I nodded along politely as she went on and on about her Instagram-worthy life and her fancy marketing job and her perfect boyfriend, who was around here somewhere.

As conversation flowed around me, all I could think about was how I was the only single girl in the group. I mean, besides Angelina. She was a kid. She had plenty of time.

It wasn't supposed to be like this.

Charlotte announced she had to go to the bathroom. Naturally, all of us stood up and made our way towards the lavatories. I didn't have to pee, so instead, I fixed my lipstick and smoothed my frizzing hair.

Nicole came up beside me to wash her hands. I offered a polite smile through the mirror.

"So," she said as she lathered. "Your boyfriend couldn't make it?"

I gritted my teeth. *Of course* she'd bring him up. No one had talked about him yet. Miranda had probably warned them ahead of time to not mention it, having filled them in on the gossip already, but Nicole couldn't resist.

"I broke up with him." *Lies.*

"Aw, sweetie. I'm so sorry to hear that." Her fake pout wasn't fooling me.

Thankfully, the other girls finished up before Nicole could ask any more stupid questions, and we all headed back out to the reception.

Nicole approached a gorgeous, unnaturally tall man whose muscles barely fit within his extremely well-tailored shirt and tasteful slacks. I didn't mean to check him out, but damn —that ass.

Nicole rested an arm on his bicep and he turned to face us, a winning smile on his face. "Becky, this is my boyfriend, Chaz. He plays for the Canucks."

Of course, he does.

"Nice to meet you," I said, offering my hand and doing my best not to blush, but failing. Damn me and my easy-to-blush pale genes. He took my hand and gave it a tight squeeze, my knuckles pushing together painfully under the pressure.

"Hey," was all he said. Great. Thanks for contributing to the conversation.

We stood there for a few painful, awkward moments in near silence until tinkling glasses saved us. Someone made a toast, and then there were some speeches. Afterwards, a dance area was lit up and a DJ hit the stage.

The absolute last thing I wanted to do was dance. Nope. As Nicole and Chaz excused themselves to the dance floor, I headed back to wherever those crab cakes were. Unfortunately, I didn't quite make it.

In front of me jumped a tall, lanky guy with a very loud shirt and shorts which came up far too high.

"Hi, there! You must be Becky?" he said. He seemed a little overeager to meet me. Had someone told him I was single? Dammit.

"Rebecca," I corrected while politely offering my hand. He took it and gave it a weak shake, hanging on too long, his grasp clammy. Poor guy was probably super nervous. I should be nice.

"I'm Hank."

Hank felt like such an old man's name. Who named their kid Hank anymore? Maybe it was a family name. Regardless, I couldn't imagine saying it in the throes of passion. And now I was imagining him naked. Why did my mind always go there?

"Hi, Hank. How do you know Miranda?" I asked, refocusing.

"I work with Derek at the charity. I'm one of his grooms-men. We'll be walking down the aisle together!"

He blushed. I blushed. Everyone was blushing. "Oh. Great." I said.

"Yeah, so we should probably get to know one another," Hank replied.

The first thing I learned about Hank was that he struggled with personal space. He was all up in my bubble. The second thing I learned about him was that he liked to look at my boobs, which was especially odd considering I barely had any boobs at all.

Despite these facts, I was too socially awkward to find a way out of the conversation. And so the next hour and a half was spent with me drinking chardonnay and eating crab cakes while he went on and on about himself.

When he asked me to dance, I respectfully declined. Looking at my phone, it was close to eleven and a totally reasonable time to bow out of the conversation with the excuse of being tired. My head was very truthfully pounding from the DJ anyway. I made my way through the maze of increasingly intoxicated people. Miranda was on the dance floor with Nicole dancing to *Barbie Girl* in what appeared to be a routine they'd made up for some drunken karaoke escapade back in their college days.

I smiled and waved, but Miranda didn't see me, so I left.

Instead of going back to my suite, I made my way to the ocean. Carrying my wedges, I walked barefoot in the sand. The breeze ruffled my hair as I dipped my freshly shellacked turquoise toes in the water. I walked along the edge, the waves sloshing up to my ankles, past rows upon rows of empty lounge chairs and the occasional couple fooling around.

That could have been us.

But you had to go and fuck it all up.

Maybe it was the stress of travel, maybe it was the chardonnay, maybe it was Nicole and Chaz, or maybe it was the fact that my best friend was getting married in two days and didn't have time for me, but tears threatened my composure. I forced them back, feeling silly.

My eyes wandered down the beach to what looked like a party going on at another resort. I listened to the deep bass for a moment and watched the coloured lights as they danced along the sand. Part of me wanted to go over there. Investigate. Have a few more drinks. But the pounding in my head and the aching in my heart told me it was a bad idea. Instead, I retreated back to my room where I could sleep all alone in my giant king-sized bed and, possibly, make good use of my vibrator.

Three

I WOKE the next morning with no hangover. I thanked myself for making the responsible choice and heading to bed early last night. Showered, blow-dried, make-upped, sun-screened, and clad in booty shorts and a flowing tank-top, I donned my bright pink flamingo flip-flops and oversized sunglasses and headed out to find some breakfast. Today called for a mimosa. Or three.

After dropping my airplane clothes off at the front desk to be dry-cleaned, I went to the buffet. I was quick to spot Miranda's sister Angelina with her parents. They waved me over, gesturing to sit with them. I pushed my sunglasses back on my head, grabbed a mimosa and yogurt, and joined them at their table. They got up and gave me a hug, Miranda's mom kissing me on both cheeks.

"Hey, Susan, Frank! What has it been, like two years since I've seen you? You weren't at the reception last night." I paused to sip my mimosa. It was delightful.

"Oh, we didn't get in till late. Our flight was delayed. Some idiot had a drone out on the tarmac or something. How have you been? Miranda told us about what happened with your boyfriend. How are you holding up? I thought for sure you'd be next!" Susan was interrupted by an elbow from her youngest daughter.

I cast a thankful glance to Angelina, who nodded and returned to her meal of bacon and eggs. I forced a smile and took another long sip. "Yeah, it just wasn't working anymore. When you know, you know, right?"

Susan nodded. "Oh, you're so right, honey. So right. Especially at your age, there's no time to waste. I told Miranda, I said, honey, you better hurry up and get that man to marry you. I need grandbabies." Susan laughed, patted the corners of her coral-coloured lips, and then took a bite of her croissant.

I got enough pressure from my own mom to hurry up and get married. I didn't need it from Miranda's mom, too.

"So," I said, eagerly turning my attention to Frank. "How's retirement treating you?"

He shrugged noncommittally then looked to his wife to answer for him.

"Oh, Frank is loving it, aren't you, darling? We're finally able to get done all of those pesky little chores around the house that have been adding up! He spends almost the whole entire day out in the garage, tinkering. He's just loving it!"

I glanced at Angelina, who rolled her eyes, and I stifled a smile in my drink. Frank was Miranda's step-father and Angelina her half-sister, but Miranda had never made the distinction, so neither did I.

I spent the rest of the day wandering bored around the resort, drinking fruity drinks with umbrella straws, hiding my pasty white ass from the sun, searching unsuccessfully for Miranda, and avoiding absolutely everyone else.

Not exactly how I'd pictured my Mexico vacation. Today

we would have gotten a couple's massage, maybe taken a trip into town to go shopping, gone snorkelling out in the ocean, or perhaps ordered room service and spent the afternoon in bed, emerging flush and giddy for the rehearsal dinner tonight.

By the time evening came round, I needed another shower. The layers of sunscreen had mixed with my sweat to form a paste, and my hair was beyond help.

Dressed to impress in a flowy dusty rose number and wedge sandals, I exited my room to see Nicole and Chaz sidling up. Great timing. Nicole looked drop-dead gorgeous in a sapphire-coloured dress that wrapped around her curves, flaunting her cleavage. Though, the diamonds around her neck and dangling from her ears were ostentatious. Who travels with that much jewelry? And her shoes—were those *real* Louboutins?

I glanced self-consciously down at my meagre b-cups, which barely filled out my bra. And my shoes; could she tell they were from Winners? I suddenly felt very plebeian.

"Nicole, you're not supposed to upstage the bride!" I said as she hover-kissed both my cheeks.

"Oh, this old thing?" She posed and laughed.

I third-wheeled alongside her and Chaz, nodding politely as Nicole went on and on about the fantastic spa they'd found, and the delicious room service they ordered, and the scuba diving excursion they'd booked for the following day.

Great. So happy for you.

At the rehearsal dinner, I was seated third in line between Miranda's cousin and Nicole, of all people. Charlotte was busy catching up with Angelina on the opposite side while Nicole engaged mostly with Hannah at the end. Which left me in the middle, sitting by myself, stealing glances at my best friend as she cooed over her husband-to-be.

The food was good. The drinks were good. The cake was good. The toasts were okay. One was pretty funny, actually. Derek's best man had some good stories about their college days together, about how they'd eaten too many pot brownies, and Derek had clogged the sink with his barf. The story reminded me of my plane ride here, of my queasy companion and our misfired flirtation.

My heart twinged, a longing ache in my chest, but for what, I wasn't sure. A feeling of something that could have been, but wasn't? Or maybe my heart hurt because of *him*. I couldn't stop looking out over the tables and noticing the empty space where he should have been.

With the formalities at an end, I pushed my way over to Miranda before she could be distracted by the other guests. All I wanted was a drink—just one drink, alone, with my bestie.

"Miranda! You look spectacular," I said, admiring her white maxi dress with tasteful glitterings and shocking bright pink heels.

"So do you! I love this dress on you. You look amazing," she said, giving me a tight hug. My heart ached, needing more than one little hug, having felt so far from her these past few weeks, but not wanting to burden her with my pain while she prepared for her wedding.

"Let's go get a glass of wine! I have to tell you what happened on my flight," I said, taking her by the hand.

She grinned and let me pull her along until some other relatives of hers stopped us to chat. A few more steps, another distraction. Then Hank showed up.

Great. More Hank.

"Miranda, can I steal away your Becky for a drink?" he said as if asking her permission was the same as asking me if I wanted to drink with him.

"Oh, sure!" Miranda said, obviously needing to talk to all of these other people.

I turned to her, mouthing *NO*, but Miranda coaxed me on, mouthing back, *he's single*!

Yeah, I sort of picked up on that already, thanks.

Hank offered his arm. I was cornered. How could I turn this guy down without making the whole rest of this wedding super awkward? I opened my mouth to say yes, but Angelina swept in and grabbed me by the hand.

"Becky! Do you have a tampon?" she asked.

I didn't, but she gave me a wide-eyed look. To any woman, it was obvious Aunt Flo wasn't really visiting her. She was an angel by both name and virtue, clearly.

"Oh, sure! Sorry, Hank. Rain-check."

In the bathroom, Angelina sat on the counter and looked at me straight. "Cut the crap. How are you really doing?"

I slumped against the wall. "Not good."

She nodded knowingly. "Why don't we get out of here? I hear there's a cool beach party close by. We can go dancing, drink tequila, find some boys?"

Tempting. "I don't know. You're the Maid of Honour. Don't you have to be here?"

Angelina shook her head. "Miranda is so busy she won't even notice we're gone. Besides, do you want to risk having to talk to Hank all night again?"

Valid point.

We were like CIA agents sneaking out of there, hiding behind various floral arrangements and ducking past wait-staff. As soon as we hit the beach my steps were lighter and my smile came easily. Angelina was in great spirits, and her mood was infectious. Arm in arm, we walked down to the beach party with its thumping bass and dancing lights.

A crowd of half-naked, drunk young people was (crowd is singular, so the verb should reflect that) dancing on the beach. I felt incredibly overdressed and, comparatively, very, very old. Angelina was right in her element, though, and within minutes she had a guy ordering us drinks. I sipped my vodka cran and leaned against the bar, people watching, as Angelina flirted.

A guy stumbled into me, his sweaty chest rubbing against my arm, his eyes unfocused from what was sure to have been a full day of drinking. I grimaced as he exhaled his nasty breath on me.

"Come dance with me!" His drink sloshed over the edge of his glass, nearly getting on my dress.

"No, thanks." I tried to take a step back, but I was already up against the bar.

"Why? You got a boyfriend or something?" "No, I just don't want to dance. But thank you for the offer."

He reached out and grabbed my wrist, evidently to pull me onto the dancefloor. I yanked it out of his grasp, spilling my drink down my arm. I tried to alert Angelina, but her view was blocked by two guys chatting her up, completely oblivious to the drunk asshole harassing me.

The guy didn't give up. "Wha-what's wrong? Don't be a— be a bitch about it. Come dance with me!"

I was seconds away from throwing the rest of my drink in his face when someone came up and intervened, a strong hand on his chest holding him back.

"Hey, Moe, leave her alone. She said no."

It took a second for me to recognize him. Dev. Moe looked from me to Dev, said something under his breath about me being a bitch, and then stumbled away.

Dev turned to me; his lips turned up in a half-smile. He wore khaki-coloured shorts, very familiar leather sandals, and a white linen shirt unbuttoned down to his mid-chest. A smattering of dark hair poked out, and his sleeves were once again rolled up to reveal his forearms.

Oh, those forearms.

"Are you stalking me?" I asked in jest, glad the darkness hid my blush.

He laughed. "You're the one at my resort. I thought you were following me!"

"Thank you, by the way. For saving me. Some guys won't take no for an answer."

Dev nodded and brushed his hand through his hair, his arm flexing as he did so. Oh my...

"Sorry," he said. "He's one of my cousins. He's not usually like that. He's been drinking all day, and he hasn't gotten anyone to dance with him yet."

I tried not to hold his asshole cousin against him.

"Can we—can we start over?" Dev asked, his eyebrows raised and forehead wrinkling the same way it had done on the plane, which was completely endearing.

I glanced down at my feet and then back up. This is why I was here, wasn't it? Couldn't hurt. I only hesitated for a moment before reaching out with my hand. "Hi. I'm Rebecca."

He took my hand in both of his hands and held on for a few seconds, looking deep into my eyes as if he was trying to see my soul. "Dev." A shiver ran up my spine, and the hairs on my arms raised in goosebumps.

He released my hand, and with it went the warmth that had been beginning to flood the base of my abdomen. I felt a little lightheaded and dizzy. It was like I'd been holding my breath while he touched me, and I'd only remembered to exhale with his release. Such a simple touch, yet it had stirred some very not-so-simple sensations. Maybe there was something special about him...

Or maybe I was drunk and lonely. Probably that.

Dev grabbed me a new drink and we headed to an area of the outdoor bar where it was a bit quieter. We stood side by side, inches apart, the thrill of latent sexual tension buzzing between us. I caught Angelina's attention, and she gave me an excited thumbs up, mouthing, *oh my god, so hot*! I rolled my eyes, but inside I was giddy. She, herself, was quite busy fighting the guys off. A natural flirt, that girl.

"So, how do you like Mexico so far?" I asked. "The weather is great. I hate tequila, though. I don't usually drink. It took me all evening to get through one beer, so honestly, I'm a bit out of my element here," he said. With the noise from the DJ, he had to lean down and talk close to my ear, his breath sending tingles down my neck.

"Are you going on any excursions?" I asked.

"I was thinking about it. Everyone else spends most of the day hungover, napping, so I've been wandering around the beach for the most part."

"You could try snorkelling or scuba diving."

He hesitated. "Honestly, oceans freak me out a bit. Plus, it's not really fun doing that sort of thing on your own."

I nodded with a sad sigh. "I hear you. I've been doing pretty much the same thing. Mexico isn't really meant to be explored on your own."

"Maybe one of these days you'll let me take you out, go exploring together."

I looked at him, his face so close, and smiled. "I'd like that."

He leaned closer, his eyes on my lips. My heart fluttered, lips parted, and stomach dropped in anticipation... but as soon as the moment came, it passed. Dev inched away, shifting his gaze to the dancefloor.

I glanced away, uncertain. *Had I wanted him to kiss me?* He was a perfect stranger! Then again, this was Mexico. The heat, the ocean, and the alcohol, it stirred... feelings. It's not that I'd never fooled around with someone I'd just met. I mean, I've had my fair share of one-night-stands before. But with Dev, there seemed to be more to it; another layer I wanted to unravel. It was alluring, yet also made me

feel a little uncertain. Was I really in the right place of mind for this? Maybe I needed to let go of all that and be in the moment, as my yoga instructor would say.

I glanced at him, eyes wandering up his body, admiring the cut of his jaw, the attention to detail in his beard and hair, his stern eyebrows framing dark eyes scanning the crowd as the people danced, seemingly lost in thought. He certainly was sexy.

I broke the silence. "I'm not usually one for dancing, but do you see the girl over there? The blonde in the dress?"

Dev looked from me and back to Angelina. She was on the beach near the DJ, dancing her heart out with two guys who both looked as equally invested in sleeping with her as they were with each other.

He nodded.

"She's my best friend's little sister." "The one who's getting married?"

I was surprised he remembered such a minute detail. "Yeah. Want to dance with me? I don't want to lose her in the crowd."

I was fibbing. I hated dancing. Sure, I wanted to make sure Angelina was okay, but I also wanted an excuse to be close to Dev to see if the feeling of wanting his lips on mine came back. It was the first time in a long time I'd felt that way about anyone, and if it helped take *him* off my mind? All the better. He reached his hand out, and I took it, my stomach fluttering. Out there with him, the sand beneath our feet, his body close to mine, I quickly forgot I hated dancing. He was such a natural at it and made me feel like I was a natural, too. Every touch on my hips and lower back was firm yet gentle. Respectful, but left me wanting more.

A few songs in, I found myself pushing the limits, seeking more of his touch. He followed my lead, and before I knew it, my arms were wrapped around his neck, my face hovering close to his.

I hoped he'd get the hint and kiss me already, but when no kiss came, I had to take matters into my own hands.

I stood up on my tiptoes and pressed my mouth against his. His beard tickled my chin, a pleasant sensation that reverberated down through my core. I'd never kissed a man with a beard before.

His lips were still, unresponsive. Perhaps I'd made a mistake, misread something. I began to lean back, but he pulled me closer. His lips matched mine in intensity, and soon our tongues were involved, flicking gently at first, explorative, but quickly becoming bolder.

He kissed like he danced.

My body arched into his as his hands pulled me closer. I could feel him hard against my hip, and that did it for me. Before I could talk myself out of it, I whispered in his ear.

He nodded.

After checking in with Angelina, we stole away from the party hand-in-hand, giggling like school kids. While waiting for the elevator in his resort, he pressed me up against the wall, kissing my neck. A moan escaped my lips, and we stumbled inside. I began fumbling with his pants. I was still struggling to get them undone when the doors opened. We tumbled down the hall. He maneuvered his keycard into the slot just in time for us to fall into his room. I unbuttoned his shirt enough for him to pull it over his head. He unzipped my dress and peeled it off of me, sticky with sweat. I tried again with his pants, but he pulled my hands away with a grin and un-did them himself. There were three buttons! *Three*!

"What are these? Smart girl pants? Some sort of IQ test before you take someone to bed?"

He grinned and then shut me up by kissing me. We fell onto his bed as he fumbled with my bra. I reached back and unsnapped it for him. "The tables have turned!" I joked.

Dev laughed and pressed down on top of me.

He pulled my underwear off, kissing along my thigh, which sent a tingling sensation up my spine and caused my back to arch. Dev's eyebrows raised at the sight of my naked body, his eyes lingering over my breasts and abdomen, then further down. I hoped he liked small boobs.

"Your turn," I said, biting my bottom lip, eager to see what he had in store for me.

I was not disappointed.

He bent back over me to resume kissing, but I stopped him.

"Condom?" I asked.

He hesitated. "I don't have any."

"What!" I sat up, nearly knocking my forehead into his.

Dev sat back on his heels. "Well, I didn't exactly think this would happen."

I looked at this naked, gorgeous specimen of a man in front of me, completely bewildered as to how he could think he could go to Mexico and not get laid.

"I think I have one," I said finally, flipping off the bed to find my clutch.

"You have a condom? Is this one of those feminist things?"

I fished it out and laughed, recalling our first meeting on the plane, and waved the condom in the air. "No, this is one of those 'being a responsible adult' things."

"Ouch," he said in mock offence.

I tossed the little square package at him and hopped back on the bed. "Suit up!"

Dev was about to rip the package open, then squinted at it in the dim light. I laid there, propped up on my elbows, and waited.

"Is something wrong?" He sighed. "It's expired."

"What! No!" I cried, sitting back up, nearly knocking my head into his again, and snatched the package away. I confirmed that it had expired over a year ago. "Sorry. I haven't had to use a condom in a long time, I guess."

"Don't apologize. I don't think either of us wants to bring home a baby as a souvenir."

I didn't tell him I had an IUD. Babies weren't the only thing you could bring home as a souvenir from a random sexual encounter, but I didn't want to be rude.

We sat there for a moment, at a loss for what to do. He was still erect, I was still more than ready to go, and I'd be damned if I was going to walk away from this without something to show for it.

I tossed the condom aside and looked at him in a way I hoped was sexy. Reaching down, I took him in my hand and then lowered my mouth towards him. He gasped as I licked along the tip, teasing him, and then took him as fully in my mouth as I could. I loved the way he tasted, the way he smelled, the way he felt.

Glancing up, his eyes were wide in shock and pleasure as if he couldn't believe this was happening.

"Wait," he said, gasping.

I paused, looking up at him, my hand still around his cock, moving slow and methodically.

"Yes, Dev?"

"I know you're a feminist and everything, but on this, I absolutely insist. Ladies first."

Couldn't argue with that.

He kissed me fervently on the mouth and leaned me back until I was lying down on the bed. His hands made their way along my body, lingering on my breasts, teasing my nipples, and then his lips followed suit. He licked the curve of my abdomen, close to where it met my hip, which brought a shocking feeling that made me gasp and push his head away, the sensation too strong.

Dev clearly made a note of this and came back to it later. His mouth, tongue, and fingers worked their magic. With some direction and guidance, he brought me to climax much quicker than I would have expected. He was a good listener. I thought he was finished, but he wasn't. He gave me a moment to recover, then went back at it again, and again, until I forcibly pushed him away and turned over, shuddering.

Snuggling up beside me as the big spoon, he brushed my hair out of the way so he could tenderly kiss my neck. I felt him hard behind me and made a move to roll over, to return the favour, but he stopped me.

"Relax for a bit. We're not in a rush," he said.

So I did. His fingers trailed up, and down my arm, his exhales tickled the hair on the back of my neck, and even though I had just met the man I was so completely, utterly at ease. My whole body relaxed, sinking into the comfortable bed, his body enveloping mine, the cool breeze floating in off the ocean...

I woke with the sun streaming in through the windows. A light sheet covered my otherwise naked body, and my head throbbed slightly from the day of sun and chardonnay prior. Dev was fast asleep. He lay on his back, one arm over his head, his long dark lashes curled against his high cheekbones.

I took a moment to admire this Adonis, with his luminous brown skin and dark chest hair, which trailed down his abdomen to his groin, hidden beneath the sheet. He was muscular, but not in an obtrusive way. It looked like he went to the gym to stay healthy but didn't spend the entire time looking at himself in the mirror with dumbbells, working out his ego.

Reaching out, I touched his bicep before leaning in and kissing him on the cheek. He stretched and groaned, then opened his big brown eyes. A smile met his lips, which mirrored my own. The way he looked at me made me blush and glance away.

"Good morning, gorgeous," he said.

I leaned in and kissed him, this time on the lips, in a gentle, tender way, as if we'd been lovers for years and not hours. "Good morning."

His body responded immediately.

I raised an eyebrow suggestively. He grinned. As I made my way down to finish what I'd started the night before, my phone rang. I paused, looking at him.

"It's okay. Answer it," he said.

I got up from the bed and found my phone. It was Angelina.

Oh shit! I'd forgotten all about her! I'd been so caught up with Dev that I'd left her out on the dance floor with those guys. I thought I'd be gone for an hour, tops, not the whole night. How could I do something so irresponsible? I was the worst friend ever, having completely abandoned her. Worry and guilt overwhelmed me as I answered the phone.

"Hey girl!" Angelina chirped. "Hey! You okay?"

"Yeah, why wouldn't I be?"

I breathed a sigh of relief. "I lost track of time and fell asleep. I'm so sorry, I can't believe I left you back there all alone."

She laughed. "I'm fine. Looked like you were busy. You still at the party resort?"

"Um. Yes."

"Good. Me, too. Meet me out on the beach in ten? Miranda's called me like ten times. I think we're late for something."

"Yes, okay. I'll see you in a minute." I hung up the phone and looked at Dev, who was lying in bed making a tent with the sheets.

"Everything alright?" he asked.

I sucked in a breath through my teeth apologetically, shoulders up around my ears. "I'm sorry, but I have to go. Raincheck?"

He laughed. "Sure. I'd walk you out, but, uh. You know."

Smiling, I found my clothes from the night before and pulled them on. Before I could forget, I asked him his number. He relayed it, and I texted him right away, his phone dinging from somewhere in the room.

Wedges in hand, I stumbled out the door, waving awkwardly as I did so.

In the elevator, I took a moment to collect myself but couldn't shake the stupid grin off my face.

What. A. Night. Just what the doctor ordered.

Four

Down on the beach, Angelina stood waiting, shoes in hand. She squealed when she saw me, and we gave each other a fierce hug. I was so, very thankful to have her there with me, a mini version of my bestie but a hell of a lot wilder. Actually, Miranda used to be wild like that. Then she grew up. We both did.

As we walked home, she filled me in on the rest of her evening, which involved two bisexual men who apparently made her feel like an absolute goddess all night. My face reddened at the lewd details. I told her tidbits about my night, about how we'd met on the plane and he'd thrown up on himself, how we both inexplicably had the same ridiculous luggage and got it swapped, and then met at the party when he saved me from his creepy cousin.

"It was a fun fling," I said, ending my story. "A fling? A fling!" Angelina scoffed. "That's not a fling, girl. It's *fate*! What I had, was a fling. A glorious, incredible, amazing fling, which you can *not* tell my sister about. What you had, it's like, the ideal meeting the love of your life story!"

"I don't think throwing up on yourself constitutes as an 'ideal' story for anyone," I said with a laugh. It wasn't exactly Nicholas Sparks.

"True. But you have to admit, it is weird you kept bumping into each other. Until, you know, you were *bumping into* each other." She winked.

I laughed. She made a valid point.

So distracted by our conversation, we didn't realize Miranda was standing out on the beach... with the entire wedding party.

Angelina and I stopped dead in our tracks, both wearing our crumpled dresses from the night before, makeup smooshed, hair dishevelled, and heels in our hands. The crowd gawked at us. I wasn't sure what was worse: Nicole's judgmental look or Hank's defeated one. Miranda looked surprised at first, but then her face broke into a grin, and she gave us a clap, which turned into applause from the rest.

I blushed, embarrassed beyond belief, but then Angelina took my hand, lifted it, and then dropped us both into a bow.

"Thank you! Thank you!" she said. Her nonchalant attitude brought a grin to my face.

More than anything, I wanted to shower and change my clothes, but they had waited as long as they could. A catamaran sat out on the ocean and began loading everyone in.

Miranda ran up and gave me a giant hug. If I'd known sleeping with a guy would catch her attention, I would have done it on the first night.

"Oh. My. *God!*" she exclaimed in a loud whisper, taking my hand and pulling me away from the group.

I smiled and bit my lip.

"That good, hey?" she nudged my arm.

Giggling, I bumped her back. "It's a funny story! I met him

on the plane, and he's the guy who I swapped luggage with by mistake. He's really nice, actually. I meant to tell you about him, but you've been so busy."

She frowned. "I'm sorry, babe, there's been so much going on and so many people I haven't seen in years. I've barely had a chance to talk to you."

"No! Don't be. Love, this trip is about you. I am so incredibly happy for you. I'm fine. Angel has been keeping me company."

"Oh god. She's a bad influence, Becky, you be careful with her."

Having apparently heard the comment, Angelina winked at me over her shoulder.

I laughed, having come to really enjoy spending time with Miranda's younger sister. After all this, she and I would have to hang out sometime.

The catamaran was incredible. They took us on a sightseeing tour around the coral reefs. The weather was perfect, dolphins jumped and splashed, and other people on boats waved to us. I love that about boats. Everyone is excited for other people on boats. It's like, "You're on a boat? I'm on a boat! Holy shit, we're both on boats."

We had lunch on a private beach. Angelina stayed by my side as if she could smell Nicole waiting for the opportunity to tease me for my walk of shame earlier. Charlotte and Hannah were good sports, both enjoying the wine and sunshine. We chatted happily, but in the back of my mind, I was still in bed with Dev, imagining what would have happened if we'd been prepared with condoms. I wasn't sure if it could have been any better, though, other than leaving the poor guy with a serious case of blue balls.

I looked at my phone, and a smile lit up my face to see he'd texted me.

I tried not to message you. Can't stop thinking about you. Hope you're having a great time! See you later, if you're free?

He used full sentences. And the proper 'you're.' Sexy.

I replied. *Glad you messaged me! Can't stop thinking about you, either. Definitely see you later.* My thumb hovered over the send icon, debating whether adding a kiss face emoji was too much. He hadn't used emojis. Maybe he wasn't an emoji-type guy? I omitted it, pending further analysis of his texting style.

"Who you talking to?" Miranda asked, bumping into me, two glasses of sparkling wine in hand.

I took mine, and we clinked our glasses. "Who do you think?"

"No! He's texting you? Let me see!"

I showed her my phone.

"He used the correct 'you're'! Hot."

I laughed. Great minds.

"You look so much better today, love. I don't know what he did to you, but whatever it was, I hope he keeps doing it! You need something good in your life, after what that asshole did to you."

I nodded and looked out at the ocean, my eyes suddenly misty. She meant well, I know she did, but I hadn't thought of *him* all day, and now with the reminder, guilt seeped into my consciousness. It was stupid, feeling guilty. I had no reason to feel that way.

He had been my longest relationship—the *one*. The person I thought would be the father of my babies. And here I was, two and a half weeks later, in bed with some other guy who was basically a stranger.

She was right, though. After what happened, I was the last person who should feel guilty getting into bed with someone else. Then the guilty feeling shifted. I should have been thinking of Dev, not my ex! Or should I not be thinking about Dev at all?

While I debated internally about why I felt guilty and for whom, my phone dinged.

Looking forward to it! *Kissy face emoji.*

Damnit, I should have gone with my gut. "Aw, you're smiling!" Miranda cooed, hugging me from the side. Then, she tensed beside me. "Holy shit. I'm getting married tomorrow."

"Holy shit, you're getting married tomorrow!" We squealed in unison.

"Hey, by the way, this guy you're seeing—" she started.

"I don't know if 'seeing' is the right word, but okay."

"Dave?"

"Dev."

"He's welcome to come to the reception tomorrow if you want. I've noticed you're kind of on your own with all of these events, and it's the last thing I want. You shouldn't be forced to hang out with my little sister or Derek's single friends. I want you to have fun here, too!"

I considered it. "Are... are you sure?"

"Of course! Besides, we already paid for the plate. It's really not a big deal."

"Thank you," I said, surprised and grateful for her offer. "I don't know, though. We'll see."

We turned and re-joined the rest of the group. Though I was physically still there, my mind was elsewhere. Last night had been fantastic, one for the books, but to bring him to Miranda's wedding reception?

A: I wasn't sure if he'd even be interested. I mean, it's the kind of thing you do when you're dating, and I didn't want to scare him off, not that it mattered, but anyway...

B: What would everyone else think? One second, they expect me to be with *him*, then he's not in the picture, then I bring my one-night stand to the party? Who does that?

And C: Did *I* want to have him there at the reception? What if I only liked him in bed?

As the catamaran took us back to the mainland, my mind and heart were troubled. Though we were on solid ground, the uneasy sensation of being aboard the ship remained. Miranda reunited with Derek, as expected. I checked the itinerary on my phone, but the schedule was blank.

I found Angelina. "What's the plan for tonight?"

"I don't think there is one."

"We can... do our own thing?" I asked, my voice raising a little higher than intended.

She smirked. "Yes, you can go find your sexy Indian prince."

I rolled my eyes but didn't correct her. I texted Dev. *What are you up to?*

He replied right away. *Reading on the beach.*

A guy? Bringing a book on vacation? Butterflies resurfaced. *You up for exploring with me?*

Definitely!

Once the wedding party dispersed for their own private evenings, I went back to my room to shower and change before meeting Dev in front of my resort.

He looked absolutely dashing in a polo shirt with khaki knee-length shorts, his well-styled hair tousled by the wind.

"Should I go change?" I asked, feeling under-dressed in my short shorts and tank top.

He shook his head, his brown eyes meeting mine. "You

look perfect." As we drew near one another, a spark of electricity danced between us, and my pulse quickened in response. The intensity of my emotions made me a little uncomfortable. I forced my breathing to slow, hoping my heart rate would follow. It had only been one night. Just one night. Settle down.

I looked away before he could kiss me. "So, what's the plan, Stan?"

He led me up to the street and into a cab, where we were taken to an avenue lined with food trucks and tourist shops. As we wandered down the lane checking things out, he reached out and took my hand. I gave it a reassuring squeeze, my heart rising into my throat at his touch.

We spent the evening filling each other in on the details people usually do on a first date, prior to the sexy stuff. He'd taken six years to earn a four-year BA degree, as he'd had to continue working in his family's various businesses. He liked the idea of continuing his education, and getting his MBA but wasn't sure. It turned out I was a few years older than him, which I tried not to let bother me. When the guy is older, nobody gives a shit, so why should it matter when the woman is? He was very impressed by my degrees in polymer and mechanical engineering and my career in injection mouldings.

I avoided talking about work. Everyone hears 'engineering' and thinks my job is super interesting, and I never want to ruin it for them. My degrees were for very practical applications. I wasn't some inventor like I'd imagined I'd be when I was a kid. Nobody wants to hear about 3D CAD programs and packaging design.

The conversation shifted to all the travelling I'd done, and how lucky I'd been to explore the world. Travel was a priority in my life and always would be. Having been so busy working for his family and getting his degree, Dev hadn't travelled much out of the lower mainland but hoped to change that.

Dev always had great questions to ask, his eyes lighting up or his smile tugging at the corners of his lips while I spoke. It was nice talking to someone and having them listen. Like, really listen. Usually, my dates focussed only on themselves, but with Dev, it was the opposite.

But damn, did I love listening to him talk. His voice was so smooth, so sensual, and I loved watching his lips move, his brow furrow, and his eyes twinkle.

I told him about my older brother who lived in Australia, and about my parents who were retired and lived in Victoria. He was shocked I only had three cousins I wasn't remotely close to, and he couldn't imagine having such a small family. He had one younger sister, so many cousins I couldn't believe it, and lived with his family on their estate, where they also grew blueberries.

I didn't blame him for living with his parents still. Given the cost of housing in the Greater Vancouver Area, most young people stayed home until they got married and moved into crappy condos. Plus, he was a student, so his finances were likely limited. I wondered about his expensive-looking clothes, the shoes he wore, and the watch on his wrist. His family owned a business, so perhaps he came from money.

Regardless of his finances, I wasn't one to judge. I lived in a tiny-ass condo in Vancouver, which wasn't much to brag about, didn't own a car, had never even learned to drive, was up to my eyeballs in student loan debt, and my savings were non-existent.

Our lives seemed so different.

For a few minutes, I considered telling him about my ex,

but why spoil our day? We were both having such a great time. The last thing I wanted was to be a Debbie Downer.

"What's with your ridiculous pink luggage?" I asked as we sat in one of the bars for a drink. I had a margarita, and he had a Sprite.

His brow furrowed and forehead wrinkled, which I was slowly becoming addicted to.

"My sister, Priya. It was a prank. She hid all the rest of the luggage in the house so I'd be forced to use hers. Her way of embarrassing me in front of our cousins, I guess. Joke's on her, I'm comfortable with my masculinity, and pink doesn't bother me."

"So, it's her fault this happened, then." I smiled and licked the salt from the rim of my glass.

Dev smiled, too. "Yeah. I guess I'll have to thank her."

The night drew to a close. Hand holding wasn't enough for me anymore, and I couldn't wait to have his lips on mine again. Before getting into a cab, I popped into a convenience store and bought a pack of condoms.

"Awfully presumptuous of you," he joked.

I rolled my eyes, unable to wipe the stupid grin from my face, and tugged him towards a cab.

The poor cab driver did his best to navigate without being distracted as we teetered closer and closer to the edge of impropriety in the backseat. My legs intertwined with Dev's, nearly straddling him, fighting against the restraint of my seatbelt. Dev's hands were on my ass, his mouth on my neck, and his gasps in my ear.

We managed to make it to my resort and up to my room, collapsing onto the rose petals and kissing swans the cleaning service so diligently set up each night, completely oblivious to the fact that I was the lone occupant.

Until tonight, of course.

We hurriedly removed our clothing, making no time for sexy stripteases. I ripped into the package of condoms, tearing the box in half and flinging little silver packages everywhere. Dev and I couldn't help but laugh, both grabbing one and racing to see who could open it first. He won, sliding it over himself before tossing me onto the bed.

Our bodies craved one another's touch, hungered for it. As our mouths collided and our bodies pressed into one another, we rolled back and forth from positions of dominance and submission, selfishly satisfying our carnal cravings before turning our attentions to the other.

We moved as one, in blissful harmony, as if we'd been rehearsing for years. He seemed to know what I needed, and if ever he was slightly off course, I felt completely comfortable guiding him to a more fruitful path. Dev was eager to please, and I returned the favour.

Breathless, we collapsed, not even making it under the covers. We stared at the ceiling, panting, our bodies flushed and tingling from our exertions.

I looked over at him, enjoying the view. A light sheen of sweat on his chest reflected the moonlight

from the window, the warm colour of his skin a welcome contrast against the white sheets.

His gaze connected to mine, and a smile lit up

his face. I grinned, an elated bubble in my chest.

I had no idea that in losing my luggage, I'd find something so unexpectedly wonderful.

Five

I WOKE up with a salty breeze stirring the white curtains through an open window, the sun streaming in. Dev was still asleep, one arm above his head again, mouth hanging slightly open. Looking at him, my heart felt heavy and my stomach light.

We'd made good use of the condoms, having gone through three before finally collapsing, exhausted and spent. The first time had been rushed, overeager as if we couldn't wait even a second longer.

Afterwards, we'd taken our time. We spent a lot of time kissing, exploring each other's bodies with our mouths and hands. I'd been on top, his hands on my hips, sitting up at first but then folding over top of him, my face tucked into his neck, allowing myself the pleasure of losing control.

The final time, we'd been asleep for a while. We'd woken at some point, the hour unknown, our lips meeting soft and tender. He was on top of me, and for a while, we moved together without kissing, simply gazing into each other's eyes, abandoning our thoughts of whether we were moving too fast or too slow, the pleasure of each other's company more than enough.

I squeezed my legs together, recalling every moment, every touch, every kiss.

A guilty feeling crept up again, glancing around my suite, knowing I'd planned for someone else to be here, not him. All the things we'd done the night before, had it been meant for someone else?

For a moment I imagined my ex lying there instead of Dev—practically a stranger. He was kind, funny, and extremely attractive, but a stranger, nonetheless.

Even if my ex had been there, the sex wouldn't have been near as good. Dev was... incredible. Surprisingly amazing, in every way.

I got out of bed to pee and checked my phone. Angelina texted. *Where r u?! Hair and makeup rm 1573! Tell ur Indian prince to put it back in his pants!*

Oh. My. God! Miranda's wedding!

I checked the time. It wasn't too late. In a flurry, I jumped into the shower and rinsed the smell of sex off me, avoiding my hair; there was no time. I pulled on my clothes and was about to burst out the door when—

"Good morning, beautiful!"

"Dev! Shit, I'm sorry, I forgot you were here." "Aw, that's nice." He rested on one elbow, chuckling.

Hovering by the door, I shrugged my shoulders up to my ears. "It's Miranda's wedding today. I have to go get ready with the other girls. I'm really sorry, I forgot to set an alarm."

He shook his head. "Don't worry about it. Go, don't be late."

I turned to leave but stopped, thinking about what Miranda had said. "I told my friend about you, and she said you are welcome to come to the reception. If you want to." I hoped I didn't sound like a weirdo.

Dev mulled it over for a moment. Then he raised his eyebrows, wrinkling his forehead. "Do you want me to be there?"

A smile met my lips. "Yes. I do." "Then I'll be there."

I stepped away from the door and leaned across the bed to smooch him quickly, the temptation far too great to crawl back in for more.

"I'll text you!" I called over my shoulder after pulling away and darting out the door.

I ran down the halls, berating myself for not setting an alarm, and burst into the room, huffing and puffing. Everyone looked to me simultaneously, in various states of readiness. My face warmed. They knew exactly why I was late. I was really giving myself a reputation.

"There you are!" Miranda said in a sing-song voice, smiling at me through the mirror while a girl attended to her hair.

"Miranda! I am so sorry. I thought my alarm was set."

Nicole, having her makeup done, raised an eyebrow.

I ignored her.

"It's fine," Miranda said. "There's lots of time. Come sit next to me. They'll get started on you."

I swept my mussed hair back and swallowed, trying to calm my breaths from my early morning exertions. Angelina swept by and deposited a mimosa and muffin into each of my hands. I grinned and hugged her from the side before sitting down in a chair to let the stylist begin going through my messy, post-sex locks.

For someone about to get married, Miranda was totally chill. The ideal bride.

We spent the morning drinking mimosas, eating pastries

and fruit, and getting ready for her big day. A playlist of our old favourites was on in the background, and we all burst into song at random intervals when the BackstreetBoys or Journey came up.

A photographer fluttered around, taking candid shots.

"So, is... sorry, what was his name again?" Miranda asked, peeking out from under her eyelashes as the artist applied her liner.

"Dev," I reminded her, trying not to move my lips as another artist outlined them.

"Is Dev coming tonight?"

"He said he'd be there."

"Great! This will be so fun!"

"Thank you, Miranda. I mean it."

"You'd do the same for me, babe."

I reached out, and she took my hand, giving it a squeeze.

The dresses were all removed from their protective cases, each one a slightly different shade of peach and cut to suit each of our body types. Best of all, they all had pockets! All dresses should have pockets.

I tucked my lip gloss and phone inside before twirling around with the others like we were four-year-olds playing dress-up. All the shoes were strappy black sandals, perfect for a beach wedding. I looked down at my bright turquoise toes and reprimanded myself for not going with something more neutral.

Miranda had been a saint, organizing and shipping the dresses so we wouldn't have to worry about it. Then again, Derek's parents had hired a professional wedding coordinator to help her organize everything. Even now, a secret-agent-looking woman was checking things off on a clipboard and speaking in hushed tones through an earpiece.

It was a little over the top. When I get married, someday, I would do it small. Like, out in the forest with only my future hubby and me, our witnesses, the person marrying us, and maybe a photographer hiding in the bushes.

Miranda was helped into her stunning ballgown dress that had buttons and lacing up the back and long lace sleeves. The thing must have cost a fortune, but damn was it gorgeous. I teared up, remembering all the times we'd spent in high school poring through magazines and planning our imaginary weddings to the boys we'd had crushes on at the time.

Now it was finally happening... for her.

Right on schedule, we made our way to the beach. A violinist played covers of songs by City in Colour as we walked down the aisle, the ocean backdrop picturesque.

Derek stood next to a white archway, gossamer curtains blowing in the breeze, looking charming in his three-piece suit with a peach-coloured rose in his lapel.

When Miranda appeared, he teared up, which made me cry, and soon everyone was a sniffling mess. Her oversized bouquet of peach roses with a trail of greenery hanging down complemented her dress perfectly.

She walked down the aisle, Frank proudly at her side. My heart swelled seeing the two of them together. I hoped I'd be able to have such a special moment with my dad someday, too.

The ceremony was lovely. Miranda and Derek's vows were heartwarming. Once it was all done, we walked back inside. I was arm-in-arm with Hank, who wouldn't meet my gaze. As soon as we were out of sight, he released me and walked away without saying anything. That said a lot about him. I commended myself on my decision that Hank was kind of a creep and was happy Dev was already solving my Hank Problem without even being there.

The huge reception room opened to a private beach. Strings of lights hung above circular tables nestled in the sand, their white tablecloths tugged by the breeze and anchored in place by centrepieces of greenery and candles. The fully stocked bar was already overwhelmed by the wedding party for a toast. The dance floor was set up, but not yet active, with tasteful ambient music in the background.

I grabbed a glass of champagne, toasted with the others, and then checked my phone.

Dev had texted me. *How formal is this wedding?*

I snapped a pic of what a group of other guys were wearing —semi-formal, nice pants and shoes, button-up shirts.

He replied. *Camera was pointed wrong direction. Winky emoji.*

I smiled and sent him a selfie.

He replied with three heart-eyed emojis.

'You can come any time, we're at the main ballroom.' I texted.

Grinning, I put my phone away as Miranda came over and gave me a big hug. "You look stunning!" I gushed, trying not to cry again.

"Don't cry! You'll make me cry." And she meant it, given her broad smile. The wedding party lined up next to the bride and groom for pictures on the beach. I hate awkward pictures like that, especially when they make you look at each other and fake laugh.

What felt like an eternity later, Miranda and Derek were swept off for private photos and the rest of us hit the bar and buffet for appetizers. With a drink in one hand and my mouth half-full of crab cake, I turned towards the entrance.

And in walked Dev.

His black hair was combed and shined, his beard was

trimmed along his jawline, and his brown eyes smouldered beneath dark brows and lashes. He wore the same clothes from the plane, freshly dry-cleaned. His shoes matched his watch, visible since his sleeves were once again rolled up to reveal his sexy forearms.

Several other women turned to gawk at him, and I hurried to swallow the crab cake in my mouth. He sidled up to me, a warm smile on his face.

His hand wrapped around my waist, so familiar, and it immediately made me feel comfortable having him there. Not for one moment did he seem out of place, as if he'd planned to be there all along. Gently, he pressed his lips to my forehead, and then I was lost in his eyes again.

"Who's your new beau?" Nicole asked, appearing out of nowhere with Chaz trailing one step behind, his hands full with a plate of food. Her smile was so phone it nauseated me.

Dev reached out and introduced himself, shaking both her hand and Chaz's.

Seeming to sense my discomfort, Dev jumped right into professional small-talk mode with Chaz, and the two delved into a conversation about hockey. Nicole grew bored quickly, as she couldn't get a word in edgewise and was clearly not used to being on the perimeter of the attention circle.

Finally, she interrupted. "Chaz, baby, would you mind getting me a drink?"

Chaz's hands were still full of his plate of food. He looked down at the plate, then up to Nicole, who met him with another fakey-fake smile.

"I need a drink, too. Dev? Drink?" I suggested.

"Sure!" he replied. Then he, Chaz, and I made our way towards the bar, eager to be away from Nicole and her judging stare.

Chaz turned out to be a super nice guy. What he was doing with Nicole, I didn't quite understand. Whatever. Not my business. I grabbed another glass of champagne, and Dev took a club soda in a short glass. When I raised an eyebrow, he said he got tired of explaining he didn't like to drink. It did, indeed, look like he was drinking vodka. I silently commended him, glad his clothes would stay vomit-free this evening.

We walked away, and I began subtly pointing out the people I knew to catch him up on relevant gossip. Eventually, we found Charlotte and Hannah, who were more than welcoming to Dev. They didn't question why I had brought my vacation fling to the party or why he had agreed to come. Dev chatted them each up, asking about what they did for work, listening to them talk about their kids. I learned as much about him from their follow-up questions as they did.

Dev's family lived on an acreage outside of Surrey, where they grew blueberries. His family also owned several automotive shops and other businesses throughout mainland British Columbia. His grandparents had immigrated from the Punjab region of India in the early twentieth century, and he was the third generation of Indo-Canadians in his family. I found that very interesting, as my father had immigrated from the United States (his father from France), and my mother was a second-generation Canadian, her family having been from Germany and Russia.

Dev joked about how his family was more Canadian than mine, but Hannah was quick to interject. Her parents had immigrated from Korea and worked hard for their citizenship and, in her opinion, that did not make them any less Canadian than others whose families had been here longer. We agreed, of course. Charlotte argued that if anyone here was more Canadian, it was her, as she was one-quarter Métis on her dad's side.

Dev and Hannah chatted a little about their experiences belonging to a minority religion in a country that, though secular, still revolved around Christian holidays. Hannah was Buddhist, and Dev's family was Sikh. I didn't know much about Sikhism, but I was curious and interested in learning. As the conversation continued, I realized how privileged I was that the cultural aspects of Christianity were respected enough to warrant national holidays, among other benefits. Personally, I didn't practice religion, but I'd been raised Catholic and still celebrated Christmas and Easter. Mostly for the gifts and chocolate, though.

We were interrupted by an announcement introducing Miranda and Derek as husband and wife. I breathed a sigh of relief; our conversation was starting to feel a bit too deep for a wedding. I hadn't expected Dev to receive the third degree on his heritage and faith.

"Sorry about that," I whispered as we watched the bride and groom enter.

"It's no problem. It doesn't look like they know a lot of brown people," he commented. I looked around the room, noticing for the first time that almost everyone who didn't work there was white, other than Hannah. It hadn't initially dawned on me as strange, but now I found it unsettling seeing it from Dev's perspective.

Angelina came up beside us.

"Hey Dev!" she said as if he was always supposed to be there. God, I was really starting to love this girl!

The two of them chatted about nothing in particular, sharing laughs. I stood by and watched, completely transfixed by Dev and his ability to feel so at ease in any situation. He was such a stark contrast to my awkward self.

Miranda and Derek worked their way down the receiving

line, finally making it to us. I hugged Derek as Miranda shook Dev's hand. Then Miranda hugged me, whispering, "He's so hot!" in my ear. She held my hands and gave them a squeeze, and then was ushered past us to more people all waiting for their moment to congratulate them.

Eventually, we made our way into the dining room. I sat at the head table and looked out across the room nervously, but was happy to see Dev seated next to Chaz. They would be fine. I relaxed. Toasts. Drinks. More toasts. Food. More drinks.

Finally, we were released from our strict seating arrangements. I found Dev. He had somehow managed to end up with Miranda's mother, who was no doubt talking his ear off. The conversation I walked in on had something to do with how she once lived in a building that always smelled like curry. *For all that is holy, Susan, please don't say anything offensive.*

"Dev! Glad I found you. Oh, hey Susan! Sorry, I have to steal Dev away," I said, grabbing his hand and tugging him along. Once I got him out of that uncomfortable situation, I apologized profusely.

All he could do was laugh.

"I'm glad you have such a good sense of humour about it," I said, still feeling embarrassed by Susan's behaviour.

I looked up at him and smiled but noticed a glint of something amiss in his eyes. Was it something Susan had said? Before I could ask, another announcement was called about the bouquet being thrown. Angelina grabbed me and pulled me into the throng. Miranda pointed at me and winked, then turned and tossed her beautiful peach-coloured rose bouquet over her shoulder.

Well, I'll be damned if I didn't catch it.

Bouquet in hand, I pivoted and looked over my shoulder at Dev. He was clapping and smiling, but the smile didn't reach his eyes. Angelina interrupted, giving me a big hug and squealing so loud in my ear that I probably lost a few of my higher frequencies.

The rest of the night went off without a hitch. Dev was the perfect gentleman, the perfect date. I couldn't have asked for more.

...so, why was there a sinking sensation in the pit of my stomach? I could sense it, in the way he put his hand on my back, to the way his eyes didn't crinkle when he smiled, to the somewhat looser grip he had on my hand when he held it in his.

Miranda and Derek shared their first dance, which began as a sappy love song and then exploded into a hilarious dance routine that probably took weeks to master. Others began joining them on the dance floor. Seeing Miranda so happy, so in love, reminded me of what was important tonight. It wasn't about me, it wasn't about Dev, it was about Miranda. I wasn't going to let anything stop me from showing up for my best friend in the whole world on one of the most important nights of her life.

Despite my discomfort with dancing in public, I grabbed Dev and pulled him out with me. The music was great, the atmosphere was perfect, and after a few minutes, everything seemed back to normal with Dev and me. I began to wonder if I'd imagined the whole thing or if I was creating a problem where there was none. According to my ex, it wouldn't be the first time. Then again, that was when he was gaslighting me...

At midnight we gathered on the beach and sent the bride and groom off, complete with sparklers and fireworks. Miranda and Derek walked hand-in-hand down the beach to their suite where they'd spend their first night as husband and wife.

I turned to look at Dev. The uncertainty was back, the look in his eyes that he wasn't sure of something.

"You want to call it a night?" I asked.

He nodded. We said polite goodnights to the few people we passed who knew us, Angelina included. Angelina begged us to stay out, to get some shots with her, but that was the last thing I wanted. Wordlessly we made our way back to my suite, the tension between us palpable, but not the sexual kind. My mind raced, wondering what had happened.

Door closed, I sat on the edge of the bed and removed my sandals, peppering the floor with sand. Dev stood by the door, hands in his pockets.

I looked up at him. "I'm sorry if Susan said something that upset you. She tends to do that."

He shook his head. "It's not that."

I stood and gathered my sandals to move them out of the way. "What is it, then?"

"Who's Graham?"

I froze, a chill running down my spine. The very name brought with it a wave of nausea. Surely someone said something. Damnit, Nicole!

"Graham?" I said, swallowing, my stomach in knots.

He pulled a piece of folded card paper from his pocket, edged in gold with *his* name on it.

Graham Hoffman.

My stomach dropped.

"Was I here to replace him?" he asked. "No, I..."

"Was this guy supposed to be here with you?"

"Well, yes, but..."

Dev looked around my suite, the king-sized bed once again sprinkled with rose petals, the towel swans kissing. "You were supposed to be here with some other guy. Where is he?"

I swallowed. "We broke up." "How long ago?"

I hesitated. "Two weeks ago."

His eyebrows shot up, startled. "Two weeks?" There was nothing I could say.

"Am I just some stand-in?"

The disappointed look on his face was heartbreaking, and tears tugged at the corner of my eyes. "I'm sorry..."

Though he must have been hurt, he didn't raise his voice. I was used to being yelled at, but this quiet anger was somehow worse. "Was I a vacation romance for you to get over your ex? A fling? Why didn't you tell me, Rebecca? You didn't even mention... you know what? Never mind. You don't owe me an explanation. I thought what we had was going to be something more. I guess I read into it too much."

He set the card down on the dresser and reached for the door.

"Dev, wait!" I said. He hesitated, looking back at me, the hurt evident in his gorgeous eyes.

And then, he left.

I wanted to run out into the hallway, to call for him, to tell him... to tell him what? That I loved him? I'd only just met the guy! And I *had* broken up with my ex two weeks ago.

Was he right? Had I been using him to ease, no, *delay* my pain during my friend's wedding, to make it easier on myself, with no consideration for Dev's feelings?

The rest of the night was spent in a drunken blur as I cried in the jacuzzi, drinking the contents of the minibar. The following morning I was hugging the toilet.

It seemed everyone at brunch was feeling similarly hungover, easing their discomfort with Bloody Marys. I sat with Hannah and Charlotte, who could not stop gushing about how wonderful Dev was. I smiled and nodded, explaining he had something to do this morning and wouldn't be joining us.

I'd hoped to catch Miranda before leaving for my flight, but it seemed she was still hiding in her newlywed glow with Derek. I sent her a text instead. *Off to the airport! Love you so much. So happy for you. Let's meet up for coffee soon. xoxo*

I didn't have the energy for emojis.

Everything was stuffed back into my ridiculous suitcase, which would now forever remind me of Dev and our short-lived vacation romance. I shoved my unused rabbit somewhere in the middle, having learned my lesson from last time.

The cardstock with *his* name on it sat semi-folded on the dresser. I tossed it into the trash. I should have thought to check the table for something like that. It hadn't even occurred to me.

At the front desk, I left my bridesmaid's dress and sandals, not wanting to take them with me, as I hadn't paid for them and didn't want to clog up my already overflowing closet with them either. I turned to leave, but the man behind the counter caught me.

"Wait! Your cleaning, miss!" He held up my airplane clothes, freshly cleaned and pressed. I took them with a lump in my throat, another reminder of Dev's kindness and my asshole behaviour. I shoved them into my bag, fighting the pressure of tears threatening to spill out once again.

In the cab, I checked my phone. No texts from Miranda. No texts from Dev. Maybe I should message him. But what would I say? He was right. I had behaved selfishly. I should have told him right away, or at least the night we'd gone out on a date. Everything had been so perfect, though, I didn't want to spend the night telling him about my break-up.

Re-living it was the last thing I wanted to do.

Six

BACK HOME IN VANCOUVER, life returned to normal. Work Monday to Friday. Running along the seawall Monday and Wednesday. Yoga Saturday morning. Grocery shopping and meal prep Sunday. Evenings spent watching Netflix. Try not to binge ice cream and cry. Fail.

What little tan I'd managed to get faded within the week, but my memories of Dev and our romance hadn't faded in the slightest. Thankfully, a coffee date with Miranda broke up the monotony of my rigidly scheduled life and would offer a bit of a distraction from my relentless thoughts of Dev.

"Call him, damnit!" she urged, setting her cup down with a frustrated clink.

So much for a distraction. I stared dejectedly at the foam in my vanilla latte. "It was just a fling."

"It's two weeks later, and you're still thinking about him. That's not a fling, Becky. If you don't do something about it, you will regret it forever. What's the worst that could happen? He ignores your call?"

"I don't want to be rejected again."

"What Graham did, that was awful, okay? Not all guys are like that. I only met Dev once, but he didn't seem like that."

I smiled a bit. No, Dev had been the perfect gentleman.

Miranda reached across the table for my hand. "Look. I know when something is real when I see it. The spark between you two, it was there! You can either chicken out and let the spark fizzle, or you can blow on it and see what happens."

I laughed. "Miranda, 'blow on it' is always the advice you give."

"Number one relationship advice: when in doubt, blow on it."

The ladies next to us glared when our laughing spiralled out of control.

"Enough about me and my failed romances. How's married life?" I asked, spirit elevated with her sitting across the table, finally getting some time with her after the chaos of her wedding.

"Honestly? Not any different."

"Really?"

"Yeah. I thought something would feel different, you know? More permanent, at least. But it's pretty much the same as before, only now instead of people asking us when we're getting married, they're asking us when we're having babies."

"So, when is that?" I smiled, giddy at the idea of mini Mirandas running around.

She shrugged. "I'm so happy with how everything is, you know? I love my job, and I love my freedom, but it would be nice to get started right away while we're still young. It would suck to be retiring and putting kids through college at the same time."

My stomach sank, doing the mental math in my head to determine when I'd need to meet someone, date the appropriate length of time, get engaged, marry, and then have babies, if I wanted not to be retiring when they were going to college. It didn't look promising.

Miranda continued. "Derek's ready to be a dad. He's been ready for a while. He wants four kids. Four!"

"How are you going to manage four kids and work?"

She half-smiled. "Maybe I won't go back to work."

I sat back in my seat, surprised. She'd worked so hard to get into the medical field, and worked as a server to pay her way through school, but now that she was married, she was willing to let it all go?

"But you love being a nurse!"

"I know, I do, but nursing is hard work. Even working part-time, I think I'd be burnt out trying to do both. And there's no reason for it."

"Aren't you worried about your independence?"

She shrugged again. "A little. Money is the last thing I have to worry about anymore. It sounds shitty to say, but it's true. There's no point in me being stressed out about a job and kids when I can relax and enjoy having a family."

That rang true. It sounded like she'd put a lot of thought into it. It still made me uncomfortable being so completely dependent on someone else. Perhaps if I had someone like Derek, I'd understand.

She must have noticed the sad look on my face because she reached across the table again and took my hand. "Hey, your time is coming. Okay? Just don't be afraid to love again. You can start by picking up the damn phone and calling Dev!"

That night, two glasses of wine in, I went for it. I didn't even text. I called. Like, actually called. Shiraz made me brave.

The phone rang twice, and then he answered. A confused, "Hello?"

"Dev? Hey, it's me. Rebecca."

"... hey."

"Hey. Um. Sorry, is this a bad time? I can call back—"

"Nope. Is everything okay?"

Classic gentleman, as always. I tucked my feet underneath myself and exhaled, suddenly unsure of what to say, the speech I'd prepared vanishing from my brain.

"Listen. I just wanted to apologize for not telling you about... about Graham earlier." Saying his name out loud brought me physical pain. "We were having such an amazing time. I didn't want to ruin it. I'm sorry. I should have told you."

A moment of silence. "Okay."

"Um." I pressed onward. Wine, don't fail me now! "Well, I was thinking, if you're up for it, could I take you out for dinner or something?"

Another moment of silence. "Are you asking me out on a date?"

"... yes."

"I don't think a lady has ever asked me out on a date before."

I smiled into the receiver. "I'm a feminist, remember?"

I could hear him smiling, too. "I remember."

"Besides," I added, "you owe me one."

"I owe you one? How's that?"

"You barfed on me on the plane."

He laughed. "That's true. I did, a little."

I paused and waited, chewing the skin off my bottom lip.

Finally, he spoke. "Sure. You gave me a chance to start over. I'll give you one, too."

My heart leapt. "Okay, great! Um, how about Saturday?

Are you okay to come out to Vancouver? I don't... I use transit."

"Yeah, that's fine. I'm excited to meet you. Again."

"Same," I said, butterflies emerging.

We said goodbye, and I ended the call before I could say anything to ruin it.

I texted Miranda quickly, who replied right away with an *I told you so!' Winky-face emoji, eggplant emoji, heart emoji.* Classic Miranda.

Saturday could not come fast enough. I'd never planned a date before, and it was nerve-racking! Most of the places I liked revolved around their fab drink menu, but with Dev, that was off the table. Ooh! I knew the best taco place. Wait. I shouldn't remind him of Mexico, not when we're trying to have a fresh start.

Then, I found it—the perfect date.

After another bland week, Saturday night finally arrived. It was raining, as per usual. It took me an hour to get dressed, snapping pictures and sending them to Miranda until she'd finally had enough. I went with my booty-enhancing Freddy jeans (I needed all the help I could get), realistic two-inch pumps, and a V-neck shirt that went well with my spring jacket and yellow umbrella. I took the Skytrain downtown and then waited for Dev in a whiskey bar, having one to settle my nerves. I'm not an alcoholic by any means, but I didn't know how Dev could go through life without the occasional drink to calm himself. Perhaps it was because he was naturally so chill.

He texted me. *Here.*

Having pre-paid for my drink, I slammed the rest of it back before stepping out into the rain to find him. I didn't have to look long.

I flashed back to the first time seeing him on the plane, how he'd taken my breath away. He turned as if in slow motion, his dazzling smile lighting up his perfectly symmetrical features. His sense of style was again on point, dressing much better than I had; dark-wash jeans and a brown jacket unzipped to reveal a navy sweater. He sidled up, black umbrella with a shiny wooden handle in his left hand, his right extended out to me.

"Hey," he said. "I'm Dev."

"Rebecca." I grinned.

For a long moment, we simply looked at one another, hands held mid-shake. *Click.* Everything snapped back into place as if nothing had ever been amiss.

I led him across the street to a restaurant where people dined completely in the dark. It initially sounded like fun but I was now a little uncertain.

"If this is too weird, we can go somewhere else," I offered.

"Are you kidding? This is awesome! Except there's one problem," he said.

"What's that?"

"I won't get to look at you."

I blushed. He had a point. We perused the menus and gave our orders to the hostess, who then introduced us to our server, who was an extremely charismatic woman who was blind. She explained how everything worked before leading us into the restaurant. They weren't lying. It was pitch black. I held onto the server's shoulders, Dev held onto my waist, and we got to our table and sat down.

Right away, Dev and I launched into a light conversation about nothing in particular. He was a natural conversationalist, the world's easiest person to talk to, as there was always the right amount of give and take— even without visual cues in the complete darkness. The drinks were tasty, and the food was delicious, though it was a little unnerving not being sure what you were putting in your mouth and being somewhat surprised by the texture. I had chicken; Dev went for the vegetarian option.

"I'm sorry, I didn't know you were vegetarian!" I said between bites. How had I not noticed before? "Is it like with drinking, you'll eat meat on occasion?"

"I try not to unless it would be extremely rude not to eat what's being offered."

"I tried to go vegan once, but only lasted a month. I lived off of yam fries and guacamole."

"Vegan isn't necessarily healthy like some people think. Ritz crackers are vegan."

"Same with Oreos."

"I love Oreos."

"Is your whole family vegetarian?"

"Most everyone. Some of my cousins are looser about it, like about drinking. My parents and grandparents are more strict."

We fell into a bit of a silence.

"You know," I said. "I hadn't really thought this date through. It sounded like a good idea at the time, but you're right, I miss seeing your face." Then I slipped my foot out of my shoe and ran it up his calf.

I could hear him smiling when he said, "I was thinking the same thing."

After the meal, which I was adamant I'd pay for since it was my date, we took a walk downtown arm in arm, hiding beneath his umbrella. The plan had been to take a stroll through Stanley Park, but the late winter storm was growing worse and our umbrellas were not doing much to protect us from the stinging droplets blowing in sideways.

"Should I take you home? I parked over there," he asked.

My mood deflated. I didn't want the night to end but wasn't sure what else to do. Most local activities I was aware of involved drinking. We headed towards the parkade. His white BMW was somehow spotless despite the messy spring roads. He opened the door for me. *Classy.* The leather interior was the colour of cinnamon, impeccably clean, with not a speck of dust in sight. Dev climbed in and started it up.

The transmission was manual. I'd never seen anyone drive a manual shift before, having grown up in Vancouver and having been raised on public transit. The way his feet maneuvered the pedals, his right hand gripping the gearshift as he clicked it into its rightful place, all while weaving through the challenging stop-and-go traffic of the downtown core, was sexier than I could have imagined. By the time I'd directed him to my apartment, I was eager to invite him up.

"Normally, I'd offer you a glass of wine. Tea, perhaps?" I asked, unbuckling and shifting in my seat to face him.

Dev smiled his charismatic smile. "Normally, I'd like to walk you to your door, but there's no parking around here."

"I have access to the visitor's parking if you want to come up."

He hesitated. "Rebecca... if we're going to do this, and I mean really do it in earnest, I want to date you properly. Respectfully. Trust me, there's nothing I want more than to come up to your apartment for, uh, tea, but I want to make sure you know that I respect you."

I rolled his words around in my head for a moment, unsure if they were respectful or condescending. After all, it had been my idea, and we'd already seen each other naked. "The invitation was for tea," I said, a little more defensively than I'd intended. "We don't have to do anything else."

He thought for another long moment, his four-way signals

flashing. "Sure. Tea never hurt anyone," he said finally, a smile coming to his face but with uncertainty in his eyes.

I directed him where to park. My building was nothing special, nestled between the less-fortunate East Hastings Street and the more well-to-do neighbourhoods. Though my place wasn't anything to be excited about, it still cost me a great deal. Worth it, though, to live in the best city in the world.

Even though the rent was expensive, I refused to have a roommate. They're the worst. I'd never had a great experience with one. I'd rather live in a tiny five hundred square foot apartment than have a bigger place with someone else always underfoot.

The elevator smelled vaguely of urine and shuddered as it carried us to the fourteenth floor. I let him in, jiggling the sticky lock. The walls were white and stark, and so thin that a second-rate comedy show's laugh track was clearly audible from my neighbour's apartment. I walked in and kicked off my shoes into the pile next to the door, which was also right next to my fridge.

"So, um. What kind of tea can I get you?" I asked, quickly flitting around the small space, tidying. I grabbed my bra and jeans off the couch I'd bought on Craigslist, faux leather scratched and sunken, and tossed them onto the heap in front of my overflowing bedroom closet. I eyed my unmade bed, the drooping mandala tapestry hanging above the plain metal frame, and far too many scented candles littering nearly every available surface.

"Chai's fine," he said, entering and taking a look around at my sparse decorations.

The space was perfect for me, but with him in there, it felt small. Cramped. Awkward. Given his new BWM and stylish clothes, he probably had a nice house—a house on an acreage, surrounded by blueberries. Having been in his spotless car made me wish I'd cleaned up a bit more before heading out for the day. I moved to the fridge for a glass of wine and turned on the electric kettle.

If Dev was uncomfortable in my apartment, he didn't show it. Instead, he looked at the photos I had displayed on a bookshelf next to the TV, where I also stored my DVD collection.

"*Silence of the Lambs, Pulp Fiction, Seven...* I expected *The Notebook*, not murder thrillers." He smirked over his shoulder at me. "I should have known better. You're the girl who caught my *Fight Club* reference."

I poured myself a glass of cheap pinot gris and screwed the lid back on, not mentioning how *The Notebook* was, in fact, still in my DVD player from the last time I'd watched it, and my collection of other sappy movies was in a drawer below the TV. I'd let him believe I was too cool for chick flicks for the time being. "It's an unhealthy obsession, I guess. I've watched all of the murder shows on Netflix, too."

"Do you listen to that podcast?"

"With the two girls talking about murderers?"

"Yeah, that one. My sister listens to it all the time. What's with our society's obsession with murderers?"

I took a sip, more comfortable with the glass in my hand, and leaned against the counter while I waited for the kettle to heat up. "I have no idea, but it seems pretty common. Maybe we just want to understand people who are different from us."

Dev picked up a frame. "Who's this?"

I walked over to him and brushed my shoulder against his, electricity jumping with the brief contact. The photo was me in a bikini on a beach with a tall, muscly, topless dude covered in tattoos. I could see why he might have been concerned and stifled a smile. "He's my brother. I went to visit him in Australia, right before my tour of Southeast Asia."

"What does he do there?"

"He's a petroleum engineer."

"Damn. I have no idea what that means, but it sounds impressive!" He laughed. His gaze shifted down and met mine. Our eyes locked, and I could feel the heat from his body as an unspoken mutual lust grew between us. We inched closer, my heart racing, the hand on my glass an anchor to the real world as my head swam, lost in his presence. He lowered his face to mine, and—

The kettle whistled. I jumped and headed back to the kitchen. I set my wine on the counter and swallowed, trying to focus, searching the cupboard for tea. "I only have earl grey and chai."

He came up behind me, his chest brushing up against my back. I tilted my head to the side as he lowered his mouth to my ear, his warm breath sending a tingle down my spine. An involuntary gasp escaped my lips as his mouth lingered by my neck. I turned my face towards his.

Dev took a step back, chai teabag in hand.

I gripped the counter in front of me, releasing a shaky exhale. I was intoxicated by his presence, an addict in need of another hit, and unsure if it would ever come.

Inviting him up had been a mistake. He had clearly been uncomfortable with the idea, wanting to 'respect' me, whatever that meant as if having sex with someone you liked was disrespectful.

But, if the roles were reversed and it was me wanting to wait before having sex, the last thing I'd want is some guy pressuring me into it.

Though, that didn't stifle my curiosity. "Are you normally like this with women?" I asked, fingernails tinkling on my glass.

He looked up from his cup, adorable brow furrow emerging. "Like what?"

"Do you have a three-date rule or something?" Dev held his cup in both hands, mulling it over, but didn't say anything.

"It's just, you didn't seem to have a problem having sex with me in Mexico, when we were perfect strangers. But now that we're here, you want to wait. I'm fine waiting, I mean, until you're comfortable, but I just want to know why." I reprimanded myself for saying 'just' so often, a permission word primarily used by women. I'd managed to rid it from my vocabulary in work settings, but with Dev, I didn't want to come across as pushy.

A smile curled the edges of his lips as he blew the steam from his mug. "If I remember correctly, you kissed me first, and then you led me to bed."

My cheeks flushed with the memories of our hot, sweaty nights together, my lips twitching into a smile. "I didn't hear you complaining at the time."

He set his mug down and approached me, his hands finding their way to my waist. As I forced myself to look into his eyes, the hint of anger that had wormed its way into my subconscious melted away.

"There's so much I want to learn about you," he said, his voice low and more seductive than he ever could have imagined. "If I take you to bed, you and I both know it's all we'll ever do. We rushed into things in Mexico. Because of that, you didn't tell me about your ex. If I'd known about him, I might have made some different choices."

"Do you regret what we did?" I asked, unable to mask my worry.

He hesitated, then shook his head. "No. But I do wish you'd told me. I still know nothing about what happened between you two, how long you were together, or anything."

"After I tell you, will you be comfortable enough for, you know—" I winked, trying to lighten the mood.

"Is this a quid pro quo?" He raised an eyebrow.

"Quid pro quo, Dev," I replied in my best Hannibal Lector impersonation.

He snorted a laugh. "I don't think quid pro quos include sexual favours."

"I don't think there's any limitation to that sort of exchange. But I was kidding. Of course, you don't owe me anything. But I do owe you an explanation." I heaved a sigh. "Well, we'd better sit down for this." I took his hand and led him to my couch. Dev set his mug on a coaster *(swoon)* before pulling my legs onto his lap.

It took a moment for me to collect my thoughts, unsure of where to begin. The breakup was still so fresh. Miranda had been busy planning the final stages of her wedding, and it wasn't the sort of thing I'd talk to my mom about, so I'd bottled it up. Not a healthy coping mechanism by any means, but it

was easier to file it away in storage than deal with it all on my own.

Well. Better get this over with.

"He cheated on me," I began, my voice flat and without emotion. "Cliché, I know. We had been together for a year and a half. I found out he had been cheating on me for the last four months of our relationship. When I caught him..."

My attempt to lay everything out as plainly as possible was already failing as my throat constricted. I had avoided talking about this for so long; locked away the pain and the hurt and the embarrassment. Opening this small hole threatened the integrity of the entire dam.

He gave my knee a squeeze. "You don't have to talk about this if you don't want to. But I'm here. And you can cry if you need to."

A man? Telling me it's okay to cry? My heart fluttered.

"No, I'm alright," I said, voice wavering past my forced smile, betraying how I truly felt. "I knew something had been wrong for a while. Looking back, it was obvious. I guess it always is. Hindsight, you know? One day he said he had to work late, like so many other days. I decided to surprise him at his office with food. I got our favourite take-out and went to his work, but he wasn't there. His co-workers, the way they—"

I choked on a sob, betraying tears running down my cheek. He rubbed my arm. I forced myself to continue, sniffing hard.

"The way they looked at me, it was awful. They all knew what was going on. They pitied me. I never felt so stupid in my entire life. I went to his desk, and I—I guessed his password, it was the same as our Netflix account, and I saw the emails."

"That must have been really hard to read."

The more tears that escaped, the less control I had over them. Like a Band-Aid, I forced myself to continue, ripping through the next part as quickly as possible. I blubbered on, unsure if he could understand me, and not really caring. "When I told him I knew, he didn't even try to lie. I asked if he was sorry. He said he was. And then— And then I told him I'd forgive him, that we could work past it, that we could— could still make it work, and he— he chose to leave me. He didn't want me at all." I pulled myself away and wiped my nose on my sleeve. "I'm just so— so disgusted in myself, how I could let someone cheat on me, and know he obviously doesn't care, and then say I can forgive him and welcome him back. What—what's wrong with me?"

Dev pulled me back into a hug, rocking me while he stroked my hair. I wept for another minute, and as I did the ache in my chest subsided, my tears dried. It felt good to finally let it out.

"I feel so stupid," I said, my voice hitching.

"You didn't do anything wrong. You see the best in people."

I wasn't sure about that but didn't correct him.

Dev continued. "He's the bad guy in this situation, not you. He failed to see what was so special about you."

Once again, I pulled back from Dev and wiped my nose.

"Can I get you a tissue?" he asked.

I laughed through my tears, nodding.

Dev got up, returning a moment later with a box of Kleenex. I wiped at my face and then exhaled shakily.

"I'm sorry I unleashed that on you. I know you must be thinking that it's too soon for me to be dating after a breakup, that I'm not emotionally ready for it, that I'm using you to get over him," I said, talking into the soiled tissues in my hand.

He brushed some hair out of my face. "I don't think that at all. Well, maybe a little, but that's why I wanted to give you some space. I've never been cheated on. To be honest, I've only had one real girlfriend before you, Sonja, and we split up amicably."

"What?" I looked up from my tissues. "You've only had one girlfriend?" Nothing about our time together had hinted at him being an inexperienced lover; in fact, the opposite. He had natural talents.

He laughed.

"Seriously! You've only slept with me and one other girl?"

He nodded, a bit bashful.

"How is that possible?" I was totally unable to fathom how this incredibly sexy human being had been able to walk through life without women throwing themselves at him left, right, and centre.

Dev picked his mug back up and took a sip, his other hand running absentmindedly along my leg. I set my tissues down and sipped my wine, watching his face as he spoke. I relished the way his eyes lit up, how his long eyelashes flashed up and down when he blinked, the twitch of his mouth as he smiled.

"Well," he started. "Many Indian families still uphold the whole 'no sex until marriage' thing, which in my generation is pretty rare. But still, any premarital activities are done in secret. And, since I live at home, there's no sneaking around happening there. Every Indian girl I know also lives at home, too, so that's definitely out."

"But the one girl, you two made it work."

He nodded, seeming hesitant. "Our families have been friends forever. We've known each other since we were kids. We dated for a while, mostly at the insistence of our mothers. I guess they thought it was serious, so they turned a bit of a blind eye, but it didn't work out between us."

"Why's that?"

"We were just... friends. I don't know."

"So, no other girls?"

He shook his head. "Nobody serious. I'm pretty focused on my studies, and it's hard to meet girls when you don't drink. My cousins are always going to bars and clubs, and that's not for me. And you can't talk in a library, so I'm not sure how I'm supposed to meet anyone."

I nudged him. "You dance pretty well for not going to clubs."

He grinned, understanding my double entendre immediately. "It's easy when you find the right dance partner."

Once again, a tingle of electricity jumped between us. Warmth flooded my abdomen, and every inch of my skin itched for his touch. Without intending to, my eyes wandered down to his pants. He obviously felt the same way.

He broke the spell, moving to stand. "Um. I'm going to grab more 'ch-ah'. Can I get you anything while I'm up?"

I handed him my glass, a little disappointed. "Sure. And *what* are you getting?" I didn't recognize the word.

He spoke with his back to me as he walked into the kitchen. "That's how chai is pronounced. 'Ch- ah.'"

"Not *'ch-eye?'* I didn't know that. *Ch-ah* tea," I said, trying out the sound.

Dev looked at me with a smirk. "Chai means tea. You don't say 'tea-tea.' It's just chai. And do you have a spice cupboard?"

I pointed. "What are you making?"

He pushed a few items around but didn't seem to find what he was looking for. "I thought I could show you how to make some real chai. This gora bagged chai isn't anything like the real stuff. Next time I come over, I'll bring what I need."

I grinned, excited that he'd already mentioned a next time. "Gora?" I asked, raising an eyebrow.

He grinned. "White people."

I laughed, and he smiled at me from the kitchen. God, I loved how he looked in there. I could already imagine him cooking me breakfast.

We spent hours sitting on the couch, just talking. We talked and talked as if time had stood still and nothing existed outside of my apartment. Though it was obvious both of us wanted more, to bridge the space between us and remove everything in our way, to unite again as we'd done in Mexico, we stayed true to his wishes and managed to resist.

I don't know who fell asleep first, but I was the first to wake up. My head rested on his chest, listening to his heart beating beneath the soft material of his shirt, feeling the rise and fall of his lungs as he dreamed.

Gently, I raised myself up and gazed at him, once again struck by his gorgeous features. Goddamn, he was perfect. I kissed his cheek lightly, my lips relishing the feel of his beard against my lips.

He awoke, eyes alighting upon my face, and smiled. "Hey beautiful."

I grinned. "Morning." He flexed against my thigh, apparently a morning person. I glanced down. "And good morning to you, too!"

He laughed, and then suddenly our lips were together.

An insatiable heat rose within my core. But, he had been adamant about not going any further than tea, and I didn't want him to do anything he was uncomfortable with. It took all of my willpower, but I managed to pry my lips away.

"Is this... okay? I mean, if we go further than kissing..." I asked, my heart pounding in anticipation.

Dev nodded, his expression equally eager. "We got to know each other, didn't we?"

All the blood rushed from my brain, leaving me speechless. My lips found his once more, yearning, pent up from the night of proximity. I pulled him to his feet and we maneuvered ourselves into the bedroom, where we began stripping the clothes off one another.

"Wait. Dev."

He paused mid-way pulling my pants down. "If the

condom back in Mexico was expired, chances are the ones in my drawer are, too."

"You didn't buy more?"

"I didn't want to be presumptuous." I smirked.

"Funny, I thought that was called 'being a responsible adult.'"

I slapped his chest. "Ha. Ha. Did you bring one?"

He shook his head. "This was your idea, remember?"

"Right. Well. If you're not seeing anyone else, and I'm not seeing anyone else, and you're comfortable with it, I have an IUD."

"Did you just ask if I wanted to be exclusive?"

My only response was to pull him in for another kiss. The rest of our clothes flew off and landed in disarray around the room. His lips went back to the places he'd found on those hot nights in Mexico, his tongue licking along the curves of my abdomen and further down. My body writhed beneath him until I could no longer take it, needing him, unlike anything I'd ever felt before.

I pulled his face back up to mine, and our bodies tangled up with one another with nothing between us and nothing to hide.

Seven

OVER THE NEXT SEVERAL WEEKS, Dev was over at my apartment almost every single night. We just couldn't get enough. When we weren't attacking one another like sexually frustrated rabbits, we were eating Oreos while catching each other up on our favourite things. He introduced me to OG Guy Ritchie, and I showed him Guillermo del Toro. He was the first season of Firefly to my Gilmore Girls, the Al Green to my Alt-J. Rarely did we wander out into the real world, save to scavenge for food at local restaurants.

As promised, Dev brought over the requisite spices to make masala chai (which I tried my best to pronounce properly). My apartment now held the lingering aroma of cinnamon, ginger, and cloves; making my scented candles unnecessary.

I was getting used to seeing his razor next to my bathroom sink, his pants draped over the chair in my bedroom, and his favourite cereal in the cupboard. I'd never had a roommate before, but this was pretty damn close.

Even Graham hadn't been this present in my apartment.

We'd spent most of our time at his place, which left mine as a personal retreat.

My love of it surprised me, as did how much I missed him when he had to go back home, and how much I relished the smell of him when I wore his left-behind t-shirt to laze around on the couch with.

A few months in and he headed into finals season at school. With exams to study for and final projects due, he went MIA for a while. I definitely understood the pressure of finals and projects, having been in those shoes a few years ago.

God, a few years ago, already. Had it been that long?

We made up for it with FaceTime calls with the occasional sexy striptease. He had yet to send me a dick pic, even though I'd explicitly asked for one. He said he wasn't the kind of guy to do that, and he didn't want that out there in the world. I'd laughed at the time, teasing him that only celebrities had their photos leaked, and I wasn't the kind of person to use that sort of thing for blackmail. Still, though, nothing. Memories had to suffice.

After his final exam, I invited him over for dinner to celebrate. I'd tried a few vegetarian recipes since we'd started dating and found some I liked and was excited to show him I was trying. On the menu: roasted acorn squash stuffed with quinoa, cucumber, and avocado salad, and cauliflower 'steaks.' I still liked meat, but tonight was about Dev and his accomplishments.

I even bought a bottle of sparkling juice.

With Vancouver's amazing craft beer scene and the world-renowned Okanagan valley just a few hours away I always had a six-pack of seasonal, local beer in the fridge and a few bottles of wine to choose from. I really didn't drink that much—one beer, or a glass of wine in the evening, no big deal. Around Dev, though, it made me feel a bit awkward to drink alone, him sipping on his chai. Never once had he commented on it, and I didn't ask if it bothered him because honestly, I wouldn't change my habits.

Okay, I *probably* wouldn't change my habits.

My home was spotless, there were fresh sheets on the bed, and the timing of the food was working out perfectly for six o'clock. I'd gotten waxed the previous day, exfoliated today, and even picked out some sexy lingerie, which I wore underneath my apron. The plan was to tease him throughout the entire dinner and see how long we could last. Finishing up the salad, my mind wandered to an imaginary scene of him bursting through the door, pushing everything off the table in one big romantic sweep, and taking me right there, unable to resist for even a moment, like in the movies.

The door buzzed, and I pressed the button to let him up.

A few minutes later, he entered without knocking. His eyes lit up when they met mine, and then we were kissing. A weighty sense of anticipation filled my abdomen as he pushed me against the cabinets.

He pulled his lips away but hovered, his thumb caressing my cheek.

"Hello," he said softly.

"Did you miss me?" I smiled.

"Not at all," he said, kissing me again.

A timer went off, and I escaped his embrace to take the squash out of the oven.

Dev held up a brown paper bag. "I got this for you," he said, pulling out a bottle of wine.

"Oh, you didn't have to do that! I got us some bubbles.

Congratulations, by the way!" I set the hot dish down on the stove and turned off the oven, examining the meal I'd concocted, wondering if it was enough.

He pulled two glasses down from the shelf and twisted the cap off the real wine, and poured me a glass, assuaging my fears that he had a problem with me drinking. I opened the non-alcoholic wine and poured him some, too. We clinked our glasses.

"This is delicious," I said, lifting the bottle from the counter. A smile stretched across my face. *Legacy Vineyards.* The label was highly intriguing and something I would have picked myself.

"Yeah, I wasn't sure what to get. This is a BC wine, though, and the guy at the store said it was really good."

"Aw, thank you." I kissed him again.

"Supper smells wonderful. What do we have here?" He put his hand on my back and then pulled it away. "Are you naked under there?"

I blushed and did a turn for him, revealing my near-nudity.

"Dessert comes after dinner," I chastised with a wink.

I served the food, and we sat down to eat. Dev was very complimentary, and I had to admit, it all tasted very good. It wasn't a filet mignon, but it would do.

"When do you get your final grades?" I asked.

"A few weeks. I'm not worried. Even if I failed these exams I'd still pass."

"What's next for you, then, Mr. Graduate?"

He pushed his salad around for a second and avoided eye contact while he spoke, his shoulders slumped. "On to work, I guess. My dad had been waiting for me to take over the business so he can take a step back. He's been working six days a week as long as I can remember."

"At the autobody shop?"

"There's a few of them I'd be helping run. Really, I didn't need to go to school for it, but I wanted to get a degree, and they were supportive, of course. Ever since I was a kid, I've been in the shops, detailing cars at first, but then he showed me how to write estimates, and I learned the basics of painting and everything else."

"Hmm. Sounds interesting."

He shrugged. "It is, I guess."

"Is that what you want?" I asked, sensing he had more to say.

Dev looked up from his food and sighed. "I really like school, you know? The atmosphere of it, the people. I got along well with my professors. I like the idea of continuing, maybe getting my MBA, but there's no point in it, and I'm needed at the business. My dad has only one son, and he wants to keep our family involved. Priya's not interested at all, so that leaves me."

I chewed slowly. "Have you talked to them about it? Getting your MBA?"

"No. I'd want to go to UBC. I've had my eye on their program for a while, but it's a long commute from Surrey."

"It's like a twenty-minute train ride from here, though. If you did want to go back to school, you could live here."

I hadn't even realized what I suggested. The words had simply flown out of my mouth. Dev and I both looked up at each other from across my dinky IKEA table.

Dev smiled and took a sip of his sparkling juice. "Did you just ask me to move in with you?"

My cheeks reddened. "Well, before your exams, you were here all the time anyway, and it would be convenient. I don't mean right away, but it would make sense."

"Do you need me to help with the rent or something?"

"What? God, no! That's not—I didn't mean that. Let's forget I said anything." I got up and began clearing the dishes. Standing at the sink, I remembered I was practically naked under my apron and turned to see him checking out my ass.

He grinned, apparently admiring the view.

I wasn't in the mood now, though, and regretted my choice of clothing. I turned back to the sink, face hot. A moment later, he was behind me, his arms wrapped around my torso, his lips on my neck.

"Trust me," he said quietly in my ear. "I couldn't imagine anything better than falling asleep next to you every night and waking up with you every morning."

I leaned into his embrace. "Surrey's a long way from here. It takes an hour drive, or longer with traffic. It's not fair to you to keep driving all this way, especially once you're working full time. And it would take me forever to get to you on transit." I closed my eyes and relished the sensation of his arms wrapped around me.

Gently, he turned me around to face him, tucking a strand of loose hair behind my ear. His eyes still made me melt.

"I'm not going to pretend that what you're saying doesn't make sense. It does. But I'm not sure if moving in together is the next logical step, you know? Meeting each other's parents generally comes before that, maybe a vacation together."

"We were already in Mexico earlier this year, so that leaves meeting the parents."

Dev looked uncertain. Then a mischievous smile brightened his face, and he reached around me to untie my apron. He lifted the strap over my head, revealing a red and black corset with ruffled black underwear, complete with a garter belt and stockings (which had taken forever to put on).

He took a step back, eyes widening. "Part of me wants to push all the stuff off the table like they do in the movies. But the rest of me doesn't want to deal with the mess," he said, fingers trailing down my chest.

I laughed. *Great minds.* "Couch?"

Lingerie is a good idea until it's time to take it off. Once Dev was finished thoroughly enjoying my little gift to him, he helped pull it off, which would have probably gotten a million views on a comedy YouTube channel.

AFTER WE HAD fun without the lingerie, we left the dishes for later and settled down, surfing Netflix, our glasses topped off with our respective drinks of choice.

Dev had changed into some grey sweatpants I'd gotten him as a gift to wear around my apartment. Really, I'd gotten them for me because his package looked amazing in them. I was wearing yoga pants and an old, faded tank-top, happy we were into a more comfortable phase in our relationship where we could wear chill clothes, and I didn't have to be done up all the time.

One of the suggested titles popped up as *Meet the Parents*. Obviously, I selected it, a coy smile flashing over to Dev, who nudged me back with a smirk.

A week after our celebratory dinner, I still hadn't received an invitation to Dev's family home.

On Friday night, I was out with Angelina at one of my favourite places. Tucked in along the wet cobblestone streets of Gastown, near the corner of Water Street and Cordova, we sat in a dimly-lit basement bar set up to look like the inside of an old pirate ship. The aesthetic was on point, with long butcher-block tables, black metal and leather stools, and lights on the wall reminiscent of portholes. There were all sorts of gems like this throughout the city, but the ambiance here always kept me coming back.

Ever since the wedding, Angelina and I had kept in contact, our friendship something I'd never expected. When Miranda and I were teens, Angelina had been the annoying kid sister, always bursting into her room and wanting to be included, followed by us shooing her out and complaining to Miranda's mom that she wouldn't leave us alone. We had more important things to do than hang out with a kid, like doing Cosmo quizzes and putting makeup on each other while eating Nibs and ketchup chips.

Angelina as an adult, though, was awesome. She feared nothing, including other people's opinions, and she gave her own quite readily and without a filter.

"Maybe he's ashamed of you," she said, sipping her Granville Island lager.

I nearly spat out my drink. "Ashamed of me? Why would he be ashamed of me? I have two engineering degrees, for Christ's sake!"

Angelina laughed. "No, about you being white. My friend Suri is Indian, and she said she *has* to marry an Indian guy. I guess her family knows other families and all the eligible boys her age, and she'll pretty much be set up on dates with whoever they approve of."

"Like an arranged marriage?"

She paused. "No, it's not arranged. She has a say in who she marries, she can marry whoever she wants, but they have to be vetted by her family, I guess."

My stomach knotted as my mind immediately went to Dev's ex.

Angelina continued. "And my Chinese friend Julie, her mom told her she *has* to marry a Chinese guy. *Definitely* no Japanese guys."

"But this is Canada!" I said, a little too loud.

"So? You still want your kids to be married to someone who has the same values as you, right? I mean, how can they be sure you can make Dev happy long term, or raise kids with him if you have no idea what it's like being Indian? I mean, have you even eaten any Indian food aside from samosas and butter chicken?"

My face went warm. "Yes!"

She waited, one eyebrow raised and a smirk on her face.

"I like naan bread, too!" I hid my smile in my glass.

"But seriously," she continued, "it's not really much different for white people. Your parents are Catholic, right?"

"Not practicing."

"What would they think if you brought a Muslim guy home?"

She had a fair point, though I wanted to deny it. As much as I wanted to believe that in Canada we all held hands and sang Kumbaya, there were still prejudices, racism, and stereotypes abound, especially amongst people from typically rival religions.

"Dev's Sikh, though, and I'm not really sure if he practices. We don't talk about religion."

"Does he know you're an atheist?"

"I haven't mentioned it."

"Have you asked him if his religion is important to him?"

"It hasn't come up."

·She was exasperated. "What do you guys even talk about, then?"

I took a long sip of my Moscow mule. "We're busy doing... other things."

Angelina laughed. "You horn dog."

I sighed, my smile fading. "Maybe I should take the first step, bring him home to meet my family. If I take the lead and show him I'm serious, maybe that will make him more comfortable introducing me to his own family. I mean, I'm sure if they meet me, it will be fine. Right?"

She shrugged. "That could work."

"He'll meet my family first, ease into it, you know. How could they not love him? My dad will be fine. My mom can be... difficult sometimes," I said, unsure if Angelina had ever met my mom.

"Trust me. I know all about difficult moms."

"I'm sorry, I've been talking about myself this whole time. How are you? How're the applications going?" I asked, flagging down the tall, buff, extensively tattooed bartender and pointing at our near-empty glasses.

"I've been accepted."

"That's great! Congratulations! Which program? Here at UBC?"

She nodded but with much less enthusiasm than I expected.

"You don't seem thrilled. I thought this was what you wanted," I said.

Angelina picked at her soggy coaster and shrugged. "I'm not sure if being a dental hygienist is what I want to do for the rest of my life. What if it gets boring?"

"It doesn't matter what you do. Everything gets boring from time to time."

"You're an engineer. How could your job be boring?"

"Well, okay, *technically,* I'm not an engineer. I didn't pass my final exam..." I trail off, my cheeks growing hot. "But maybe someday I will. I love my job, but even then, it does get boring from time to time." That was an understatement. I hadn't felt challenged in my job in years. I failed the final exam not once, but twice. Re-taking it was pretty low on my list of priorities, even if it would open some doors for me.

"Well, I'm glad you've found something that makes you happy," Angelina said. "All I want to do, really, is travel. I want to see the world. But that takes money, and at least I'd be making a lot of it." The bartender set down our fresh drinks and removed our empty glasses, nudging at the menu before us. Angelina picked it up and eyed it half-heartedly.

"True enough," I agreed. "I spent the first half of my twenties travelling. You won't regret it. And you can totally do something else down the road, you know? It's not like you're married to your career."

"Not like with a person," Angelina said, nudging me under the table.

"Oh, please! We've been together like, what, four months?" I blushed.

"You've probably already thought about marrying him, and about what your kids will look like, and what you'll name them, and about your Goldendoodle named Sparky, and your white picket fence," she teased.

"Sparky? Really? That's the best name you could come up with for my imaginary dog?" I laughed.

"It was spur of the moment. What can I say?" She glanced over the menu. "Want some hot wings?"

"Naw. I can't do spicy food."

"How about nachos?"

"Hell yeah!"

But even the giant plate of nachos we devoured couldn't

distract me from the truths she'd uncovered in our conversation. She was right, of course, the wise nineteen-year-old that she is. I *had* imagined it all already.

And now, it could be banking completely on whether or not his family would approve of me.

Eight

BEFORE MEETING each other's parents, Dev and I decided to test the waters and introduce me to his friends. The perfect opportunity arose on his twenty-fifth birthday.

Damn. Twenty-five. He was so much younger than me.

I'd learned about our age difference back in Mexico. I told myself it didn't bother me, and if our genders were reversed nobody would bat an eye, but a lifetime of social conditioning for women to seek older men and men to seek younger women was difficult to suppress. Our age difference didn't bother me day-to-day. Hell, he was more mature than most thirty-year-old men I'd met.

Around others, though, the nagging worry of being judged wormed its way into my stomach.

I checked my reflection in the selfie mode of my phone for the hundredth time as the Skytrain jostled its way east towards Surrey, riding to the end of the line. Despite Dev not being a drinker, I was meeting him and his friends at a pub. It was Friday night, and I was looking forward to having a drink or two. Yoga and my runs around the seawall can usually fuel me to get through the monotony of my week, my day job dragging by, but by Friday, I'm in need of something a little stronger.

At the last Skytrain station, I descended to see Dev waiting for me. A smile lit up his face, vanquishing any jitters I had about meeting his friends. We wrapped our arms around one another, and he kissed my forehead.

"Happy birthday," I grinned, lifting up on my toes to smooch his lips.

The rear window of Dev's car rolled down.

"ooOOOoooh!" someone catcalled.

I looked over, blushing, not having noticed his car parked right there and two guys grinning from the back seat.

Dev shook his head at them, then took my hand and led me to the passenger side of the car. Always the gentleman, he opened the car door for me.

"Becky, this is Sanjay and Ravi. Guys, Becky." I greeted them politely as I buckled my seatbelt. The two in the back seat continued their previous conversation as Dev navigated to the pub. Something about... Stonks? Tendies? I couldn't follow the conversation at all, though I wasn't sure if it was because of the age gap, our opposing genders, or our different cultures. Instead, I let Dev's confident hand ground me as he moved from shifting gears to my thigh.

We wound our way through the busy weekend traffic to the pub. The dimly lit building smelled of deep-fried food and stale beer. The music blared, its heavy bass making it difficult to think properly. A whole crew of people shouted boisterously at our arrival. Holy hell, he had a lot of friends. It didn't surprise me, but still.

Dev released me, giving half-hugs and hand slaps to a huge group of young guys and a few girls.

As he introduced me, I couldn't help but feel out of place.

Everyone was so... young! Not only his friends but everyone else in the building. This pub must be close to the University because almost everyone looked like they'd just turned nineteen and were eagerly using their real IDs instead of their fake ones.

On top of that, I was probably one of only like three white people in the whole building. It wasn't often I found myself in the situation of feeling like a minority, even though the Greater Vancouver Area boasted a beautiful tapestry of people from all over the world. I took a deep breath and embraced the feeling, though. Dev probably felt like this whenever he left the city limits of Surrey. I wondered if he still faced discrimination based on the colour of his skin or his religion.

We sat amongst the crowd at a sticky, bar-height table already littered with half-empty glasses and plates of mostly eaten food. The servers must have been overwhelmed because it took forever for us to get a drink.

Dev was busy talking to people he hadn't seen since classes ended, so I turned my attention to a group of young women before me.

"How'd you and Dev meet?" a girl asked after introducing herself as Neetu. Three or four other girls halted their conversations and turned to me with assessing eyes.

I leaned in and shouted over the music, going over the story about the plane and Miranda's wedding up to now.

"Moe told me Dev met a stranger in Mexico." She wagged her eyebrows at me, a grin on her face.

"Yeah, I was that stranger." The girls exchanged glances.

"You're the reason he's always driving into the city, then?" Neetu asked.

"I live in Vancouver, yeah." I smiled despite the uneasy tension in my stomach, recalling the conversation I'd had with

Dev the first night he'd stayed over at my apartment about keeping premarital activities quiet.

The girls' gazes seemed judgmental, with cocked eyebrows, but they continued to be polite and made small talk. I tried my best to keep conversations flowing, but it was challenging. My throat hurt from shouting over the loud music, so I gave up, letting the girls return to their own conversation.

I sipped my vodka cranberry and tried to suppress the migraine forming in my frontal lobe. From afar, I watched Dev as he interacted with his friends, his charismatic smile lighting up the room.

Sanjay and Ravi returned from the bar carrying a flight of shots and set one in front of each of the girls, myself included. We clinked our glasses and drained them. I was pleasantly surprised it was whiskey, not tequila. The other girls coughed and gagged, but I, an expert whisky drinker, drained it without making so much as a face.

I licked my lips. "Crown Royal?"

The boys raised their eyebrows, impressed. I smiled. "Next round on me?"

We probably had like, three or four more rounds. It all started blurring together. I'd been having so much fun drinking with the guys that I'd lost track of time. Dev interrupted Sanjay and Ravi's argument about their stock trading schemes, me nodding along dumbly, and decided it was time for all of us to go home.

Quite intoxicated, I had to agree. After paying our tabs, we all headed outside. The crisp night air and cool rain were refreshing, sobering me up a bit. The boys took turns hugging me and slapping Dev on the back, telling him I'm a 'keeper,' before climbing into a cab. After ensuring the cab driver knew the correct address, Dev led me to his car.

"Whew," I said, fumbling with my seatbelt. "Did you have a fun birthday?"

"Yeah, it was good." He started the car up and headed back towards Vancouver.

"Good? Only good?"

He shrugged noncommittally.

"Well then, I guess it's time for your birthday present."

He glanced towards me, trying to keep his eyes on the road. "What would that be?"

I grinned devilishly and tugged on my seatbelt to give me some room to maneuver. Leaning over the gearshift, I pawed at the buttons on his pants, relieved they weren't the smart-girl ones with the three buttons. I was too drunk for that.

"What are you—" He tried to interject, but I was quick.

Before he could protest, my mouth was on him.

He gasped in both surprise and pleasure as my tongue and lips worked their magic.

It had been a week since we'd seen each other last, so he finished unwrapping his birthday gift quickly— which was good because having my head down in a moving vehicle was making me dizzy.

I grinned and sat back in my seat, wiping my mouth. "So *now,* how was your birthday?"

Dev chuckled, doing his pants back up with one hand, and flashed a grin in my direction. "Perfect."

Nine

I MUST HAVE PASSED some test because after Dev's birthday it didn't take much convincing to get him to meet my family.

He'd never been to the island before, so we took advantage of the next long weekend to check it out. We stood outside on the front deck of the ferry in our heavy coats even though it was spring, holding cups of hot tea and hoping for a whale sighting.

"Wait, you don't get motion sickness from boats, too, do you?" I asked, stepping away, only half-joking.

He laughed and shook his head. "I promise it was the tequila that did me in."

I stepped back beside him and rested my head against his shoulder. "Are you nervous?"

"A little," he admitted.

"You've never done the whole 'meet the parents' thing before, eh?" I asked, recalling his very limited dating history.

He shook his head. "My plan is to do the exact opposite of what Ben Stiller did in that movie."

I grinned. "Good plan."

"Is there anything I should know about your family?" He looked down at me, his brow-furrow betraying some mild discomfort.

"My brother can be an asshole, but he won't be there. Just my mom and dad."

"Your mom Karen, your dad Steve."

"Right, good memory." I commended, trying to remember the names of his parents and failing. I'd have to find a way for him to mention them before we went to his house, which he still hadn't offered to do. Hopefully, this weekend would change things.

"Have you told your parents much about me?" he asked, staring out across the water, the wind whipping at his jacket.

"Of course! I didn't tell them you threw up on the plane, but I did tell them everything else. They know you're a vegetarian, and you don't drink, so I'm not sure what my mom's going to try to cook for dinner. They're a 'meat and potatoes' kind of people."

"I'm sure it will be great." He smiled, though I could still sense his uncertainty. We watched the waves for a long moment, the noise of the motor and wind filling in the gap of our conversation.

"What about you?" I asked, sipping my peppermint tea. "Do your parents know about me?"

When he didn't answer right away, a knot of anxiety formed in my stomach. "You've told your parents about me, right?"

He answered hastily. "Of course! Of course. Rebecca, I'm at your place almost every night and sleeping over most of them. They'd be terrible parents if they didn't care where their son always was. They're excited to meet you."

A smile came to my face. This was the first he'd brought up

meeting his family. Perhaps my plan of taking the lead was working, after all. The ferry landed at the terminal and we went below deck to prepare to disembark. The atmosphere in the car was a little tense, though if it was from Dev or me, I couldn't be sure.

Spring had come early to Victoria, and everything was lush and green with dazzling displays of flowers. We drove through the city centre past heritage stone buildings, down narrow streets, and then finally to View Royal, where my parents lived. They had retired and moved into my Grandma's house after she passed away, which was eight years ago now. I still missed my Nana, with her ginger-snap cookies and strawberry-rhubarb pie. I had spent most summers here with her when I was young, where the freedom of the island was incomparable to the stifling Vancouver city where I spent the rest of my time. I had many summer friends I still kept in contact with through social media.

As we drove down the familiar streets, ghosts of my childhood played around every corner, sitting with the neighbourhood kids on electrical boxes and gossiping, walking to the store for a Slurpee, and playing grounders on the playground 'til it was past dark.

The twenty-minute drive was too quick and passed in silence save for my directions. The narrow road wound past various private residences and ended with us pulling into a driveway of an open-beam log house with cedar shingles. He parked.

Neither of us got out of the car, both staring at the house through the windshield.

I reached over and took his hand. He gave it a squeeze and then offered a reassuring smile. I should have been the one reassuring him, not the other way around, but his calm demeanour soothed my nerves.

"Are you ready?" he asked.

Was *I* ready? I looked into his warm brown eyes, admired his perfect smile, and relished in his extraordinary sense of peace that washed over me when I needed it most.

Hell yeah, I was ready.

We left the bags in the car and headed up to the side door, which was already open and waiting. My mom rushed out and embraced me in a hug, her box blonde pixie cut hair sprayed to the point of crunching where it pressed against the side of my face.

"Oh, Becky! It's been so long! It takes you bringing a boy home to come visit your mama, does it?"

"Hi, Mom." I gasped, the air being squeezed out of my lungs.

She released me and turned her attention to Dev. "Oh, Becky, he's so *handsome!*" she gushed and then ignored his extended hand and went in for a hug, too.

I mouthed *'sorry'* at Dev while he patted my mom on the back.

"Come in, come in!" she said, releasing her hug only to grab him by the hand and pull him inside. I followed close behind, second-guessing if this was a good idea.

The side door entered into the kitchen, which hadn't been updated since the seventies. It looked just as it had in my childhood: plain white cabinets with white laminate countertops, faded yellow linoleum floor, white appliances, and a fridge absolutely covered in tacky magnets and old photos. Even though Nana had passed away, they hadn't renovated; my mom was adamant about keeping it the exact same, as if it could preserve her memory within the space.

I sniffed the air. "What are you cooking, mom?"

"Oh, your dad's favourite! Hawaiian chicken with rice," she said, rushing over to the crockpot to peek inside.

My stomach dropped. "Mom, I told you Dev's a vegetarian!"

She turned on the spot. "No, you didn't! I'd remember something like that!"

"It's fine," Dev started to say.

"I called you last week, remember?"

"You did call me last week, but you didn't mention the vegetarian thing. I'm sorry, Dave. At least you can eat the rice."

I face-palmed.

"Rice is delicious, Karen. Thank you. I'll go get the bags," he said before escaping back outside. I couldn't blame him. I wanted to run away, too.

I closed the space between my mom and me as she got to work chopping carrots. "Mom, his name is Dev."

"Oh! Short for Devon?"

"No, Mom, it's not Devon or Dave or... whatever. It's Dev. Please, try to be nice."

"Becky, I'm always nice."

I tried not to roll my eyes. Coming here had been a mistake. Poor Dev was probably working on an excuse to leave as soon as possible. "Where's Dad?" I asked, suddenly realizing he wasn't there.

"Down by the dock. Can you take him another beer? Grab one for Dev, too."

"He doesn't drink, which I also told you on the phone last week."

"If you say so, Becky." *Chop, chop, chop.*

I left mom to her vegetables, forgetting the beer, panic starting to rise in my chest. Outside, Dev was texting on his phone. The trunk was popped open, but the bags were still inside.

This was it: the excuse of something awful happening and him having to leave right away. I'd go with it, honestly. I approached, hesitant.

"Hey, I'm sorry. I promise I told her you're a vegetarian. And I don't know why she keeps getting your name wrong. If you want to leave, I totally get it. You don't have to make an excuse. We can just pack up and go home."

Dev slid his phone back into his pocket and embraced me in a hug with a light chuckle. "Rebecca, it's fine. Your mom seems nice. And this place, it's beautiful. I can't believe you got to grow up here."

I rested my chin on his chest and wrapped my arms around his waist, relaxing with his touch. Of course, he wouldn't take anything personally. Though, if I were in his shoes, I definitely would have had a different response. A smile met my lips and the excitement returned; the weekend activities I'd planned were back on the agenda.

"Thank you for being so great about everything," I said and then reached up on my toes to kiss him lightly.

"Hey, Squirt!" said a familiar voice said from behind us.

Dev separated from me, and we turned to see my dad approach. He was middle-aged and balding, his faded t-shirt was tucked into high-waisted shorts, and white socks protruded from his sandals. I cringed inwardly at his atrocious sense of style, hoping Dev wouldn't judge him by his over-the-top 'DAD' attire.

"Hi, Dad! This is my boyfriend, Dev." I hoped reiterating his name would reduce the possibility of him getting it wrong.

"Hello, sir," Dev said, reaching out his hand. "Steve! Call me Steve." My dad shook his hand enthusiastically, his other holding an empty Coors Light bottle. "Is this an M-3?" he asked, turning his attention to the car.

"Yeah, it is," Dev replied.

My dad whistled and stepped to the side, appreciating it. "Turbo? Straight six?"

"Good eye, yeah. You a car guy?" Dev tucked his hands into his pockets and stepped up beside my dad to appreciate the white sedan.

I took the bags and left the boys to talk cars, glad they had a common interest. Maybe it wouldn't be so bad. I'd order us a pizza later so he could eat something more than rice.

Instead of heading inside, I walked to the separate garage that had been converted to a suite. The wooden, moss-covered shingles gave it an earthy, almost hobbit-like vibe. Inside it was just as quaint. There was a vintage armoire in the corner, a beige and green patchwork quilt on the bed, and a mini-fridge and coffee machine next to the tiny bathroom with a stall shower.

The slight musty smell transported me back in time to slumber parties, scary movies, and, of course, boys. I'd lost my virginity in this room. Dev didn't need to know that. I left our bags on the bed, used the washroom, freshened up, and headed back outside to see Dev and my dad making their way down to the dock, each holding a beer bottle in hand.

Knowing he was too polite to turn down such an offer, I sighed and wondered which parent had handed him the bottle. My guess would be my mom. She's not the kind of person to take no for an answer. As overbearing as she was, she meant well. I left the two men to get to know one another and headed back inside to chat with her. Waiting for me was an open bottle of wine and two full glasses.

"Welcome home, darling," she said as we took up our glasses and clinked them together. "Scrabble?"

Wine in hand, we entered the living room, where the board was all set up and ready. The sun streamed in through floor-to-ceiling windows, illuminating the burgundy sectional and emerald green carpet. I sighed, wondering when they'd finally tear the old carpet out and reveal the perfect hardwood underneath like on all those HGTV shows my mom watched religiously.

"Well, darling, he sure is handsome! You met him down in Mexico. Is he from there?" she asked, grabbing her letters.

"No, he's Canadian. His family was from India originally," I said and then explained to her that his family has resided within Canada a lot longer than ours had. She found that interesting, laying the first word down as I eyed my strange assembly of vowels. Three 'I's. Not off to a good start.

"As long as he treats you well, that's all that matters to us. It sure was nice of him to go with you to Miranda's wedding. How's work?"

I caught her up on all the boring details of my job and could feel her eyes glazing over as I did so. Halfway through our game (which I was losing), the timer went off, and mom got up to finish dinner. I wandered outside to alert the guys.

Outside, the fresh air blew in off the water. I inhaled deeply, the smell of forest and saltwater a combination no candle could ever compare to. Though I descended the stairs as quietly as possible, I wasn't able to catch what my dad and Dev were talking about. The pair stood on the dock as the sunset, an orange glow illuminating the sparse cloud cover and gentle fog that had begun to roll in.

My heart leapt in my chest, and a smile rose to my face

upon seeing Dev there with my dad, both so relaxed and engaged.

"Hey, boys!" I said. The two turned to look at me, both of their faces alight with a similar expression. "Dinner's ready."

"Thanks, Sweetheart! Come down here for a second, let me get a picture of you two while the light is good," my dad said, setting his beer bottle down on the dock and unclipping his phone from his belt.

Dev set down his beer, still nearly full. I grabbed him by the hand and pulled him toward the railing. He released my hand and took a step back before turning to look at my Dad and the camera.

"Scooch a little closer, guys!" Dad encouraged. Grinning, I grabbed Dev by the waist and stepped up close, our chests touching. He looked down at me, surprised at first, but then he relaxed into a smile. His hand settled tentatively on my mid-back, thumb caressing in slow circles. The setting sun highlighted his gorgeous eyes and rich brown skin, the breeze tousling his black hair. Our eyes connected, and I was lost. For a moment, the world stood still, as if we were the only souls inhabiting it.

If I could bottle a moment, keep it forever, pour out a little bit at a time and taste it for the rest of my life, this would be one of them.

"Got it!" Dad announced, breaking the spell. "I'll meet you two up there," he said, leaving us alone on the dock. What a brilliant man.

We turned and faced the water. The forest on the other side of the harbour began to disappear behind a layer of fog. Coal Island stood in the middle of the water, peaceful and untouched. A flock of geese took off and flew past, calling out to one another. Seemingly more comfortable now that we were alone, Dev wrapped his arms around me from behind and nuzzled his face into my hair. I held onto his hands, my body aching for more of his touch but resigning myself to wait.

"Have a good chat with my dad?" I asked.

"He's a great guy," he said, softly kissing my neck.

I smiled. "Glad you think so. He's not usually that talkative. You have a gift with people."

"That's nice of you to say."

I turned around and rested my arms on his chest, looking deep into his eyes. "I'm serious." I smiled. "I've never met anyone like you before. I'm so lucky."

He closed his eyes and kissed me. Our lips moved as one, soft, gentle as if they had all the time in the world and planned to take it. He pulled his lips away but rested his forehead against mine, his thumb tracing the edge of my jaw.

"I'm the lucky one."

We withdrew from our little moment of paradise and made our way back up to the house. Dinner was served, and Dev took a small piece of pineapple-flavoured chicken to be polite even though I told him it wasn't necessary. He was very complimentary about everything, which made my mom blush (I got my blushing genes from her). As always, conversation flowed naturally as my parents got to know him. I sat there, mostly quiet, watching my parents as they interacted with Dev, how he answered their questions and returned many of his own.

"I got dishes tonight, honey," Dad announced, standing. "Want to help me, Squirt?"

I nodded. Dad kissed my mom on the cheek, and the two of us began clearing the table while my mom escorted Dev to the living room. I wasn't totally comfortable leaving him with her unsupervised; I tried to pick up pieces of their conversation in case I needed to interject and change the subject.

Judging by the laughter on both my mom's and Dev's account, I didn't have to worry. Whatever those two were talking about, it was obvious they were having a great time. Dad and I stood next to each other at the sink in relative silence, enjoying each other's company without needing to talk. My dad was a quiet guy like that.

Everything was going great. Why had I been worried? My parents were both good people, and Dev had the incredible ability to make any possibly awkward situation feel totally and completely relaxed.

Once the dishes were finished, my dad served Nanaimo bars for dessert. I helped him carry the little squares out to the living room, only to find that my mom had fished out the family photo albums. That was what they'd been carrying on about! It was too late now; they were already into my elementary school years. I had not been an attractive child. If Dev had ever considered making babies with me, surely this would dissuade him.

Dev sat between my mom and I as she flipped through laminate pages of a geeky girl with short-cropped bangs and braces, wearing a teal and pink windbreaker and pig-tail braids. It was the 90's. We didn't know any better.

Teenage Rebecca wasn't much of an improvement. There were pictures of Miranda and me riding bikes, down on the water in kayaks, and standing together with cheesy grins at the school dance. I took a few shots on my phone and texted them to her.

"Oh hey, look at that!" I said, tapping a picture. It was me at the science fair. It still stung that I'd lost to Aaron Weiner, of all people. "My eavestrough water turbine. Too bad it didn't work. I'd have won first place, for sure."

"What is it?" Dev inquired, leaning in to get a better look.

"It's like a little hydro dam. You replace the downspouts on your eavestroughs on your house and when the water runs through it the little turbines inside turn, generating electricity. We get so much rain here that solar panels don't work as effectively, but I figured we could take advantage of all the rain and take houses off-grid."

Dev raised his eyebrows. "Sounds impressive."

Dad looked thoughtful. "I think I still have it somewhere."

"Do you think you could make it work now?" Dev asked.

I shook my head. "I'm not an electrical engineer."

"Pshh," Dad interjected. "You never let that stop you then!"

"Maybe your brother could help!" Mom piped up.

I gritted my teeth and turned the page. My brother had teased me relentlessly for losing at the fair. He was the last person I'd turn to for help. I had been the first to declare to my parents that I would be an engineer when I grew up.

Later, my brother decided that he was going to do the same thing. It stung that he'd gone out in front of me and forged the path, with better grades and a better degree. He'd passed the same test I failed twice, and he did it with a hangover. It was hard to remain excited about something when my brother cast such a huge shadow.

The photos continued. After many a laugh shared (mostly at my expense), one bottle of wine down, and four and a half beers drank (four by my dad), it was finally late enough for us to excuse ourselves to the suite.

Hand-in-hand, we stole away into the darkness across the cobblestone patio and into our little hobbit escape.

"This place is cute," Dev said, removing his shoes while I lit a few candles.

"Yeah, I love it. Miranda would come to the island with me

in the summer sometimes. We'd have sleepovers out here."

Before I could finish lighting them all, he had his arms around me. He brushed the hair away from my neck and kissed from my earlobe down to my collarbone. I set the candle back on the table, safety first, and then turned in his arms to meet my lips with his.

A little overeager, I pushed against him, and his legs hit the bed. He fell backwards with me landing on top, and we shared a giggle before the kissing continued.

I lifted off of him a moment so he could slide further onto the bed, removing my shirt and bra in the process. Then I crawled up and straddled him, our lips meeting. In between short gasps for air, I managed to pull his shirt off. My fingers trailed his chest hair down to his belt buckle, which I unclasped without effort. By touch, I recognized the pants he was wearing, the pair with the three buttons. I nibbled his bottom lip and undid each one, a professional by now.

With one strong, swift movement, he flipped me over and kissed down my neck. His hands massaged my breasts, and I arched my back towards him. His lips and tongue found their way to my abdomen, and I gripped the bed, biting my bottom lip to keep from moaning prematurely, him all-too-familiar with my erogenous zones.

Finally, he tugged off my pants and underwear, spreading my legs apart as he kneeled by the edge of the bed, his beard tickling the insides of my thighs as his mouth worked its magic on my most sensitive areas.

I writhed, one hand gripping his hair and the other the bedspread. He doubled down, and I came, black spots swimming in my vision. He let off, thankfully, and I pulled him up towards me. He wiped off his beard, a grin on his face, and then lay next to me while I recovered.

A few moments later, we were kissing again, this time with less urgency. I reached down and took him in my hand, feeling him hard and ready. Pushing him over onto his back, I made my way down towards his cock, an alluring grin on my face. I loved the way he looked at me, his eyes wide and somehow astonished by what was about to occur, even though it had happened many, many times.

I teased him with my tongue, listening to his breath hitch, and then took in as much of him as I could. Some women don't enjoy oral, but I did. It made me feel incredibly powerful, like a goddess, able to give so much pleasure with an act that is so simple.

After a few minutes, he was getting close, so I moved on top and let myself sink down onto him slowly, gasping as I did, feeling myself squeeze around him in response. For a moment, I allowed my body to relax and then closed my eyes and began rotating my hips. Slow, methodical at first, but before long, I was arched over his body, his hands gripping my waist, and our movements grew in speed and intensity, both of us climaxing at the same moment, his breath hot on my neck. I collapsed on top of him as he finished pulsing inside me. He wrapped his arms around my body in a tight hug, like he didn't want to let me go.

Then, he whispered in my ear, so soft, so gentle, barely audible over the beating of my own heart.

"I love you."

A mist of tears sprang to my eyes. My lips found his again, and he rolled over on top of me, the weight of his body nearly sending me to climax once more. I managed to pull away for a moment and look at him.

"I love you, too."

Ten

I WISH we could have spent the day lazily in bed, but my mom woke us up bright and early by knocking on the door.

"Hot coffee and fresh croissants!" she announced.

"Be there in a minute!" I shouted, groggy, then rolled onto my side and rested my head on Dev's chest. He stretched and groaned before checking his phone for the time. Nine fifteen. So, not that early, I guess. It was actually late for my mom. The two of us got dressed into our family-appropriate pyjamas and exited the little cottage into the crisp morning air, the sound of geese out on the harbour greeting us. Inside the house was fragrant with fresh baking, coffee, and... bacon?!

"Mom! Are you making bacon for breakfast?"

She stood over the stove, the sound of popping and crackling betraying her. "Dev doesn't have to eat it."

I looked up to Dev and mouthed 'Sorry' to which he shrugged and went for the coffee. He handed me a cup first, and I added a generous pouring of Baileys.

"Want to sit outside?" I asked, worried that the smell of meat cooking offended him.

He nodded. I grabbed a throw from the couch and a plate where I piled up three croissants before heading down to the dock.

We sat together in silence for a while, like two old people, drinking coffee and eating breakfast. Did I want bacon? Of course, but not enough to make Dev uncomfortable.

"What's the plan for today?" he asked. I wondered if he was really asking how much longer he had to stay here.

I licked the flaky crumbs from my fingertips. "Nothing we have to rush for. I thought we'd explore downtown a bit, maybe grab some lunch. Our ferry is at eight, so that gives us lots of time for supper with the folks. You must be starving; I don't think you ate much last night, and now apparently, we only have croissants for you. Want to shower and leave sooner rather than later? Hit up a cafe or something?"

He smiled. "Sounds great. Are your parents coming?"

I shook my head. "God, no. I think two evenings with them is enough."

Dev laughed and reached for my hand. "Are you always like this with your parents?"

"What do you mean?"

He shrugged, taking a moment to choose his words. "You don't seem excited to spend time with them, is all. If I only got to see my parents a few times a year, I'd want to spend time with them. You don't have to worry about entertaining me. We can stay here if you want to."

"No, that's not it," I said, tucking my feet underneath me. "I guess I'm nervous having you around them too long."

His brow furrowed adorably. "Why?"

I sighed, looking out over the harbour, my anxiety rising at my lame attempt to express my emotions. "When it's just the two of us, it's so perfect. I don't want anything to ruin it."

He reached out and took my chin in his hand, gently directing my gaze back to his. "Hey. I don't like you. I love you, remember? And your family is part of who you are, which means I'll love them, too. And if you think your family is weird —" He shook his head and exhaled sharply.

I kissed him, tasting coffee. "I'm sure your family is great. If I ever get to meet them, that is."

He smiled. "How about next weekend, then?"

I kissed him again, lingering, my heart soaring. My plan had worked!

After cleaning up in the tiny, cramped little closet that passed as a shower in our suite, Dev and I packed up and said goodbye to my parents, agreeing to meet up for dinner later.

As we finished loading the car, my dad jogged up to us. "Wait a second, Squirt! Look what I found." He was carrying the downspout water turbine I'd built in high school. It looked the same as it had back then, kept in pristine condition. I was flattered he still had it after all these years.

Dev took it from him and turned it over in his hands, clearly interested.

"There are hinges on it, so you can see the inside mechanisms." Dad indicated.

Dev pried the thing open to see a neat line of little turbines.

"This is so cool," he said. I shifted uncomfortably back and forth, uncertain if he was being honest or polite.

"Thanks, Dad," I said, taking it from Dev and setting it in the trunk amongst our baggage.

I hugged Dad and then climbed into the car, my stomach rumbling for more than light, fluffy pastry. With my direction, we made our way to downtown Victoria and parked.

It was a gorgeous day, the weather was warming up, and people were out in droves. We waited in line at a cafe for several minutes before taking a seat. Dev and I ordered giant plates of waffles and fruit, chai tea for him, and a vanilla bean latte for me, and played footsies under the table as we chatted about everything and nothing at all.

Stomachs full, we walked out into the sunshine to explore. One of my absolute favourite places in the world is Fan Tan Alley— it's like if the magic of Diagon Alley and Chinatown had a baby. There are tiny, twisting walkways and pass-throughs, little shops with intricate wooden signs hanging above bright red doorways, and address signs written as fractions. We popped in and out of the shops, both of us equally excited about the treasures they held, as we had nothing but time on our hands. After Chinatown, we meandered down the streets, greeted on either side by old red brick buildings and a slight breeze off the inlet.

Afterwards, we jumped back into Dev's car and went to Craigdarroch Castle, another landmark everyone should visit their first time to Victoria. It was getting closer to five, so I dialled my mom to see what the plan was for dinner, hoping and praying she'd figured out something that didn't involve meat.

"Hey, sweetheart!" Mom said on the other line. "Are you two hungry? I made a reservation at this Indian place. I have a coupon!"

I hesitated, looking up to Dev. Never once had my parents ever suggested going out for Indian food. They were doing this on Dev's behalf. Inwardly I was cringing.

Dev nodded, and I replied that it would be fine. Mom was adamant about relaying the address to me despite my explaining that we could Google the location. I rolled my eyes, smiling at Dev as I pretended to take down her instructions.

Once we got into the car, I couldn't stop myself from

fidgeting. The more time we spent with my parents, the greater the likelihood of them doing or saying something embarrassing. We'd had a good visit so far. Short and sweet, the way I liked it. Why chance ruining it with more time together? I was working up the courage to cancel, to pretend I wasn't feeling well. Picking up on my anxiety, Dev wordlessly reached over and placed his hand on my thigh, giving it a squeeze.

I exhaled, trying to relax.

This was Dev we were talking about, the king of making any possible uncomfortable situation feel perfectly at ease and natural. The man had a gift. I found myself smiling as we pulled up to the restaurant.

Inside, my parents were already waiting, drinks set before them. I'd hoped my dad would have dressed a bit better, but I think he threw out all his decent clothes when he retired.

"So, Dev," Mom said, looking up from her menu. "What's good here?"

My optimism of everything going smoothly with her getting Dev's name correct vanished. I can't believe she implied that Dev should know what was good at a restaurant he'd never been to, simply because his ancestry was from the same continent as the food being served. If it bothered Dev, he didn't show it. It made me wonder how much casual racism he had to put up with on a daily basis to allow it to run off his back like water off a duck.

"Do you like spicy food?" he asked, picking up the menu to peruse.

The server came, a young girl with gorgeous brown skin and wide, dark eyes. She checked Dev out, and rightly so. He was sexy as fuck, and stuck out amongst the sea of white that was our table. I ordered a Coke, and Dev something called a mango lassi.

"Is all the food here spicy?" Mom asked, concern plaguing her brow.

"You could get vindaloo or Kashmiri. I'd stay away from the madra options," Dev said.

She shook her head with a smile. "Well, it's good to try new things!"

"Dev, you work in the car industry, right? You mentioned that yesterday," Dad said, setting his menu down.

"Yes, my family has a few businesses in the automotive industry. I've been working between them since I was a kid. Now that I've graduated, my father wants me to start taking things over for him."

"That sounds nice and secure!"

Dev's smile faded, but only for a moment. "Yes, I'm lucky. My family's worked hard for me to have such a great career path laid out."

"Is that what you want to do?" Mom asked. He hesitated. I was about to change the subject, move on to something less personal, but Dev spoke up. "I'd be a fool to turn down such an opportunity. My dad worked his whole life to build this business with the intention of his son taking over one day. I'm grateful for it."

It didn't take a genius to see through Dev's well-practiced speech. I could see my mom opening her mouth to talk about it more, but thankfully the server was back with our drinks. We relayed our orders. Dev got the veggie madras, me the butter chicken with naan bread, my mom chicken Kashmiri, and my dad the beef vindaloo. I tried Dev's mango drink, which was like a delicious yogurt smoothie. I wished I'd ordered the same, eyeing my Coke with regret.

"Dev, dear, you said you recently graduated college. You must be a few years younger than our Becky, hey?" Mom asked.

Why, oh, why did she always have to ask such awkward questions?

I placed my hand on his knee under the table. "It's only a few years difference, Mom," I said, eyes wide as if I could telepathically encourage her to talk about something else.

"Well, twenty-nine and, what, twenty-six?" Mom sipped her tea.

"Twenty-five," Dev corrected quietly.

"Twenty-nine and twenty-five is quite a difference when the woman is older."

"Mom, it's fine." My glare intensified.

She looked at me as if she were the victim. Once again, she opened her mouth but shut it in a rare demonstration of self-control.

I was beginning to sweat.

My dad broke the silence, setting his elbows on the table. "I've always wanted to restore an old car, you know? Something classic, like a Chevelle or a Stingray."

Dev hid a smile in his drink. "Those are a lot of work to keep running."

"Well, I have nothing but time on my hands. How much do you think it'd cost me?"

"Probably more than it would be worth, to be honest. But it's not about the money. Restoration is a labour of love."

The men prattled on about cars for a while, either missing or ignoring the tension between my mother and me.

In her eyes, I'd missed the mark as a daughter. Ever since I was twenty-four, she'd been pressuring me to date, pressuring me to get married, and pressuring me to have kids. She'd had her first baby at twenty-two and her last at twenty-five, so for me to be unwed at twenty-nine gave her endless anxiety of ever getting grandkids at all.

Did my brother receive the same pressure? Nope. He lived in Australia, living the ultimate playboy bachelor lifestyle, surfing and partying like he was still in his twenties. But he was a boy, thus no clock ticking, and he visited Canada so rarely that when he did, it was as if Elvis Presley had entered the building.

Our food arrived, four plates of colourful steaming dishes that smelled and looked fantastic. I glanced up from my plate to see the uncertain looks on my parents' faces. Why didn't they order the butter chicken? Everyone likes butter chicken!

I took a bite, and it was delicious, as always.

"How's your, um. What did you order?" I asked Dev.

"It's called Madras. Potatoes, cauliflower, peppers. Want to try?" he slid his dish towards me.

I took a bite. "That's so good!" I said, helping myself to more.

"How do you like yours, Karen?" Dev asked, trademark adorable brow-furrow appearing.

She'd taken maybe one bite. Mouth pressed into a firm line, she shook her head. "I don't know what spice is in there, but it's going to make me ill. The smell, I can't— waitress?" She snapped her fingers. Holy hell. She actually snapped them. I wanted to disappear.

The server approached. "Yes, ma'am?" "Honey, I'm sorry, I can't eat this. Can you take it back?"

The server went to take the dish, but Dad interjected. "I'll eat it. Can you pack it up for us, please?"

She nodded. "Of course. Can I get you something else?"

Mom shook her head. "No, thanks. I'm not hungry anymore."

I spoke up. "How about some naan bread, Mom? Try some of mine. It's really good."

"No," she said, waving her hands. "I'm fine. Please take it."

The server looked concerned, probably worrying that her tip was going from marginal to nothing, and left with my mom's uneaten plate.

"Sorry for the recommendation," Dev said.

"No, it's fine. It's the spices or something. I can't place it. I'm going to go to the washroom." She pushed her chair back noisily and left the table.

Deflated, I looked at my dad. "How's yours?"

He gave me a thumb's up, his plate already half empty.

Well, at least *he* was enjoying the food. Internally I berated myself, wishing I'd suggested we go somewhere for dinner where I knew Mom wouldn't complain. Like Olive Garden. Or White Spot.

When Mom returned, she looked paler than usual. My dad rubbed her back, a sweet gesture. "You okay, dear?"

She nodded, forcing her lips into a smile.

We ate quickly, my mom sitting across from us with clasped hands. As soon as Dev and I were finished, we asked for the check. Dad jumped up and handed the server his bank card.

"Dad, please, let us pay!" I urged.

"It's the least we can do for your hospitality," Dev agreed.

"No, it's my treat," he said.

We backed down, the polite thing to do.

"Oh, I almost forgot," Mom said, producing a coupon from her purse. She handed it to the server once she'd returned with the check.

The server eyed it, and then handed it back, apologetic. "I'm sorry, ma'am. This coupon expired last month."

"What?" Mom took it back, squinting without the glasses she refused to wear. I glanced from my mom to the poor wait-ress, cringing, knowing what was about to happen.

"Oh, honey, it's only a week past," she said, showing the server.

The server nodded slowly. "Yes. It's expired."

"Well, *barely*. Really, can't you do something?"

"No, I'm sorry." The server apologized, glancing around the table in obvious discomfort.

I gritted my teeth. "Mom, it's fine."

"No, Becky, it's not. Where is your manager?"

I wanted to disappear.

"Karen, it's alright. I'll pay," Dad said, reaching for the handheld debit machine.

My mom snatched it away. "That's not good service, and I know the manager would want us to have good service. I'd like to speak to the manager."

The poor girl looked like she was going to cry.

She walked away from the table, leaving us in an awkward silence. A moment later, an older man approached, the girl hiding behind him. "Can I help you with something, ma'am?"

"Yes, you can," Mom replied, nose in the air. "I told the girl my coupon only expired a week ago. This is our first time here, and we were waiting to use it to take the kids out to eat."

The manager took the coupon and inspected it, speaking in another language to his employee.

I leaned over to Dev and whispered, "What are they saying?"

He leaned towards me and whispered back, "I don't speak Hindi."

My face flushed. I shouldn't have assumed.

The manager looked back at my mom and forced a smile. "I'll get this taken care of right away, ma'am. My apologies."

I was so uncomfortable that I got up with the excuse of

using the washroom. Instead, I found the server on the way to the kitchen.

"I'm so sorry," I began. "My mom can be difficult. You gave us really good service and the food was great. Here—" I fished a ten-dollar bill out of my purse and handed it to her, knowing my dad was a shitty tipper even when everything went smoothly.

The girl nodded without saying anything, tears looking like they could spill over at any minute. I remembered my early twenties, working as a server and busting my ass to fund my travel addiction. The forced smiles, the miles worn into my heels, rushing after ungrateful people almost every evening and weekend, and envying the time they got to spend with their families and friends while I worked. Knowing what it was like, I always went out of my way to tip well and be grateful for decent service.

I returned to find my parents and Dev waiting for me at the front doors. We exited the little restaurant, spirits diminished. I knew it would happen. I should have listened to my instincts and let one good day be enough of a visit. My mom always found some way to spoil everything.

When we walked outside, my mom said, "whew! Fresh air!"

If looks could kill, she'd be dead. How did she think that would make my boyfriend feel?

"We've gotta go. Mom, Dad, always a pleasure," I said, hugging my dad tight and then giving a short, clipped squeeze to my mom.

Dev shook my dad's hand and accepted a hug from my mom even though she'd been so rude over the past hour.

I took Dev's hand and pulled him away.

Without a word, we climbed into his car, both releasing a slow exhale. We opened our mouths to speak at the same time.

"Sorry, go ahead," I offered, still trying to figure out how to apologize on behalf of my mother.

"I was going to ask if you could map us back to the ferry terminal." He smiled, but there was no twinkle in his eyes. He looked worn out, like a single meal with my parents had been the equivalent of a ten-hour study session for a final.

I couldn't blame him. I nodded, pulling up the map on my phone. As I directed him, I wished he'd reach over and put his hand on my leg or take my hand or something, but he didn't. Perhaps he needed his hand free to shift. I tried telling myself that, but the sinking feeling in my gut told me otherwise. If he hadn't had second thoughts about us and the possibility of a future together before, he definitely did now.

My plan had backfired miserably.

Now I was sure he'd never want me to meet his family.

How much longer did our romance have left? An unknown expiry date materialized at the back of my mind, and my heart withdrew from him, slinking back behind the walls I thought I'd torn down. After what it had been through, it had learned when to protect itself.

Eleven

"So, did you guys talk about it?" Miranda asked, filling my wine glass before topping up her own. We were in my apartment the night after returning home from my trip with our sweatpants on, hair up in messy buns, no makeup, with a Mindy Project rerun on in the background.

I sighed and ate another all-dressed chip. "No. The ride back was pretty quiet. I should have said something, I guess. Or at least apologized for how my mom behaved. I don't know why I thought introducing him to them would have improved our relationship."

Miranda settled back onto the couch. "Better to find out sooner than later."

"It felt so right, you know? Thinking back to how things were with Graham, even when they were good, they weren't this good. With Dev, everything feels so natural. He gets me."

"I know what you mean, it's like you two click, and it's effortless."

"Exactly. Like what you and Derek have. I want that."

"Well, I could talk to him about becoming sister wives." She nudged me while reaching for the chips.

"I'm not drunk enough for that conversation." I laughed and sipped my wine.

"From everything you've told me, it sounds like you're the one doing all the work to propel the relationship forward. Like, back in Mexico, you were the one who initiated sex. Here you did, too. He's always at your place because you invite him. You suggested meeting each other's families. Maybe it's time to sit back and see if he tries to move the relationship forward."

That made sense. Had I been too pushy? I did, after all, imply that I wanted him to move in with me after only dating for a few months. Then I remembered something my mom had brought up, something that had been scratching away in the back of my mind despite my best efforts to quell my fears.

"Do you think he's too young for me?"

She was hesitant, weighing her words. "He's young. Fresh out of college. Not a lot of dating experience, as you said. What were we doing when we were his age?"

"Oh god, I don't remember much of that time in my life." Honestly, we were lucky to have survived our youth with all the partying and binge drinking we did. I distinctly remember getting alcohol poisoning in a field in the middle of nowhere at one point.

"Exactly."

"But Dev isn't like that. He's so much more mature than we were," I argued.

"But does that mean he's ready to settle down? You're almost thirty. All your friends are either married with kids or close to it. You're looking for a commitment. Maybe he's not."

"I invited you here to make me feel better, not worse." I looked into my glass, a weight heavy in my chest.

"You're my best friend. Telling you what you want to hear is like, what regular friends are for. Best friends give it to you straight."

"Well then, what should I do? Break up with him? I really, really like him, Miranda. I mean, we said we loved each other, didn't we? I can't break up with him after that!"

Miranda sighed. "Then talk to him!"

"You said to wait and see if he made the first move."

"You don't have time for that. You're almost thirty."

I had to laugh. "You are the absolute worst advice giver ever."

She shrugged. "I know you're just friends with me for my looks." She crossed her eyes and stuck out her tongue. I rolled mine with a grin and turned back to face the TV.

My phone lit up with a text. I looked down, expecting Dev, and did a double-take.

"Holy shit," I muttered.

"What?" Miranda asked, mouth full of chips. "Look." I showed her the phone.

"Holy shit!" She said, spraying crumbs.

"I know! What the fuck?"

"What the fuck!" It was Graham.

"What does it say?" She said, edging closer to me.

I wasn't sure I wanted to know. My palms were suddenly so sweaty I could barely grip my phone. Setting my wine glass down, I took a deep breath and unlocked it.

Hey.

That was it. Just, 'hey.'

"What the hell is that supposed to mean?" Miranda said, suddenly furious. "What an asshole, messaging you out of nowhere. Why isn't his number blocked? Here, give it to me." She reached for my phone, but I pulled it away.

"No, wait! Don't do anything."

She looked at me, eyes wide and mouth agape. "You're not thinking of messaging him back, are you?"

"I don't know! He hasn't talked to me since... since he left." My head swam with confusion as the chips began working their way back up my throat.

"He cheated on you. There's no coming back from that."

I shrugged. "Yeah, but, I mean, I kind of get why—"

"Nuh-uh. Don't even go there, girl. Don't make excuses for him. You can do so much better. Becky, for the love of all things holy, do not message him back. Block him. Delete the text," she implored.

"What if it's a sign?" I whispered. "You don't believe in signs!"

That was true. "Fine. Fine! You're right. Here, see?" I deleted the text and then blocked his number. Admittedly, it did feel good. I don't know why I hadn't done it earlier. I suppose I'd been secretly hoping he'd come to his senses, realize he'd made a terrible mistake, and spend the rest of his life trying to make it up to me. Once Dev and I started dating, I'd thought of him less and less. Until now.

Miranda relaxed back on the couch and took a big gulp of wine.

"What an asshole," she muttered.

Then, mocking his voice, "'Hey.' Who says that? Not, 'I'm sorry for being an asshole, Becky. I'm sorry for cheating on you. I'm sorry for taking you for granted. I'm sorry for wasting a year and a half of your life.'"

"Geez, I think you're madder at him than I am," I said, nudging her with my foot before reaching for my glass.

"Damn right I am. Nobody treats my bestie like that!" She was going to be a fierce mama bear someday.

Miranda and I stayed up late catching up and watching TV. Before she was married, she would have slept over on my couch, but I guess she and Derek had plans because she was out of my condo by eleven o'clock.

Thankfully, the wine put me right to sleep, and I didn't ruminate on the ominous text from Graham. The next morning, though, it was all I could think about. I went through my usual routine in a fog of hangover and confusion. My palms itched to unblock Graham and message him back, to at least know why he'd messaged me. Having the question hanging over my head was too much. Miranda was right, though. I owed him nothing. I'd moved on, as he'd apparently done months before our relationship even ended.

By DINNERTIME, Dev still hadn't messaged me. He hadn't called or texted since dropping me off. This much radio silence was completely unlike him and further cemented the idea that my parents had ruined the good thing we'd had going.

One second we were making love and exchanging "I Love You's." The next, he was running away as fast as possible to avoid joining my ridiculous family. He was probably afraid I'd eventually become my mother.

That night as I settled down in front of the TV, finishing off the last of the bottle of wine I'd opened with Miranda, I held my phone in my hands. My fingers moved between Graham's contact and Dev's.

Sitting idle and waiting for things to happen was not my strong suit. My entire life, I'd chased after what I wanted, made plans, set goals. Now, nearing thirty, that wasn't about to change. Then, I realized, why not do both? I could inquire as to what Graham wanted from me *and* message Dev. It wasn't like I was cheating on Dev or anything. What if Graham had left some important item at my place and only now realized it?

That explanation sounded false even to my own inner monologue.

Ah, what the hell.

I unblocked Graham and messaged him back, doing my best to channel some of the righteous anger Miranda had impressed upon me the previous night. *What do you want?*

Send. Ha. There. Take that.

Then, to Dev. *Hey babe. Haven't heard from you... Everything ok between us? I'm sorry for how my mom behaved at the restaurant. We should have just gone home.*

I sat back and waited, a rerun of *Friends* on in the background. I was interrupted mid-sip with two dings, mere seconds apart.

Graham texted back, *was just thinking of u. u doing ok?*

Dev text arrived right after. *Sorry love. Been busy with family and work stuff. Don't worry about it. My family can be difficult too.*

Holy hell. What had I done?

I texted Graham, *I'm doing great. Is there a reason you're messaging me, or???*

The messaged Dev, *are you still thinking of introducing me to your family soon?*

So much for letting Dev take the lead in our relationship. There was a long pause in both text conversations, bubbles appearing and disappearing many times.

The suspense was killing me! I needed to bring in an expert.

I texted Angelina. *I fucked up. Graham messaged me and I replied and now he's texting me and so is Dev. What do I do?*

She responded immediately. *y would u text him back?*

I just needed to know what he wanted.

Angelina messaged quickly again, *'what does he want?*

'I think he misses me???'

well fuck him.

what?!?!

no no no i mean like he can go fuck himself. She followed that up with several laugh emojis.

Graham replied, *just been thinking a lot. can we get together to talk?*

I started and stopped texting a couple of times, wondering how to respond.

Dev replied. *Of course! This coming weekend still work for you?*

I texted back. *This weekend works for me!*

Only after I sent it did I realize my error. It had gone to Graham, not Dev. I nearly spilled wine all over myself in shock. I set the glass down before continuing, apparently needing the use of both my thumbs.

Before I could undo what I had just done, Graham had already replied. *great! meet u saturday at starbucks at 7, the one by ur place.*

I stared at my phone, panic rising in my chest. My fingers hovered numb over the screen.

Graham messaged again. *this really means a lot to me. Can't wait to see you.*

I knew I should reply back immediately that I'd made a mistake, that the text had been for someone else, that I was seeing a guy and it was serious, that he could go fuck himself, as Angelina had put it.

...but another part of me wanted to see him, too.

I texted Angelina, hesitant. *don't tell ur sister but Graham wants to meet next weekend to talk or something.*

Angelina replied, *wtf? y??? ur not going, r u?*

Why, indeed. That, my dear, is the question of life, is it not? Unsure of my motives, I pressed on with what sounded most realistic. *I just need closure.*

It wasn't an outright lie, since so many questions had been left unanswered. Where had we gone wrong? What could I do differently?

Maybe this could be a good thing. I'd talk to Graham, get the answers to my questions, and then be able to move on with Dev, having learned what had gone awry with my last relationship. Just one coffee and an explanation. He owed me that much.

My phone chimed again with a text from Angelina. *mood. don't do anything stupid*

There was zero chance of *that* happening. I rubbed my temple against a headache beginning to form and drank the last of the wine in my glass, suddenly remembering how early I'd have to be up the next day. It had been a long weekend, which was a much-needed respite from my job. It would be the Mondayest Tuesday ever.

I used to like my job. I used to look forward to going in there, seeing all the guys, and chatting with them about their weekend. Usually, the projects we worked on were at least mildly interesting. But now, the thought of going in there and sitting down at my desk and writing up the code to program the machines made me want to call in sick. You can only do the same thing for so long, day after day, before it grinds on you.

As I tidied, my eyes wandered to the corner where my failed downspout turbine sat on the floor. Part of me wished it wasn't there. Not only was it a reminder of coming in second at the science fair, my brother's impossibly huge shadow, and of failing my exams twice, but it was also a reminder of why I'd gone into engineering in the first place. I wanted to change the world, not churn out cheap plastic parts that were likely going to end up in a landfill.

An idea struck me.

After I got up, I dug out my old MacBook from my closet and plugged it in. In the bottom corner of my closet was also a box of old papers and textbooks, which I pulled out, too. One of them had a module on electrical engineering that might be helpful. I flipped it open and began reading, memories of my college days wafting up along with the dust of my neglected books.

If I could get the turbine to work, maybe it would hold a solution to all of this. I could be the next contract at work. I could hire the team to build models, and maybe get them working on some buildings downtown to collect data. Instead of dreading going to work, I'd be eager to go there. I'd be able to move up into a management position without re-taking that awful exam.

It seemed like a far-fetched pipe dream. But I had to do something.

After studying for a while, I checked the time and then left the books and charging computer next to the turbine to get ready for bed. I was still mulling over the project when my phone rang.

Dev. *Shit!* I hadn't texted him back.

"Hey babe!" I answered, a little too perky. Rein it in.

"Hey," he said. "Everything ok?"

"Yeah, why?" My heart pounded and my chest felt hot, guilt washing over me as I recalled my brief texting conversation with my ex. *Tell him about Graham. Just tell him. Why aren't you telling him?*

"You didn't text me back. We still on for next weekend?"

"Yes, next weekend should be good. Um, can we make it for Friday night? I have plans for spin class with Miranda on Saturday night."

And now I was lying!

"Friday would be perfect. They're excited to meet you. I told my mom not to make anything too spicy."

I forced a laugh, hoping it didn't sound fake. "That is probably for the best."

He paused for a moment and I held my breath. "Is everything okay?"

"Yeah. I mean, is everything okay with you?"

"... yeah. You seem a little distant, is all."

"Sorry, I'm just tired." I picked at the fabric pills on my comforter, guilt washing over me anew.

"Okay. Well. Love you. Get some sleep."

"You, too. Goodnight." I hung up the phone and held my head in my hands. I didn't say I loved him back. 'You, too?' What was that!

Graham had texted me, like, two sentences, and already he was ruining my relationship. I had to cancel on him. Whatever he had to say wasn't worth it.

I put my phone on silent and rolled over, wishing I could do the same for my brain.

Twelve

THE WEEK WENT BY QUICKLY, and before I knew it, it was Friday. I was so nervous about meeting Dev's family that I'd had a hard time focusing on work. Though, on the best of days, I struggle to focus on work. I think I slip into a sense of disassociation from pure boredom.

I FaceTimed Miranda to help me decide on which outfit to wear, going with a grey dress I'd bought ages ago for a work Christmas function. It was flattering around the waist and flared out below. I matched it with some grey suede wedges, apparently the only type of heels I owned. Probably for the best. I wasn't great at walking in heels, and the last thing I needed was to fall flat on my face in front of his family.

After curling my hair and obsessing over my make-up in an attempt to look casually beautiful and not like I was trying too hard, I was finally ready. Five minutes later, Dev arrived, letting me know with a text. As I descended in the elevator, I found myself thinking of last-minute excuses to get out of it, my nervous anticipation presenting itself as nausea.

My previous 'meet the parents' event had gone so well.

Graham's parents had taken to me, and our families had even met and got along great. I'd been able to envision Thanksgiving dinners, Christmas mornings, and even summer vacations altogether.

But with Dev's family, I didn't know what to expect.

Stepping out onto the street, my thoughts refocused. I had to keep my head in the game. Dev leaned against his car, his beautiful skin and dark features a stark contrast to the white BMW and grey Vancouver afternoon sky. He grinned at me, eyes lighting up. Like cotton candy on my tongue, all of my worries melted away. I closed the distance between us and wrapped my arms around his neck, planting a kiss on his lips as my fingers traced the edge of his beard along his jaw.

We pulled away from one another, and he gazed into my eyes, my heart tap dancing. Even though we'd been together for months, he still had the same effect on me that he had when I first saw him on the plane. Perhaps more so. Now I knew there was more behind his dazzling smile, gorgeous eyes, and calm demeanour. He was the real deal.

A warm sensation glowed in my lower regions as he flexed against my hip.

"I missed you," he said.

I giggled. "I can tell." It had been a long week, both of us busy with work and our separate lives in different cities.

We kissed again, but only briefly, and then he opened the door for me.

As we drove through the busy rush-hour traffic, he placed his hand on the bare skin of my thigh whenever shifting gears allowed, apparently enjoying the dress I was wearing. His hand on my bare skin, so close but not close enough, was making things damp. I normally wouldn't mind, but given that we were on our way to meet his parents, I took his hand in mine and squeezed it.

"Sorry," he said. "Like I said, I missed you."

"Maybe you should have come up to my apartment for a few minutes so we wouldn't be so distracted during dinner."

He grinned at me before adjusting himself in the seat. "That probably would have been a good idea."

We were silent for a few moments while he navigated.

"Are you nervous?" he asked.

I exhaled, nodding.

"It will be fine. My parents are very nice. Priya can be... a bit much. She has a weird sense of humour."

"Oh shit, should I have brought a bottle of wine or something? I don't have a gift. Can we stop off somewhere so I don't arrive empty-handed?" I don't know why I hadn't thought of it sooner.

He shook his head. "It's fine. They don't drink. I didn't bring anything to your parents, did I?"

I shrugged. "No. I guess you're right. I just want to make a good impression."

"You will. Don't worry." He offered me a reassuring smile.

By the time we were out of the city the sun was beginning to set, lighting up the mountain ranges still covered in snow. We drove east on the Trans- Canada Highway, Mount Baker in the distance across the border in the USA. Without having a car, I rarely ventured this far out of the GVA and was awestruck by the natural beauty. Eventually, we turned off the main road and drove into the country. Several minutes later, we pulled up to a long driveway circling around a fountain in front of a stone mansion with a triple garage and a wide burgundy door. Several sedans were parked outside, all of them higher-end models. I gulped.

The magnificent house was set on an acreage next to other giant houses with their own fleets of expensive cars. Out behind, I caught a glimpse of the rows of blueberries that stretched on indefinitely, foothills growing into mountains, a gorgeous backdrop to it all.

If it hadn't been apparent before, now it was obvious. Dev and I were from completely different worlds. What did he think of me and my tiny, plain apartment? Of my working-class, blue-collar parents and their old log house in desperate need of a renovation? I looked down at my shoes, suddenly hyper-aware of the scuff on the toe. My dress was probably out of style since I'd bought it a few years ago. I should have splurged on something new. I should have gotten a haircut. I should have spent more time on my makeup.

My car door opened and Dev was standing there with his hand out. I took it, dizzy. *Breathe, Rebecca. Breathe.* Everything would be fine. He said his parents were nice. His sister sounded like fun. This was a casual meeting—dinner and dessert. All I had to do was not fuck it up.

Easier said than done.

The white crushed stone driveway crunched beneath our feet as we walked to the front door. Before he could open it, the door swung inward. A petite girl that looked about eighteen burst through the doorway and hugged me before I could even realize what was going on.

"Welcome!" she chimed.

I patted her on the back and looked up to Dev, who was scratching his beard with an apologetic smile.

"Rebecca, this is my sister Priya. Priya—"

"I know who she is. Come inside! Wow, you're gorgeous! Pictures don't do you justice." Priya pulled me by the hand into their home.

The entryway was wide with honey-coloured wood floors and a rounded staircase that wound its way up to the second floor. To my left were French doors opening to an office with large, ornate wooden furniture and heavy drapes framing the windows. Down the hall was a living area with giant south-facing picture windows, catching the last rays of sunlight that lit up the expansive backyard. An impeccably maintained lawn met the blueberry fields in the distance. The smell wafting down the hall was fabulous: fresh bread and curry.

"Leave your shoes on," Priya ordered.

I glanced over my shoulder at Dev, who shook his head in disagreement. I kicked off my shoes while Priya continued pulling me along.

"Mama! Papa! She's here!" she shouted, her voice echoing.

The kitchen was massive, with white marble countertops, a matching backsplash, and muted walnut cabinets that complimented the floor. Behind the giant island, stirring a pot on their six-burner gas stove, was Dev's mom. She was wearing tasteful black slacks and a deep navy blouse, her gold jewelry a perfect accent. She turned from her cooking, her eyes quickly scanning up and down my dress. I averted my gaze, nervous under her scrutiny. I should have picked something less revealing.

Priya released my hand as Dev came up beside me. I prepared for a reassuring touch, something I'd grown used to, but instead, he stood about a foot away, his hands behind his back.

"Mom," he said, "this is Rebecca."

I forced my shoulders to relax and conjured the best smile I could.

She set down her spoon, wiped her hands on a dishtowel, and then made her way around the island to greet us. Dev kissed her on both cheeks, and I held out my hand for her to shake.

"Very nice to meet you, Mrs. Singh," I said. "Oh, please call me Shawan," she said, and then moved past my hand to kiss both of my cheeks as she had with her son. "Can I get you something to drink?" she offered, stepping away.

"Um, sure. Water, please, thanks."

Dev gestured towards a stool next to the island, and I sat gratefully, not entirely trusting my legs. Priya was perched on the countertop with a grin, looking from me to Dev. She was dressed casually, in tight jeans and a long-sleeve t-shirt with some

sort of anime pictures on it, making me feel silly and over-dressed. At least Dev still had his business- casual clothes on from work. He sat next to me as his mother set down two cold glasses.

Shawan moved back to the stove. Before an awkward silence could fully set in, a large man with a purple turban and long black beard with a grey stripe down the middle entered the room.

"Hello, there!" he greeted, his arms out, welcoming. Aside from his turban, he was dressed as most older middle-aged men I knew would be— other than my father whose taste in clothes ranged from 'about to mow the lawn' to 'going on a trip to Walmart.' A purple button-up shirt matched his turban and was complimented by dark grey slacks and slippers. His eyes were identical to Dev's, and his presence filled the room with warmth and comfort. I liked him immediately.

Standing, I held out my hand.

He jokingly pushed it aside and opened his arms, beck-oning for a hug. I obliged, his embrace feeling like home.

Releasing me, he held me at arm's length. "Oh, Jagdev, she is a beauty, this one!" he said, his eyes twinkling.

I blushed and tucked a strand of hair behind my ear. Dev appeared behind me, and my heart swelled at the proud look on his face.

"Rebecca, this is my father, Jagraj," Dev introduced.

"You can call him Jag," Priya called from her perch.

"That's why you go by Dev," I realized.

Dev shrugged. "Otherwise, it gets confusing."

"Mama usually yells everyone's name when she gets mad." Priya laughed.

Shawan tutted from her place at the stove, then spoke a string of words in Punjabi. Priya responded in what sounded like a snarky, teenage tone. Then, suddenly everyone was speaking Punjabi. I looked from face to face as this went on for a minute or two. Finally, Dev broke it up. "Everyone, please? English?"

"Call the others for supper, Priya," Shawan said.

Jag began escorting us to the dining room. "Mama has prepared a wonderful meal for you, Rebecca. You will enjoy it very much!"

"I'm sure I will," I said as we walked down the hall and into a huge formal dining room, the furniture once again made of fine wood with intricate carvings. As we passed through I looked at all the photos on the walls, one of which was a young Dev graduating high school. I wanted to linger, noticing him standing next to a beautiful girl with long black hair and wide brown eyes. A slight knot formed in my stomach. Was it his ex? Sonja? They had a picture of them together on their wall?

Dev ushered me along.

Pushing my questions to the back of my mind, I focused on the evening ahead. There'd be time to ask Dev about it later.

I sat next to Dev, Priya beside me. Jag was at the head of the table, and after a moment, others began filtering in. An old couple entered dressed in traditional clothing, matching yellow turban to yellow saree, who Dev introduced as his paternal grandparents. Then, an even older woman, who Dev introduced as his maternal grandmother, also dressed traditionally in green, joined us. They all smiled politely but didn't say anything.

The table was really long, and half the settings were still unaccounted for. I thought it was odd but let it go.

Shawan entered a moment later carrying a big, steaming pot. "Priya. Help, please?" she chastised, followed by a string of Punjabi.

Priya muttered something, also in Punjabi. Dev's name was in there, for sure.

Soon the table was filled with dishes, each one fragrant and colourful. Before we dished up, Jag offered a prayer in Punjabi. I followed along, holding my hands together and lowering my gaze, but snuck a look up to see Priya's eyes were open, too. She gave me a small smile before I looked away, embarrassed I'd been caught peeking.

Not familiar with the food, Priya explained each of the dishes and served me. All the while, Jag asked questions. It was hard for me to focus on exactly what Priya was saying while trying to hold a conversation, which dishes were which, and the spice levels she thought would be fine for me. Aloo baingan, sabzi, rajma... it all started blending together on my plate, my ability to discern each item lessening with each addition.

"So, Rebecca, Dev says you're an engineer?" Jag asked.

"Not exactly, no." I didn't expand on why, and my face flushed with shame. I was trying to endear his parents to me; failing my final exam wasn't going to help my case.

"But she has two degrees in engineering," Dev added, keeping the conversation flowing. I gave him a thankful look.

"That's wonderful!" Jag said. "What made you want to get into engineering?"

Shawan glanced up from her plate, but the look she gave me, one eyebrow slightly raised, was not entirely encouraging.

"Well, I was always interested in how things worked and why. When I was a kid, I'd take things apart to see if I could put them back together again.

Once I broke the family TV. Couldn't put that back together, though. Mom was pretty mad about that," I paused as Dev and his dad chuckled. "My dad is an amateur mechanic, and my brother and I spent a lot of time out in the garage with him. My older brother went into engineering, too."

Jag smiled. "Ah, so following big brother's footsteps?"

I forced a smile. Now wasn't the time to delve into the painful and somewhat embarrassing history between my brother and me. "Yeah, something like that."

"Your father is a mechanic?" Jag asked, moving the conversation along.

"Um, no. He worked for the City of Vancouver. In the waste management department." I knew it was nothing to be ashamed of. He'd worked very hard to provide for his family and retired with a full pension. Even so, I hated seeing the look on people's faces when they realized what it meant, or if they reiterated asking, 'Oh, he was a garbage man?'

"And your mother, what does she do?" Shawan asked.

"She worked in the local elementary school." "A teacher?"

"A teacher's assistant," I corrected.

"Amazing they managed to put two children through University on such modest incomes," Shawan stated between bites. Dev tensed beside me.

"Actually, I put myself through school. Working, and loans." I placed my hand on Dev's thigh under the table.

Gently, he took my hand in his, gave it a light squeeze, and then removed it from his leg back to my own before returning to his meal.

A little confused, I looked over at him and noticed disapproving glances from his grandparents across the table. I shifted uncomfortably in my seat, wondering if I'd done or said something to upset him, and took a bite of what looked like kidney beans in sauce.

"Engineering, that's interesting. Not enough women go into STEM fields." Shawan stated.

I nodded in agreement. "There weren't many other female students when I was in school. I'm the only woman in my department."

"Do you plan on getting your professional designation?" Shawan asked.

I hesitated. The memories of sitting in that room, the ticking clock mocking me, the scent of number two pencils, everyone else standing and turning in their papers while I struggled with page two... Nope. I couldn't do it. My palms got sweaty even thinking about it. On top of that, I was trying to focus more on my personal life.

Shawan's question felt weighted to me, though. I couldn't help but think she was questioning how I'd have time to look after a family with a career going on and the possibility of more school coming up.

"No," I said finally. "Maybe one day in the future, but I'm happy where I'm at right now."

"I think it's so cool you're an engineer!" Priya said excitedly. "Do you get to build stuff?"

I smiled, encouraged by her enthusiasm. "I wish. I thought

that was what it would be like. But it's a lot of software and computer stuff."

She shrugged. "I still think it's cool."

Dev looked at me, beaming with pride. "Rebecca has been working on a model to turn eavestroughs into miniature water turbines to take houses off-grid."

I glared and nudged him with my foot.

"Is that right?" Jag asked, eyebrows shooting up.

I didn't know him well enough to tell if he was actually interested or just pandering. "It's something I'm playing around with after work. I'm working out all the kinks, making sure the math is sound. I don't think anything will come of it. I'd need machines to make a prototype or at least a 3-D printer. And for that, I need cash."

"Couldn't you use the machines at work?" Dev asked.

I shook my head. "If I worked on it during work hours, they'd have a right to it. I have to get it patented first, secure funding, maybe apply for grants." My mind drifted for a moment, imaging all the work ahead of me if I did intend to pursue it in earnest.

"It would be amazing if it worked, hey Papa?" Priya chimed in. "How much rain we get, maybe it could lower the cost of energy in your shops."

"Exactly what I was thinking," Jag said, looking thoughtful. "I could reach out to some people who may be interested in investing. I will arrange the meeting, and you can pitch your project to them."

"Now there's an idea," Dev agreed.

I paled at the thought of standing in front of a bunch of people, telling them about my dreams and ambitions for green tech that hadn't even been properly hashed out yet. Before I could object, noise erupted in the hallway as the front door opened and a crowd of people piled in.

"Ah! There you are!" Jag said, greeting the group as they walked in.

Four guys and two girls entered, all around Dev's age.

My heart sank, recognizing one of them immediately.

Moe.

Thirteen

MOE and I studied one another.

He had a look in his eye that made me uneasy. I didn't trust him, not after how he'd grabbed at me in Mexico or called me a bitch for refusing to dance with him. Though, he had been quite drunk at the time.

Everyone deserves a second chance, right?

I tried my best to smile at him and make it seem genuine.

Moe and the others made their rounds kissing the cheeks of their relatives and introducing themselves to me before taking their seats. Conversations erupted around the table amongst the new group, everything loud and boisterous.

With a start, I recognized one of the girls from the pub. What was her name? Neetu? Damnit. I'd pretty much told her Dev and I were banging on a regular basis.

She smiled at me, but it did nothing to make me feel better. I'd forgotten to tell Dev about my slip-up.

I leaned over to Dev and spoke quietly in his ear. "These are all your cousins?"

He leaned in too. "Not all of them, no."

That wasn't what I meant. I tried again. "I thought this was going to be a meal with your family. I mean, the family you live with."

"It is. They live in the other wing, but we spend a lot of time together."

My eyes widened. The... other... wing?! How big was this house, exactly? I eyed the huge table laden with piles of food, all the people talking over one another boisterously, most of it in Punjabi.

To be honest, it was overwhelming having so many people at a family meal. I was used to my little family of four from childhood, so having twelve there, plus me, as an average family meal was a lot to take in. I gave up trying to follow along with the conversations and focused on keeping a pleasant look on my face, turning instead to my food.

Unsure of where to start, I picked one thing and spooned a huge mouthful in.

Holy hell. It was spicy as FUCK.

I sipped my water. It didn't help. I took a bite of naan, which was fresh and piping hot, and only made things worse. Unable to handle the fact that my mouth was on fire, I pushed myself back from the table, chair squealing in protest, and walked quickly out of the room to the kitchen.

Dev was close behind. "Sorry, Rebecca, please—what's wrong?"

I gestured at my mouth, my face by now a deep shade of red, sweat prickling out of every pore in my body.

"Oh!" He said, cluing in. A moment later, he had a glass of milk in my hand, which I chugged gratefully.

He gave me a moment to recover. "You okay?" "Yeah, I'll be fine."

He shifted on his feet. "We can leave if you want to."

"What?" I reached out and squeezed his arm. "No. It's fine! That one dish was super spicy, caught me off guard. I'll just eat the other things and bring some more milk with me."

"No, I mean, if you're not comfortable here." He looked a little deflated.

I set my glass down and then took his face in my hands, fingertips coming to life with the prickle of his beard. He placed his hands around my waist and then lowered his forehead to mine. I closed my eyes and sighed.

It was nice escaping the chaos of the big family meal for a minute, enjoying the relative quiet of the kitchen with Dev, grounding me.

"Everything's fine. I promise. Your family is great." I pulled away to look into his eyes. The uncertainty was back, the questioning. I wished I could read his mind but was also grateful that I couldn't. He was probably wondering how much of a future we could have if I couldn't even eat a simple home-cooked meal at his family's house.

The sound of someone's throat-clearing disrupted the moment. Dev stepped away from me quickly, looking embarrassed.

Shawan stood there, arms crossed. "Everything okay, dear?" Her concerned voice did not match her expression.

"Yes," I said quickly. "I needed a glass of milk. Delicious food, Mrs. Singh." Glass in hand, I left Dev with his mom, took a steadying breath, and made my way back to the table.

The cousins eyed me as I walked in. For the first time since coming to Dev's house, I felt very much aware of my pale white skin. I practically glowed in the dark next to everyone else. I sat down and turned to Dev's little sister, feeling most comfortable talking to her.

"So Priya, you're graduating this year, right? Any plans for when you're done school?"

Her back straightened. "Well, I really want to go into this awesome arts program."

"You're an artist?"

She nodded, excitement bubbling out of her as she wiggled in her seat. "I really want to be a tattoo artist. Do you have tattoos?"

"Yep, two. One on my lower back, and one here," I said, showing her the little Douglas Fir on my ankle, a homage to my love of British Columbia.

"I love it!" she gasped.

"Do you have any?"

"No. Because *someone* won't let me get one!" She glared over at her father.

Jag sighed, having apparently gone through this conversation many times and had long since tired of it. "We do not desecrate our bodies, Priya."

I cringed at the word 'desecrate,' wishing I'd kept my tattoos to myself. The table quieted at the unfolding drama, watching Jag and Priya with interest.

"It's *art*, Papa!" she argued.

Jag set down his fork and pointed a finger, switching to Punjabi. The whole table joined in on the argument, obviously some for and others against tattooing. Even the grandparents, who hadn't said much of anything, were in on the heated debate.

Well, shit.

Dev and Shawan came back and took their seats. Dev's eyes darted from person to person, trying to catch up on what he'd missed.

"Sorry," I said.

He looked at me quizzically.

"I might have mentioned Priya's art school, and the topic of tattoos came up."

"Ah. Thank you for coming," he said, feigning sarcasm.

"Any time," I replied. "This is great." I grinned into my glass of milk, and Dev stifled a laugh.

The argument seemed to reach a crescendo as Priya suddenly stood and left the room.

Everyone collectively exhaled, the silence palpable.

"My apologies, Rebecca." Jag shrugged. Then, with a chuckle, he added, "teenagers!"

"It's totally fine." I nodded as if I knew what having a teenager was like.

Taking advantage of the lapse in conversation, Moe leaned in across the table. "You're the girl Dev met in Mexico, right?"

Dev coughed, choking on his bite of food.

Shawan looked from Moe to Dev, to me. "I haven't heard this story."

Dev was quick to interject. "We swapped luggage, remember?"

"That's not the only thing you were swapping." Moe laughed under his breath. The other cousins tittered. I eyed Neetu, who was whispering something in the ear of the girl next to her.

"Enough," Jag said in a warning tone, eyeing his nephew.

Thankfully, Moe backed down.

My ears burned. I couldn't help but glare at Moe. I was already struggling to win his family over. The last thing I wanted his parents and grandparents to be thinking of right now was all the things we'd been *swapping* in Mexico.

The rest of the meal passed in relative peace. For the most part, the cousins spoke amongst themselves, only asking me occasional questions to be polite. The grandparents were quiet. Shawan kept to herself. Jag mostly talked business with Dev.

I managed to make my way through most of the food, leaving the spiciest dishes behind. When Shawan got up to do the dishes, I joined her, taking plates and carting them back to the kitchen. When I noticed that Dev stayed seated, I nudged him.

"Hey, want to do dishes with me? Give your mom the night off?" Surely that would get Shawan on my side, at least. The entire table looked at me as if I'd lost my mind.

Dev stood. "Absolutely."

Together we worked side by side at the sink, me washing as he dried and put things away. He seemed a little lost as if he hadn't spent much time in there, opening two or three cupboards before finding the right home for everything. Despite that, having him next to me was perfect.

Dinner had been a bit of a fiasco.

On the one hand, it was a relief to see that even a family like Dev's, with their gorgeous mansion, sprawling estates, and traditional Indian culture, still had squabbles like my family did. The amount of times dinner conversations had exploded into arguments at my house was more frequent than I'd ever want to admit, often because of my brother and me fighting about something petty.

On the other hand, his family was so much bigger than mine. So many people lived in this house, interacting with one another constantly. It wasn't only him, his sister, and his parents, but three grandparents and five cousins all under one roof.

But standing next to Dev at the sink, an inch between us, laughing and joking and talking as if nobody else in the world existed, everything else seemed to fall away.

In the end, that's what mattered.

Dev and me.

After all the dishes were washed and put away, Dev took me on a tour of the house while Shawan got to work preparing chai and setting out dessert.

The main floor had the expansive kitchen and attached great room with giant windows overlooking the blueberry fields. His cousins were lounging on the couches, watching TV, and staring at their phones. The dining room was down the hall, across from the office, beside the entryway with a curved staircase to the second floor.

Down another hallway was the garage and a door that went to a separate wing where his cousins lived.

"Have your cousins always lived with you?" I asked.

Dev shook his head. "No. The new wing is an addition we built about six or seven years ago now. It's closer for them to get to work. Sometimes fewer people live with us, sometimes more. Our family's quite close. My cousins are more like siblings."

I couldn't comprehend living with so many people. After being around so many people for this one evening, I definitely felt the need to escape back to my introvert lair with my sweatpants, comfort food, and junk TV.

I took Dev's hand as he led me around. A door near the garage led down to the basement suite, if you could call it that. It was a walk-out with a view of the fields, and paired with the high ceilings it didn't feel like a basement at all. There were two main bedrooms, another room currently set up as a gym, as well as a gourmet kitchen. The living room alone was bigger than my whole apartment.

I whistled. "Holy shit, this is so nice!"

Dev's grandmother appeared at the doorway of a bedroom

and eyed us. Dev dropped my hand. His grandmother shook her head subtly and then went back in her room, shutting the door.

"Oops," I said, cringing and turning to Dev.

Dev's expression was hard to read, making me nervous. "Come on, I'll show you upstairs."

The landing at the top of the stairs had two closed double doors, which belonged to his parents' main suite. Down the hall was a spare room, occupied by one of his female cousins.

Priya's door was obvious, decorated in fantastic comic book style artwork.

"Did Priya draw these?" I asked, pausing to admire it.

Dev nodded, a proud look on his face. "You should get her to show you her graphic novel sometime. She's a little shy about it, but it's really good."

Impressive.

We continued down the hall to Dev's room, the last one. His king-size bed matched his dresser in dark wood, which was opposite the giant window overlooking the front driveway where his car and several others were parked. Opposite his bed was a walk-in closet and ensuite bathroom. Each bedroom in this house had its own bathroom, apparently. Like his car, everything was spotless. His bed was made, his clothes were hung, and not a speck of dust was to be seen on any surface.

The door clicked shut, and Dev came up to stand beside me as I looked out the window. We both exhaled in relief, glad to have a moment alone. "Is everything okay?" I asked, feeling insecure after what could only be described as a less than perfect first impression with his family.

He smiled. "Of course. Why?"

"You've felt really cold and distant ever since we got here. I try to hold your hand, you let me go. Did I do something wrong?"

"Ah. Right. Indian families are generally uncomfortable with public displays of affection. We're lucky they didn't have us sitting on opposite ends of the table," he explained.

I slapped his arm. "This is the sort of thing that would have been helpful to know *before* I got here. I thought I'd done something to piss you off!"

He laughed. "You're right. I'm sorry. I should have warned you."

"You also should have warned me Moe was going to be here," I said, crossing my arms.

He frowned. "I didn't think he'd bring up Mexico. He's still sore you turned him down. Don't worry. I'll talk to him."

"Your mom probably thinks I'm a hussy, partying in Mexico, hooking up with a stranger, and getting tattoos." I thought about bringing up the conversation I'd had with Neetu but refrained. If they were going to gossip, there wasn't anything I could do about it.

Dev hugged me from behind, resting his chin on my shoulder. "She's not judgmental like that. And she's used to Moe's big mouth."

I sighed and turned in his arms, pressing my ear against his chest. It was so nice to have him alone for a moment. He held me in his arms and kissed the top of my head, embracing me in a hug. I breathed in his scent. My hands found their way to his beard, fingernails running along the long stubble.

He looked down at me, meeting my gaze, and caressed the edge of my jaw with his thumb.

I smiled. "Do you still love me even though I can't eat spicy food?"

He laughed and pressed his forehead into mine. "I still love you."

His muscles tensed under my fingertips. I pulled away, noticing an uncertain shadow in his eye.

"Something's wrong."

Dev's brow furrowed.

"Oh shit, something *is* wrong!" I pulled away from him.

"No, it's nothing. Well, it's not exactly nothing. We should sit down." He pulled me over to the bed, and we sat on the edge, hand in hand. It took him a few moments to gather his thoughts, and I waited for him to do so, barely breathing. Finally, he spoke, avoiding my gaze.

"I've been thinking a lot about us. About our future."

Oh hell. This is it. He's breaking up with me. My heart began pounding in my ears as my mind raced through the afternoon, settling on every detail that could have gone better.

He exhaled slowly. "I applied for the master's program at UBC."

My eyes widened in surprise, and my pulse quickened. I stayed quiet, sensing he had more to say. He let the silence hang, both of us holding our breath.

"I was accepted."

"Dev! That's amazing!" I nearly leapt into his arms. "Congratulations!"

He grinned, but his smile didn't meet his eyes.

"You're worried, aren't you?" I said, finally cluing in. His parents already had one child going down her own, somewhat questionable path. Dev was their sure thing, their shoo-in, the person they were counting on continuing their legacy. I could see that now. The whole family lived here together, their future dependent on Dev and his ability to keep the family businesses running. And now he was turning away from it to pursue a master's degree, and with my encouragement.

"Of course, I am," Dev said. "But I can't live my life for other people. Spending the last few weeks working solely in my father's shops, without classes to look forward to or studying to do... I couldn't imagine myself doing it every day. I miss everything there is about school, and I want to find a job that's more 'me.' Is that selfish?"

"God, no! Your life is about you. It's not like you're abandoning your family and backpacking Australia for the rest of your life."

"True."

"You can still be successful and happy on your terms. They will understand."

"I hope so." Judging by his tone, he wasn't convinced.

I squeezed his hand, my pulse quickening. "So, does this mean you're moving in with me?"

He inched closer. "If the offer is still open."

"It's more than open," I said, bridging the gap between us. My lips found his, hesitant at first, but after a moment, he relaxed. I pulled him closer, and then when he wasn't getting close enough, I climbed up on top of him, straddling his lap, arching my back, and pressing my breasts into his chest. A moan escaped his lips, his bulge hard against my thigh. I pushed him down, laying on top of him, my pelvis grinding against his. My dress rode up past my thighs, and Dev's hands found their way to my ass, where he gave it a tight squeeze.

The door swung open. "Jagdev, dessert is—Oh my goodness!"

Shawan was at the door, mouth agape, eyes wide in shock. She turned and left without another word, leaving the door open.

"Oh teri," Dev said under his breath.

I pulled my dress down and climbed off. He stood, grabbed my hand, and then looked me dead in the eyes. "Well, we may as well get this over with."

He pulled me out of his room and down the hall.

"Do you think this is a good idea?" I whispered hoarsely as we passed Priya's room, her door now open and head poking out, as if she could sense drama unfolding.

"It's like a Band-Aid, Rebecca—let's just rip it off. Trust me, it will all blow over."

Thirty minutes later, I sat on a stool in the kitchen as Punjabi was shouted all around me.

Thankfully, the cousins and grandparents had retreated to their areas of the house, leaving the four of us. Moe did give me a sideways smirk when he left as if entertained by the turn of events. I tried to ignore him.

The argument had started off in English. Dev apologized to his mom for having walked in and seen something she shouldn't have. Then, he declared that we were moving in together, and he was continuing his education in the city.

After that, everything was in Punjabi. My face reddened, knowing that most of what they were saying was likely about me. Luckily, I had my phone on me. I pulled it out and began recording, catching the last part of the conversation for later interpretation. I didn't trust Dev to give me a complete, unfiltered recap of the proceedings.

At first, it was uncomfortable being unable to understand an argument that pertained a lot to me and my involvement in Dev's life, but after that wore off, I became... bored. It was odd.

Everything was muted and distant while a pleasant, glowing sensation blossomed in my chest. Dev was a grown man, capable of making his own decisions. He was also the kindest, sweetest, most alluring person I'd ever met. And he wanted to be with me. Me! In my crummy little apartment. He'd rather live with me in my tiny apartment downtown than here with his family in their mansion on a sprawling blueberry estate.

Part of me felt guilty that I was partially to blame for such an uproar, but the other part of me felt pretty awesome, I had to admit.

I had to remind myself it wasn't only about me. It was about his education, his future. And he'd decided he wanted it to be with me.

Finally, Dev seemed to have had enough. I hastily pushed my phone back into my clutch and stood as he took my hand and led me to the door. I looked over my shoulder, his mother's expression furious and his father deeply saddened. Priya peeked out from her spot on the steps where she'd been eavesdropping, her forehead bearing the same worried wrinkles that Dev's did.

Outside, the door slammed behind us. The crisp cool air and light evening drizzle brought with it some clarity. He led me to the passenger side of his car and opened it for me. I shut it, turning to face him.

"Dev," I said, stern. "Not now."

"We have to talk about this."

"Please, can we just go?"

The look on his face was one I hadn't seen yet. He was hurt. My body went rigid, and my fists clenched at my sides. I wanted to walk back into that house and give them a piece of my mind, but I had no idea what exactly I should be angry about. I wiped a tear from my face, opened the door for myself, and climbed in.

We drove in silence back to my place—silence, except for my intestines that rumbled noisily. The spicy food was not sitting well. I began to sweat, clenching as tight as I could as my stomach rumbled louder and louder. It would be forty-five minutes until we got home. I held it as long as I could, but it just slipped out.

I farted.

It sounded like a confused balloon animal. I glanced over at Dev.

He glanced over at me.

Then the smell began to permeate the air. I sheepishly rolled down the window. "Sorry," I muttered.

A chuckle broke the silence, and I looked over to see a grin splitting his face in half. His laugh triggered my own, and suddenly we were both roaring. The tense evening we'd gotten through all seemed so far away now, with the two of us laughing like elementary school kids over the silliest thing.

We were going to be living together— it was only a matter of time before one of us broke the fart barrier.

Fourteen

THE FOLLOWING morning we lay in bed, post lovemaking, him with his head on my chest and me twirling my fingers through his hair. Vancouver rain pounded against the window-pane. I watched the droplets run down the glass, choosing one to race against the other at random. Though the day was dreary, it was as if sunshine were streaming in, alighting me from within. I sighed, barely able to contain my deep sense of contentment.

Dev mumbled something.

"Hmm?"

He moved his head back to the pillow and looked into my eyes, his brows knitting together. "We can't move in together."

Suddenly my mood matched the weather. "But you said..."

"I know what I said." He sighed, rubbing his hand down his face. "There's a lot I have to think about. A lot to consider." Dev rolled out of bed and sat on the edge, facing away from me, his shoulders hunched.

I sat up and pulled the blankets over myself. "So, what then? What about your master's program?"

He rubbed his hand over his beard. "I don't know."

I inched closer to him and kissed his back. "What is it that you want? You. Not what everyone else wants."

He was silent for a moment, and I gave him time to gather his thoughts. "I want many things. I want you. I want us. I want to forge my own path in life. But I also want my family, and to look after them. I don't want to neglect my responsibilities."

My throat felt as if it was closing in on itself, betraying the tears brewing beneath the surface.

He stood, leaving me alone and cold in the bed, and began pulling on his clothes from the night before. I watched him dress, a sinking feeling in the pit of my stomach that this was the end of the road for us. We'd come as far as we could go.

"I need some time to think." He turned, his mouth forming a half-hearted smile that did nothing to reassure me.

"Is this about what your parents said last night?"

He ignored my question. Bending down, he kissed my forehead and hovered a moment. "I love you," he whispered. I could tell by his voice that he meant it. And then he walked out of the room.

I sat with my knees tucked up to my chest and listened as he rummaged around the apartment for his things, the door squeaking open and then shutting behind him.

My bottom lip trembled. I allowed the tears to escape. Holding my head in my hands, my heart ached as previous wounds warned me of impending danger.

But I didn't have time to wallow in self-pity. Today was the day I'd planned to meet with Graham. First things first, though, I had to get a complete picture as to what was going on with Dev.

I got up, wiped away my tears, and jumped in the shower.

Feeling somewhat refreshed and energized, I sat down in front of my computer with a hot cup of coffee (with lots of Baileys) and made an ad on Craigslist.

'WANTED: Punjabi Interpreter'

The rest of the day was a tense blur, anxious nausea surfacing and retreating in waves. I made myself busy going out into the world to grocery shop, cleaning my apartment, doing laundry, and working on my turbine project. I didn't want to talk to Miranda, lest I accidentally bring up my coffee date with Graham. *No, not date.* Coffee … rendezvous? Did that sound more innocent? I also didn't want to talk to Angelina until I had more information. And I *definitely* didn't want to talk to my mom. Geez. I needed to branch out, get more friends or something. How do adults even go about doing that?

My phone vibrated with an incoming text in response to my ad. We messaged back and forth to confirm details before deciding to meet at a mid-way point in a bar. It was nearing five o'clock anyway, and I needed a drink to calm my nerves before my coffee *rendezvous* with Graham.

It took me longer to get ready than I cared to admit. I'd be heading right from my meeting with the interpreter to see Graham, and I wanted him to see me and think A: I was totally over him and didn't care what he thought, and B: I was still super attractive, and he was an idiot for letting me go.

I pulled on my Lululemon pants, knee-high tan boots, and a comfortable (but not too comfortable) sweater. I walked the three blocks to the meeting point and entered the dimly-lit bar, already bustling with people ordering their cheap happy-hour drinks and appetizers. A tall, lanky college student with a fledgling beard, a black turban, and a grey Simon Fraser University hoodie flagged me to the booth where he sat.

Reaching across the table, I shook his hand. "Hey, I'm Rebecca."

"Jagmeet," he said, his grip confident but not too tight.

I ordered a Caesar, sans tabasco, and he ordered a tea. Then we got down to work. I passed him my phone and played the recording.

"Wow, they're really angry!" he commented, laughing.

"What are they saying?"

He listened for a while and then paused it. "Do you want the gist, or like, a completely accurate transcription?"

I hadn't brought anything to write on and felt silly about it now. "The gist is fine, I guess."

"I'll try to be as accurate as I can. What's the context here? Who's talking?"

"My boyfriend and his parents."

Jagmeet pressed play. "So. The father says, 'I can't believe you would make a decision like this, such a big, important decision, without even talking to us first. What were you thinking? You didn't even consult the family! Decisions like that involve everyone, not just you acting on a whim.' The son, your boyfriend, says, 'It's not a whim. I've put a lot of thought into it. And I'm talking to you about it now.' The dad says, 'that's not the same thing, and you know it.'"

"The mother's chiming in: 'People have been gossiping. They know all about your sneaking around. It is ruining your reputation. And not only yours, but your whole family's. Do you not care about your family?'"

I gulped. I should have been more careful when speaking to Dev's cousins on his birthday.

Jagmeet continued. "The son says, 'of course, I care about the family.' The mom's back at it saying: 'We've tried to give you space, to let you come to your senses, but you can't keep behaving this way. Sleeping over at a woman's house, both of you unmarried? It's completely disrespectful, and it's gone on long enough.'"

"The dad's back. 'We've been preparing for months, years, for you to take over the businesses. You didn't stop to consider what this will do to us, this going back to school.' The son says, 'I thought you'd be proud of me. Getting into the UBC master's program is a big deal.'"

"The mom interrupts now saying, 'of course we're proud. But we also know the local university has a master's program and you're only moving away to be with this gori—' that means white woman— 'and we won't be fooled into thinking otherwise.'"

I wince as he continues.

"The dad interrupts her, they're talking over each other a little, asking if he even plans on going back to work in the shops after. The son says he

doesn't know. The dad's furious now: 'After all we've done for you, you're going to throw it all away. For a girl.' The son replies, 'No, not for a girl.'"

By now, my palms were sweating. I flagged the server down for another drink.

Jagmeet continued. "He's cut off again by his mom. 'Your actions affect all of us. All the years of work we've done to build this family, and you're behaving this way? How do you expect to attract a nice girl from a good family when you're ready to settle down? No wonder things didn't work out with Sonja. You need to stop fooling around.'"

The mention of Sonja's name nearly made me choke on my drink.

"The son says not to bring her into this and that he isn't

fooling around, he's serious about her. I mean you. The dad's now yelling that the son is trying to abandon his responsibilities, but it's time to grow up. Your boyfriend is saying that if he doesn't have the support of the family he will take out loans, get a job if he has to, like Rebecca—I mean like you did. He seems to really admire you."

I tapped the table, not wanting to miss anything on the recording.

Jagmeet went on. "The mom is saying: 'What happens after school? What happens to the family? What will become of his grandparents? Is he going to abandon them all in a nursing home, like white people do?' No offence."

I cringed inwardly but shrugged.

"The dad says: 'If he's going to behave selfishly and like a child, and make decisions without even speaking to his family, without consideration for their future, then he may as well not be part of the family at all.'"

The recording was muffled and then went silent.

I rested my face in my palms.

Jagmeet fidgeted and then finally spoke up. "Is there anything else I can help you with?"

"No," I said and fished out a fifty from my clutch. "Thank you."

He hesitated before taking it from me. "Are you okay?"

I nodded and took a long sip from my Caesar. "I have a lot to think about... He didn't even fight for me. For us."

"Yes, he did."

I slumped back in my chair, disappointment seeping heavily into my chest. "Didn't feel like it."

"Arguing with your elders isn't something you do in an Indian family. There's a lot of respect and reverence," he tried to explain.

Priya didn't seem to have a problem arguing with her parents.

"Listen," Jagmeet said. "These big families, they're complicated. There's a lot of politics involved, a lot of moving parts. Everyone cooperates, works together. Well, most of the time. But I'm sure it will all work out." Jagmeet offered a kind smile and then stood and made his way out of the bar.

I wished I had his confidence. Somehow, I didn't think Dev's decisions lately were part of the family's plans at all. And who was at the centre of it all? Me.

I checked the time. Twenty minutes before my coffee *rendezvous* with Graham. Also, an unread message from Miranda popped up. *So how'd dinner at his parents house go??? Call me!!! Kiss emoji, excited emoji, nervous emoji.*

I left it on read, unsure of how to answer that question. Overall, though? Not well. Not well at all. Usually, the constant rain I dealt with as a Vancouverite didn't bother me. I'd grown up with the dreary sky and cold, wet droplets that fell most days of the year. Tonight, however, I'd have given anything for a bit of fair weather. My mood was despondent enough as it was.

I walked the few blocks back towards my apartment to the Starbucks where I'd agreed to meet Graham. Though I hadn't eaten, I wasn't hungry. Caesars were kind of a meal unto themselves, for one, and for two, the anxious ball of stress in my stomach was taking up a lot of room.

My mind was all over the place, tumbling between Dev's family's argument, our apparently crumbling relationship, and wondering what Graham could possibly have to say to me after so many months of radio silence. The most prominent question in my mind, though, was whether or not I cared.

The scent of freshly roasted coffee swirled out to greet me

as I opened the door. Conversation hummed in the background; tables were crammed with people chatting, reading, and studying.

Graham was across the room, sitting at a table with two cups in front of him. Our eyes met. My chest tightened, and my palms began to sweat. I hadn't seen him since the day he left. I'd stuffed his things into my old suitcases and thrown them into the lobby for him to retrieve rather than allowing him back into my home.

He looked the same. Sandy brown hair cut close, face clean-shaven. He was dressed in a grey sweater with a black jacket over top. The bags under his eyes were a little darker, perhaps; his rounded baby face a little pudgier.

As if in a dream, I walked forward and took a seat. We stared at one another for some time. I kept my expression in its standard resting bitch face and waited for him to make the first move.

"I got you a vanilla latte," he said, his memory of my typical order accurate.

I flicked my gaze down to the cup and then back up to him. "Thank you."

He fiddled with his cup, heel bouncing up and down under the table.

"Is there a reason you brought me here, or...?" I asked, glad my tone implied I was braver than how I truly felt. Miranda would be proud— after she got over being angry at me for meeting with him in the first place.

"Look, Becky. I made a terrible mistake," he began.

I took a sip of my lukewarm latte and raised an eyebrow. "Obviously."

"What I did to you, it was awful. I was an asshole. I see that now. Hell, I saw it then, too. What we had? It was amazing. I've never loved another person more than you. And that's why I did what I did."

I glared at him. "That makes zero sense."

"I was scared, Becky. When I looked at you, I saw my future wife. The mother of my children." He reached across the table and touched my hand.

I withdrew it, my throat tight.

He slid his hand back and took a deep breath. "I was turning thirty. I was starting to get fat. You know I have a complex about that. The kids at school? How they used to call me Chunkalunks? Now it's all I see when I look in the mirror. I was going bald—am going bald, I mean. It all hit me at the same time, how my youth was behind me."

"For the record, I never cared that you're going bald or that you're overweight."

"I know, I know. It's an insecurity thing, and I've been working on it with my therapist."

"This isn't about your insecurities or about your therapy— which, I'm glad you're getting help—this is about the fact that you cheated on me."

Graham sighed. "I know. I feel like such an idiot. I guess when Victor expressed interest... It was an opportunity I never had before. In high school, I didn't want to consider the fact that I might be queer. I mean, you've met my parents. And now, as an adult, I know I'm bisexual, but I'd never had the... chance, you know? To see that side of myself? It's hard even talking about it."

He lowered his head as if ashamed. I reached over and took his hand, giving it a squeeze. I wish he hadn't grown up in such a controlling household. No one should ever feel shame for their sexuality or gender or for not adhering to society's binary idea of what 'normal' is. If he'd been given the chance to embrace who he was at a young age, we wouldn't be here right now.

I swallowed the lump in my throat. "I don't care that you're bisexual, Graham. In fact, I'm proud of you for admitting it and being true to yourself."

Graham looked up, the dimples on his cheeks showing with his smile. "That's why you're so great, Becky."

I withdrew my hand. "But it doesn't change the fact that you cheated on me and hid it from me for months. You gaslit me and made me feel like I was crazy."

He sighed and leaned back against his chair. "I know."

I continued, anger building. "Then when I found out about Victor and confronted you, told you to stop cheating and just pick one of us... you chose him. Graham, you chose him." A wave of nausea struck me, and I pushed my cup away.

He stared down at his hands, slouching in his seat. "I had to see it through. Everything with Victor was so new. I had to process those feelings, as well as my feelings for you. I've gone over it with my therapist, and I think deep down, I was scared. Scared of leaving my youth behind, scared of never exploring that side of my sexuality, and... scared of being a father. My family life was so fucked up. I didn't want to repeat that."

Graham looked up at me, his bright blue eyes misty. "But I'm not scared anymore. I want to settle down, and get married and have kids, and... and I want to do it with you. I want to spend the rest of my life making it up to you. I love you, Rebecca."

My chest ached. It was as if he'd read my diary, if I'd had one, of what I'd hoped he'd say. Now that he had said it, though, I didn't feel any better. No sense of smug satisfaction, just the cold icy grip over my heart that said, *'Don't you do it, Rebecca. Don't let him back in.'*

I cleared my throat, fighting to keep the tears at bay. My mind was a tornado of conflicting emotions, and I couldn't listen to him anymore.

"I'm sorry, I have to go."

My chair squealed as I pushed back and got up to leave. He stood, grabbing my wrist. I turned to look at him, my glare evident that his touch was uninvited, and I had no problem causing a scene.

He released me, his face reddening. "Rebecca. There are no words for how sorry I am. I know what I did is unforgivable, but I'm hoping with some time, perhaps we can start over. We could still have a future together. You know it as well as I do: there's no one in the world who's better for you than me. All I want is a chance to be the husband you deserve, to be the father of your children you need. I'm ready. And I know you are, too."

I turned and left, the pressure of tears threatening to spill down my face as the pain he'd caused months ago resurfaced anew. The last thing I wanted was for him to see me cry.

Once I was back outside I called Miranda. I needed to hear her voice. She'd be mad, of course, but it didn't matter.

She answered right away.

"Hell-oooooooo!" She sounded like she was singing in a musical.

"Oh, he-hey," I stammered, caught off-guard by her over-the-top happy mood, especially when I was feeling so miserable.

"You wanted me to call?"

"Becky, ohmigod, I wanted to wait to tell you, maybe take you out for dinner or something, but I just CAN'T! Becky! I... I'm pregnant!"

I stopped in the middle of an intersection.

"... Becky? Hello? Did we lose... Becky?"

"I'm here, I'm here," I said, my feet somehow finding their way in front of each other, horns blaring.

"Are you okay? Shit. I knew I should have told you in person. I peed on the stick like an hour ago, and I couldn't wait! I'm sorry!"

"Of course, I'm okay!" I sniffed, my eyes blurring. I stopped walking and leaned against the closest building.

"You're crying!"

"I'm just so... so happy..." I sobbed, tears running down my face.

Now it sounded like she was crying. "I'm so ha- happy, too!"

"You're going to be a mom!" I wailed.

"I'm gonna be a momma!" she echoed.

We both cried on either ends of our phones, snorting, slobbery messes. When I finally found my words, I managed to croak out something along the lines of needing to celebrate, of going to brunch on me, or maybe a spa day.

And then, the call ended, and I was walking down the street in a state of partial zombification back to my apartment, where I collapsed on the floor and bawled until there were no tears left.

Fifteen

I SPENT the rest of the night in a stupor of self-pity. I'd managed to crawl into the shower and then onto the couch, still damp and naked, and turn on the TV to a random show to provide enough background noise so I could pretend I wasn't completely alone. I'd left the wine in the cupboard. The last thing my body needed was a depressant. Though I hadn't eaten all day, I wasn't hungry. I let my stomach growl to itself, the physical discomfort somehow lessening my mental anguish.

My brain rolled over the day again, and again, and again. Dev didn't want to live with me. His family didn't approve of me. Graham wanted me back in his life. And Miranda was pregnant.

I'd felt it creeping up—being left behind.

All my other friends from high school had either moved away or were married with kids. We'd stopped hanging out after that, having nothing in common anymore.

It had been just Miranda and me.

At her wedding, it had all come rushing back. I was the only one who showed up without a boyfriend when everyone else was either married with kids or soon to be. Even Nicole, with all her fake-ness, was further ahead in her love life than me.

Where had I gone wrong? What had I done to deserve this?

I'd had a plan. School. Travel. Job. Date. Marry. Kids. I was a modern woman. I could have it all, right? I didn't think it would take me until thirty to get this far, though. Had I wasted too much of my youth travelling, studying, and partying when I really should have been looking for a husband? Had my mom been right this whole time?

Maybe all the good ones were gone. Dev would move on and marry his ex Sonja, who his parents loved and respected. Would I be with Graham? That, or endlessly scrolling Tinder trying to find someone halfway decent who'd probably cheat on me anyway. At least with Graham, I knew what to expect. I knew the signs. I'd be able to tell sooner if something was going on.

If it hadn't been for him cheating, we'd be engaged by now. We'd be on our way. A quiet, peaceful wedding in the forest. Two-point-five children. Move out of the city, into the suburbs. White picket fence. A minivan. I'd learn to drive, to get the kids to hockey practice.

We'd been happy, hadn't we? I tried to remember, my memories shrouded, as if I'd covered them up like they did to furniture in old houses to keep the dust at bay. I remembered sitting on the couch in his apartment. Small, like mine, but well finished. Granite countertops. Gas stove. Real furniture that hadn't either been purchased from Ikea or from strangers on the internet. Tasteful yet safe art upon the walls, not wanting to make too much of a statement.

He'd cooked for me. Chicken breasts, Sidekick Noodles,

and boiled peas. At least he'd tried, right? He even watched *The Bachelor* with me. Not many guys would do that!

The sex was... sex. Some kissing beforehand, not much during. It was good, but, you know. I'd had better. It was like cereal. Yeah, cereal is good. You can eat it every day. But it's not like waffles and bacon, smothered in maple syrup, with powdered sugar sprinkled on top.

Which brought me to Dev.

Jagdev. Jagdev Singh.

Rebecca Singh.

What would we name our kids? Carter Singh. Penelope Singh.

Or maybe their names would be completely different from the ones I picked out in third grade.

But our future was up in the air. I'd made myself out to be the enemy, single-handedly driving him away from his family, the businesses they'd expected him to take over, and his responsibilities as a son. On top of that, there was a better, more suitable option for him to marry, someone his mother apparently not only approved of but was actively encouraging him to date.

Even if I was what Dev wanted, maybe he'd make a different choice. Maybe what his parents had said was sticking for him, making him think what we had was only a brief, sexual fireworks show, which would eventually fizzle out and leave him wishing he'd made a different choice—a more responsible choice.

Then, I realized, what Dev wanted was out of my control.

What was it *I* wanted?

I wanted what Miranda had. A loving husband, and a baby on the way. Her whole future was set before her now, every-thing bright and bubbly and shiny. When we were teenagers, we'd planned on getting married and having babies around the same time so our kids would grow up together, like we did.

Now those plans were out the window.

It was a surreal feeling, being so happy for someone, yet so sad it wasn't happening for me. I tried not to be jealous at first, but then I realized

there was no one around to judge and I let the feelings wash over me.

Miranda and her perfect, fairy tale wedding. Her husband with the good job and the good family and their nice house and their new baby on the way and the Pinterest-worthy nursery they were bound to have.

Angelina, her whole life still ahead of her, with so much gusto and confidence about who she was and her place in the world, a stark contrast to my own awkward self.

Even Nicole, with her perfect job, perfect rich boyfriend, perfect *everything*.

Ugh.

As I prepared for bed, I glanced around my apartment. It had always been enough for me. But, of course, Dev didn't want to live here. There wasn't even room in my closet for me, let alone him! I had been stupid even asking him.

Crawling into bed, I fell into a deep, exhausted sleep with no more tears left to cry.

THE FOLLOWING morning I woke with just enough time to make the early yoga class and busted my butt getting out the door and down the street in time to get there.

Somewhere between the third vinyasa flow and warrior three, I had an epiphany.

Never once in my life had I sat around and waited for something to happen. I made plans. I went out, and I took control—always had, always would. Waiting for life to happen wasn't my style.

Call me a control freak or whatever, life is too short to sit around waiting for other people to make decisions for you.

After class, I didn't even wait to go home and shower. All fired up from a sweaty flow class, endorphins flooding my body, I called Dev. No time to think. Just Do It. I channelled my inner Nike commercial and dialled.

The phone rang three times, and I was about to give up lest risk going to voicemail when he answered.

"Hey, Rebecca. I was just thinking about you." The sound of his voice made my heart sing, only to sink a moment later, remembering my reason for calling.

"Hey," I said, searching for the words I'd planned to say.

Dev filled in the silence. "I'm sorry for leaving so suddenly yesterday. Especially after... you know. It's been a lot. Can we talk? Not over the phone. In person?"

I nodded, even though I was on the phone. "I was thinking the same. A lot has come to light recently, and I think we need to take a look at our relationship."

I could almost feel him nodding on the other end of the line, too. "You're right. Things have been put into perspective. This week is busy for me. Can you wait until next weekend? I want to see you, but with everything going on—"

"That's fine. I understand. Next weekend works. Gives us both some time to think, to clear our heads."

"Right."

"Dev?"

"Yeah?"

I reached my apartment and stopped outside the entrance,

looking up at the sky on a rare, clear day. "I love you. I want you to know that."

His voice cracked. "I love you, too. I'll call you later, okay?"

"Okay. Bye."

We hung up. A lump was forming in my throat again, but I controlled it. Enough tears had been shed already. Enough time wasted on silly boys and silly emotions. I ran up the stairs to my apartment and spent the rest of the day scrubbing, reorganizing, and clearing my closet of all the stuff that no longer suited me.

At the end of the day, I poured myself a tall glass of cheap wine and was about to turn on the TV but turned to my little turbine project instead. It was a good distraction, and it was starting to give me

hope. The 3D CAD program I used was old and clunky, but the math was sound. It should work, theoretically.

I jotted down a few notes based on some research I'd done. One downspout per twenty feet of eavestroughs, so the average home would have six downspouts. Most houses are thirteen feet tall, so that's seventy-eight feet of my turbines.

Based on how much energy one foot of my turbines could generate, times seventy-eight, multiplied by the average rainfall in Vancouver over the course of one year...

Holy hell.

We could take the whole city off the grid.

I mean, at least through the rainy season. But it was something. Paired with solar panels in the summer? This could make a huge difference. And not only in Vancouver, but in other parts of the world that needed clean energy but didn't have enough sun.

But was it cost-effective enough to work in other parts of the world?

Based on similar projects we'd done at work, I calculated what I figured I might be able to make my turbines for.

It was doable. This could work. Really, the main thing holding the technology back was home batteries. Luckily, that was being worked on.

Lithium batteries had come a long way in the last few years.

I looked over the diagrams once more, eyeing them. Then, I opened a few more browser windows. I'd never filed for a patent before, but luckily there seemed to be several online businesses that could help. Though, did I really want to spend five hundred bucks on it? I chewed on my lip.

Leaving that window open, I navigated to the Government of Canada website. They had a whole page devoted to clean technology advancements. There was a grant available for green energy research and development...

I took another long sip of my wine. Dare I? Ah, what the hell. If you don't ask, the answer is always no. I began filling out the online form.

With the wine catching up to me, and Monday fast approaching, I closed my computer and headed off to bed. It felt like I was actually working towards my goal of doing something better for the world like I'd planned on doing so many years ago when I went to school.

At least I had that to look forward to. One glimmer of hope in all this mess.

On Wednesday night, I met up with Miranda for dinner to celebrate the wee clump of cells quickly multiplying within her uterus.

"Cheers to you and your incredible fertility!" I said.

She laughed. "I didn't think it would happen so fast! I thought that when you got off birth control, it would take months, maybe years to conceive. But apparently, that's not accurate because two months later, and bam—pregnant."

"Is that how it happened? Bam!" I giggled.

She shrugged. "Well, it wasn't as romantic as I'd always pictured it. You know? Like I thought it would have been a super lovey, missionary position, lots of eye contact, and petting deal. Nope, we banged on the couch mid-way through a Peaky Blinders episode."

"I can't say I blame you. Cillian Murphy is sexy as fuck."

"Always gets me going, that guy."

I looked at the menu. "So, I guess sushi is off the table for a while, hey?"

"Oh, god, I already miss it. And wine! Ugh, I miss wine. Once this is over, let's go on a wine tour. Like, to Penticton or something."

"Deal! So, when are you making it Facebook official?"

The waitress appeared and took our orders. Miranda got a burger and fries, and I the chicken strips. Leave it to us to go to a classy establishment and order plain crap.

Miranda answered my question. "We aren't telling like, *everyone* everyone, until three months in. That's what they recommend. God forbid anything happens, but generally, that's when it's safe."

"Who all knows, besides me?"

"Well Angelina, obviously. Hannah, my cousins, Nicole. Do you talk to them, anyway?"

"Nicole, lord no. Angelina and I text now and then," I said, which reminded me that Angelina knew about Graham and Miranda didn't. I should have brought it up, but the last thing I wanted was the wrath of a hormonal, pregnant lady bearing down upon me.

"What's your deal with Nicole, anyway? You two are my best friends. It kind of bothers me you don't like each other."

"Oh, she doesn't like me?" I raised my eyebrows in mock surprise.

Miranda's expression remained serious. "I don't get it. You're both great. It would make things a lot easier on me if we could all hang out together. Which reminds me, I have to tell you something."

Oh, god, what was it now? "What's up?"

She bit her bottom lip. "Nicole's already offered to do the baby shower for me. And I agreed. I hope you're not mad!"

Of course, I was. "No! Not at all! Babe, as long as you get a baby shower, that's all that matters to me." So now I had *that* to look forward to—a perfect, over-the-top baby shower put on by Fakey- Fake McGee herself.

"Good! Good, okay. I was worried it would bother you for some reason. Don't know what I was thinking. Actually, you know, I was wondering if you could give me an early baby shower gift."

"What's that?"

"Can you try to be friends with Nicole? I know she can come off as kind of arrogant sometimes, but it's a façade. She's really sweet when you get to know her. You just have to get past her walls. It would mean the world to me, especially now that I'm going to have a kid and have even less time for friends. If you two got along, then we could do girls' nights and stuff, and it would make the baby shower a whole lot less stressful for me."

I forced a smile. "Of course. Anything, for you."

The waitress returned with our food. Miranda took a bite, and with a mouth full of half-chewed burger, said, "I am so sorry! I've been so wrapped up in my own life I completely forgot to ask. How was dinner with Dev's family?"

I sighed. "It didn't go well. There was a lot of yelling."

"What? Why were they yelling?"

"Well, it started off fine, but then Dev's mom walked in on him and me... you know. And then he decided to tell them he's moving in with me."

"He's moving in with you? Becky, that's great news!"

I shook my head. "No, he's not. The next morning he changed his mind. We're meeting up next weekend, but it doesn't look good. I've been thinking about it a lot. I think our relationship has reached its end. I... I don't want to get any closer to him if it's not going to work long-term. I don't have time for that, and honestly, I don't want to get hurt again."

Saying it out loud to another person made me lose my appetite. I wanted to be with Dev, of course, but there was no sense in prolonging our inevitable break-up. Dragging it out would only make it hurt worse. This time, I told myself, I would be in charge. Perhaps that would make me feel better.

"Aw, Becky. I'm sorry. Everything was going so well! Why were his parents yelling? Because he wanted to move out? He's a grown man, for Christ's sake."

"It's not that simple. They have like, a huge family with his parents and grandparents, and they all depend on each other. It's complicated.

Anyway... you promise you won't think I'm a creep?"

Her eyebrow raised at the possibility of juicy gossip. "No promises. But tell me anyway."

I blushed a bit at the confession. "They were arguing in Punjabi and... I recorded it."

"WHAT?" she said, far too loud, attracting the attention

of the other diners nearby. She continued at a lower volume, leaning over the table, rapt. "What did they say?"

"Remember how I told you Dev had only dated one person before me? Well, I guess she's the person his family set him up with in hopes they'd get married. I think I saw a picture of her on the wall at their house. And—"

Miranda picked up her phone. "What's her name?"

My shoulders slumped. "Don't do it."

"Do what?"

"The creepy thing where you track someone down and stalk them on the internet."

She ignored me. "Sonja? Right? Let me see..."

I shook my head and leaned back in my chair. She was like a bloodhound on the trail of an escaped inmate. Now that she had the scent, I had to wait it out.

"Aha!" Miranda exclaimed a minute later. Her expression switched from excitement from the thrill of the hunt to doom, her eyebrows worrying.

"What?"

"Nothing." She tried to tuck her phone away, but I snatched it from her grasp.

I scrolled through the Instagram feed, full of perfectly curated snapshots of Sonja's life. Generally, I avoided Instagram. It gave me anxiety, and this was no different. First of all, she was fucking gorgeous. Second, there was a whole block of her and Dev together. Both of them had the same radiant white smiles. Oh my god, they looked perfect together.

And here was one of him kissing her cheek!

Squinting, I tried to zoom in and expand on the picture, but a little white heart popped up.

"Fuck..." I whispered, eyes widening.

"What?" Miranda said, snatching the phone back. She

gasped. "You *liked* it?! Becky! She'll know I've been spying on her!"

I panicked for a moment but swallowed it down. "It's fine, right? She doesn't know you, right?"

Miranda raised an eyebrow. "I'm sure she can figure it out."

"But she has like, what, a hundred followers?"

Miranda's lips twitched in a bemused smile. "Try a couple hundred thousand. This girl is like, Influencer status."

I crossed my arms. "I'm sure lots of people go back and... like pictures from... years ago...?"

Miranda laughed. "Only new girlfriends checking out ex-girlfriends do that. Trust me, you're on her radar now."

I groaned. "You're not making me feel any better."

She tucked her phone away. "Sorry, you're right. It's probably fine. You don't have Instagram, maybe she won't cross-reference with Facebook, and even if she did, your account is private. And, I un-liked the picture right away. Maybe she won't see the notification."

Shaking my head, I tried not to imagine Sonja laughing about me creeping her Instagram account with my best friend.

Miranda took a big bite of her food. "Okay, so, you were saying you recorded their argument, which is super creepy, by the way."

"I know," I groaned. "I had to get it translated. Basically, they said they would disown him if he moved in with me."

Miranda sat back in her chair, abandoning her burger for the moment. "That's seriously fucked up."

"It's nothing against me, personally. He has responsibilities to his family. You know? Like, he'll be giving up the job his dad worked his whole life to guarantee for him. And their home, they have older grandparents who need care, and that's on Dev to look after."

She nodded. "I guess it makes sense. But it sucks."

"You can say that again."

"But would you really want to be part of that, anyway? You moved out as soon as you could and worked your ass off to get through school on your own, and the great job you have. You don't even have roommates in a city where rent is like more than half your wage. You're stubbornly, almost stupidly independent. Do you think you'd be able to deal with having a family that close? Up in your business all the time? I mean, his mom walked *in* on you. Did she even knock?"

I sighed, having already given it a lot of thought. If Dev and I were going to be together, long term, did that mean we'd always be at his family's house, having big family dinners like the one I'd been to? Would we have to live with them someday, too? Sometimes I liked eating Kraft Dinner on the couch in my underwear, and living with his family would definitely put a damper on that. The idea of being constantly surrounded by people felt claustrophobic, even in a mansion.

I turned to my fries, dipping them in ketchup. "All I know is that I love Dev. Maybe part of loving him is letting him go. Letting him be the person he was meant to be, without me distracting him."

Miranda reached across the table and touched my hand. "You'll find someone, Becky. Trust me. Dev is great, but he's not the only fish in the sea."

Sixteen

I HAD LIMITED contact with Dev throughout the week, just the bare minimum texting required to arrange a meeting on Saturday night. Dev wasn't letting me in on exactly where we were headed, only giving me general directions. I told myself that it was one last date, one last night dancing in the ballroom with the prince before the clock struck midnight and everything turned back into pumpkins.

I'd decided not to tell Miranda about Graham. The conversation hadn't gone in that direction, and I didn't want to add more items to her growing list of reasons to feel bad for me. Angelina hadn't texted me about him, either, having probably forgotten all about it with the news of becoming an aunt. I didn't want to bother either of them with my problems, anyway. I still wasn't sure what to make of what Graham said, but I hoped that after this final date with Dev, it would be clearer.

When Saturday came, I was beyond nervous. My anxiety was once again presenting as nausea, rolling in waves on and off throughout the day. If it hadn't been for getting my period, I'd be worried about being pregnant, too, as if Miranda's fertility could rub off on me.

I'd decided to dress somewhat casually, probably putting too much effort into it than I needed to. My hair was up in a carefully crafted halfway messy ponytail, my eyeliner was perfect, and the jeans I wore were specifically designed to make my ass look amazing.

Though Dev offered to drive, I told him I'd rather meet him there. The idea of being in a car with him both there and on the way home when our relationship was at its breaking point did not sit well with me. It was nice having the time on the Skytrain to think, organize my thoughts, and go over the speech I'd prepared earlier in the shower. It was so much easier in the shower. Next time I'd record myself and replay it for whoever was to be on the receiving end.

I got off the train, and he was there waiting. He leaned against his car, painfully attractive in his jeans and V-neck shirt, exposing a smidge of chest hair. The sleeves were pushed up halfway, revealing those sexy forearms I loved so goddamn much. The way he smiled at me made my stomach jump into my chest, pushing my heart up into my throat. Suddenly I didn't trust my legs to hold me up, but somehow I managed to make my way to him without tripping over my feet.

I stopped about a foot away. He took a step towards me, the smell of his cologne wafting over with the breeze, combining with the aroma of cedar coming down from the forests on the mountains. It was intoxicating. The way his deep brown eyes drew me in, framed by his long lashes and serious brows, it wasn't fair. I was helpless.

Dev took another step, closing the distance between us, electricity dancing between our bodies like jumper cables connecting two batteries. He reached up and tucked a strand of loose hair behind my ear, his caress so gentle as if I were made of porcelain. Then, he bent down ever so slightly and pressed his lips to my forehead. My whole body tingled at his touch. My heart pounded against my rib cage as if trying to break free.

Then his arms were around me, pulling me close, and I could feel his own heart pounding in sync with mine. I wrapped my arms around his torso and leaned my head against his chest, breathing him in, wondering why the hell I didn't spend every single waking moment of my life in his embrace.

The pressure of tears formed behind my eyes as I remembered why I was there. I blinked them back and loosened my grip. He released me, wordlessly opening the car door.

Sitting there, I clenched my fists, steeling my nerve to do what I needed to do. We drove in silence. The silence wasn't uncomfortable, though. With Dev, it never was; his uncanny superpower had a universally calming effect no matter the circumstance.

I was going to miss it.

Glancing at him as he maneuvered through the city streets, I admired the way his hands gripped the steering wheel with gentle confidence, the same way he put his hands on my body. He caught me looking and smiled. I blushed and turned my gaze out my own window, wondering where we were headed.

Finally, we reached our destination: the Capilano Suspension Bridge. I hadn't been there since high school—weird destination for a date, but whatever. At least we would be outside, instead of some stuffy restaurant. Even so, all I could think about was my heart aching and the bittersweet feeling that this was our final date. I tried to ignore it so I could enjoy these last few moments together. I got out of the car and wrapped my jacket a little closer around my body, the shadow of the mountains sapping any warmth left from the day.

Dev came around to my side of the car, his hand on my mid-back.

"Something's bothering you," he said. Was I so easy to read? Or did he know me that well? He took my hand and we walked, my gaze down at the gravel pathway in front of me.

Given the opening, I took my strength from the giant trees around me, inhaled a shaky breath, and began.

"I did something I'm not proud of. I'm not sure what you will think of me, but please let me finish what I have to say."

He stiffened and then squeezed my hand.

"That night at your parent's house, after you told them you wanted to move in with me, while everyone was yelling... I recorded it. I'm sorry. I know it was a creepy thing to do, but I had to know what they were saying. I had someone translate it for me."

He didn't say anything. I continued, my heart pounding in my ears, my throat dry. We stepped out onto the bridge, old-growth forest surrounding us, cool fog rolling down below like a river. My stomach dropped, not only because of the ground falling away beneath our feet while the narrow bridge swayed in the breeze but because I was about to break my own heart.

And his.

"I appreciate everything going on in your life. I know how hard this must be for you, feeling like you have to choose between me and your family.

The last thing I wanted was to take you away from them, to cause a divide there. Your family really loves you, and they also depend on you. Before I came along, you had everything all figured out. Your dad had the business for you to take over, and it sounds like your mom had a girl lined up for you to marry, who, judging by the picture I saw, is beautiful. You two look great together."

He tried to interrupt, but I plowed on, knowing if I didn't use the momentum I'd gained, I'd never be able to finish.

"I love you. I want what's best for you. That's why I think we should end our relationship. What we have is amazing. I've never felt like this before with anyone. But there's more to... to a lifetime commitment than that. You need to be with someone who can help you be the person you were always meant to be. I love you enough to realize it's probably not me."

He pulled me to a stop. I had been so focused trying to recall the speech I'd prepared, trying to convey what was in my heart, that I didn't realize how far out we'd made it. We were in the middle of the bridge, suspended between two mountains, a deep ravine beneath us. I glanced back the way we came, then towards our destination, wondering which direction to head. Having said what I'd said, perhaps it was time to turn around and go home. There was no point in continuing on.

"Look at me," he said, his voice quiet yet commanding.

I didn't want to. So far, I'd kept the tears at bay, kept it cold and clinical, separated my heart from my words, shielding it from further damage.

Gently, he tilted my face up towards his.

Our eyes met; his a soft, warm, brown of infinite depth. His brow was furrowed in that heartbreaking way. My bottom lip trembled. For a moment, his hand remained on my face, caressing my cheek, his thumb running along my jaw. I leaned into him, my whole body yearning for more of his touch, to close the space between us and never separate again.

I pulled my face away, the tears I'd been suppressing threatening my composure. He held my hand tighter and pulled me farther along the bridge, deeper into the forest.

"Now it's my turn," he said. "I'm surprised you recorded us, but I'm not mad. It was rude to argue in front of you, and

I'm sorry. I shouldn't have used that moment to bring up moving in with you. It was poor timing on my part, but I don't regret it. These past few months with you have made me think. A lot."

It was his turn to take a deep breath.

"My whole life has been planned. My parents had two kids, a boy, and a girl. They raised me with the expectation that I'd continue the legacy they'd grown. My grandfather had moved to this country at a time when he was not wanted, was not welcome, and scraped and saved and built a business and a home and a community. His children, my father one of them, took that and ran with it, bringing wealth and prosperity to our families through six-day workweeks and twelve-hour days."

He sighed. "For me, all I have to do is keep the ball rolling. But I see things differently now, with you in my life. When I met you, from that first moment on the plane, you shocked me with how different you were: loud, outspoken, and not afraid to say what you wanted and to go out and get it."

I grimaced and looked up at him, unsure if those were good qualities to have. His smile told me he considered it a great compliment.

Dev continued. "You put some things into perspective for me, for who I wanted to be, for what I wanted my life to look like. You showed me it's okay to want something different and to chase after it, even if it means going against your family's plans. In the end, I still want to be there for my family, to look after them and continue the legacy they've grown."

He stopped and turned to face me, taking both of my hands in his. We'd reached the other end of the bridge, surrounded by trees taller than skyscrapers and older than the city itself.

"You also showed me how deeply I can love someone else.

I'd sort of resigned myself to the life my parents had lived. It is a good life. They're very happy. But the sort of passion between us? Now that I've tasted it, I can't live without it. I can't live without you. You're all I want, Rebecca. I know you love me, too. The fact that you're willing to leave what we have out of respect for me, for my family, is the greatest act of love I could ever imagine."

My heart was pounding so hard I was worried I'd crack a rib. Then, he slowly descended onto one knee. My head swam, unsure if I was dreaming or hallucinating or what.

"Rebecca. Will you marry me?"

He looked up at me. His eyes reflected so much hope, so much promise.

Over the next fleeting seconds, my mind raced for an answer, his proposal so unexpected that I hadn't had time to consider any possible future for us other than an ending.

He loved me. He wanted to be with me. He wanted to make it work.

What did *I* want?

I wanted him. More than anything in the world, I wanted him. Everything else floated away, like dandelion tufts in the breeze.

"Yes," I managed to squeak, tears running down my cheeks.

And then I was in his arms. He held me tight as if I were more precious than diamonds but likely to vanish at any moment. I pressed my face against his chest, listening to his heart pounding, and allowed myself a quiet sob. He kissed my temple, the feeling of his beard against the side of my face drawing tingles along my spine. I lifted my face to his, and he kissed me, his lips enveloping mine. It was as if my soul wanted to leap out of my own body and be one with his.

After a moment, he gently pulled me away. His eyes were

red-rimmed, cheeks wet. I laughed and wiped at his tears with my thumb, caressing his face. He grinned and pulled a small box from his pocket. I collapsed against his chest, barely able to hold myself up on my own two feet. He chuckled and pulled me back again, forcing me to look at the box.

He opened it. A giant diamond ring sat there, framed in white gold. With a slightly trembling hand, he slid it over my finger. I gaped at the huge diamond and then back up to his face.

He looked as if he'd won the lottery.

We were engaged.

Seventeen

WE COULDN'T STOP GIGGLING and stealing glances at each other the whole way back to my apartment. Soon to be *our* apartment! Once we arrived, we barely had time to take off our clothes before consummating our engagement. Just knowing Dev was mine, that he wanted me to be his, made everything one thousand times better. I couldn't believe merely hours ago, I'd planned on never seeing him again. Honestly, I didn't really remember what had been going through my head. It felt like a different person's problem.

We lay in a tangled, sweaty heap on the rug in my living room, clothes strewn about, fingers tracing patterns on each one another's bodies, memorizing each curve and dimple. I stretched out my arm, staring at my hand and the giant rock adorning it. It was way bigger than anything I would have picked for myself. Gaudy, in a way.

"Do you like it?" he asked.

"I love it. Are you hungry?" I kissed his cheek "Yes, but there's no way I'm leaving this apartment."

"Pizza it is!"

I smooched him and then pried myself away to use the washroom and order food, donning my robe afterward. In the mirror, my reflection was of a woman so completely happy, so beside herself with glee, I wanted to reach through the mirror and hug her.

My elation was like a helium balloon in my chest, and the only thing to stop me from floating away was sitting on the floor in the next room.

Looking back out at him, I relished the image, capturing the moment. That gorgeous, intelligent, caring human being was there, and he was there for me. Forever.

I started the pot on the stove and gathered the ingredients to make chai. "It's a good thing I cleaned out my closet the other day. There's actually space in there for you!"

After putting on his sweatpants, Dev came into the kitchen and leaned against the counter behind me. "Actually, that's something we need to discuss."

I glanced at him. "My lease will be up in a few months if you want to look at other places. But we should stay in the area for transit. It's not far from UBC and my work."

"Well, the thing is, I don't think we should live together until we're married."

I frowned, fishing a spoon out of a drawer. "So, we're still only going to see each other on weekends for a year plus until we get married?"

"Years? No. We'll get married in a few months before my program starts."

The spoon fell out of my hand and clattered to the floor. "A few... *months*?"

"Like I said, something we need to discuss."

I grabbed the counter behind me for support. "Dev. This is like, unprecedented. Miranda and Derek dated for two years before getting engaged. *Years.* We've been together like, what, five months? And mostly just on weekends! People usually live together before they get married, test it out, you know?"

He opened his mouth to start talking, but I interrupted.

"I thought we'd move in together first, enjoy being engaged, and then take our time planning the wedding. I mean, I don't have anything like what Miranda and Derek did in mind. Something small, you know? In the forest, like where you proposed. That was beautiful. But even then, we have to book the photographer, and the person who marries us, I have to get a dress, I have to pick out the bridesmaids' dresses, and then the reception—"

Dev grabbed my shoulders. "Relax. Breathe. It's all going to be fine. You don't have to worry about planning anything. My family's already gotten started. They've contacted our Gurdwara for the ceremony, my cousin's a photographer, and you can rent dresses."

"You've contacted the... what?"

"The temple. For our wedding."

I raised an eyebrow. "We're having a... Sikh wedding?"

Dev looked confused. "Of course."

I broke free of his touch and turned around to remove the boiling pot from the stove. I stared at it, unable to remember the next steps of making chai, my head spinning. After a steadying breath, I said, "Um. You know I'm not religious, right?"

"I gathered that, yes."

I exhaled, relieved, and turned to face him. "And, just so we're clear, you fall where, exactly, on that spectrum?"

He smirked. "Well, I'm sure you've noticed I trim my hair and don't wear a turban."

"I did pick up on that, yes." I couldn't help but smile.

"I love my family, and our culture, and our traditions, but to me, it's not much more than that. I guess you could say I'm an agnostic when it comes to the actual spirituality of it."

"So then why are we having a religious ceremony?"

"Don't a lot of people get married in churches even if they don't go to them on Sundays?"

"I guess that's true. Sometimes."

He rubbed my arm. "Part of joining my family is also joining the culture of my family, which means a traditional Sikh wedding. It would mean a lot to me."

I mulled it over, staring into his eyes as he waited for my response. How could I say no to him? I wasn't religious, and he sort of was. Well, his family was. I took a deep breath. "If it means that much to you, then of course."

He kissed my forehead and then embraced me in a hug. "Thank you."

I allowed myself to relax into his body, against his chest, appreciating his closeness when earlier today I thought I'd be saying goodbye to him forever. A traditional Indian wedding. In a matter of months. I'd been to Catholic weddings before. Couldn't be much different than that, could it?

The buzzer rang, and I jumped. Dev chuckled. "I'll get it."

He paid for the pizza while I paced the living room, my thoughts spiralling once more.

"There's so much we don't know about each other yet! Like, for example, you're vegetarian. We got a vegetarian pizza, which is fine, but I eat meat when we're not together. Do I have to be a vegetarian now, too? I love bacon, though. I would seriously miss it. Can you deal with me cooking meat in the house? Wait, do our kids have to be vegetarian? How many kids do you want? What will we name them? Is there religious stuff we have to do with the kids, too? Like baptisms? What if—"

Dev cut me off. "Woah, woah, woah. Time out! Breathe."

I swallowed.

"Rebecca, whatever comes up, we will handle it. Together. Let's take it one day at a time instead of being overwhelmed. What is the first thing we need to do?"

"We have to pick a date. Have you already picked a date? We have to reserve a place to do this thing. Did you say you already did that? You mentioned a Gurda-what? A temple. Right. I have to get a dress! Or do I? What will I be wearing? Oh, shit! I have to tell my mom! I have to tell my friends. I have to—"

"Calm down, relax! I've already spoken to your parents."

I stopped, my mouth falling open. "You did what?!"

"I called and asked your parents' permission," he said as if it were the most obvious thing in the world.

"Oh, because I belong to them?" I grimaced.

"What? No! Not like that. It's respectful, isn't it?"

"It's old-fashioned, that's for sure. It's leftover patriarchal bullshit."

"Is this one of those feminism things?" he joked.

I slapped his shoulder. "Dev!"

He laughed. "Sorry! I mean, if you think about it, marriage in its entirety is leftover patriarchal bullshit. I didn't mean to undermine you, Rebecca. I thought it was the right thing to do." He popped open the pizza box and offered me the first slice.

"I don't know, Dev. It's a lot to think about." I grabbed a slice of pizza and took a huge bite.

"Well, we don't have to talk about it right now. Our temple's reserved and we put out some feelers to a few places for the reception. I've spoken to my parents about everything, and as long as you said yes, we were going to have it all lined up and ready."

His parents had reacted poorly to the idea of him moving in with me. I could only imagine what kind of argument they had over him proposing. His mother, especially, could not possibly be excited about this. She seemed pretty set on him marrying someone else. Now she was bound to have a white daughter-in-law who knew nothing of their culture or customs and couldn't even eat a simple home-cooked meal at their house without having major digestive issues after.

We moved over to the couch, and I sunk into the cushions with a sigh.

Dev eyed me. "You're not having second thoughts, are you?"

"What? No!" I hesitated, then reached for another slice. "I mean, maybe. A little. I don't know. It's just sudden."

He looked at me, unable to hide the disappointment in his eyes. "Then why did you say yes?"

I set down my half-eaten slice of pizza and cupped his face in my hands. "I'm not having second thoughts about *you*, okay? I love you."

Dev leaned in and pressed his forehead to mine, smiling. "I love you, too."

I nuzzled into him. "I can't wait to wake up with you every morning and go to bed with you every night."

"Only a few months to wait."

I pulled away and frowned. "Your parents weren't concerned about us getting married so fast? Mine, either? People will think I'm pregnant."

He chuckled. "Why should we care what other people think? Let them gossip. I didn't tell your parents the timeline; I asked if they'd be okay with me proposing to you. As for my family, my grandparents met each other once before agreeing to get married. My mom and dad only dated for several weeks. They've all had successful, happy, long-term marriages. Living together or having a long engagement doesn't mean a lower chance of divorce, you know."

"I guess not. It's so different than how I planned things in my head."

"Don't let the plans of how you thought your life should be, get in the way of what's happening. Everything is good. We're happy. We love each other. We want to be together. That's all that matters, right?"

"How are you so wise?" I kissed him and then went back to my pizza, glancing around my small apartment. It was pretty small, which was fine for me, but with another person around, always underfoot? No matter how much I loved Dev, I was sure I'd need my own space now and then.

"What do you think? Should we rent a bigger place? I guess it would make sense to stay here, save up, buy a house."

"No need for that. After I graduate, we'll move back in with my family. We'll raise our kids there, and they can grow up in the same house I did." He had a faraway, dreamy expression on his face.

I choked on my pizza. "You didn't think to mention that *before* you proposed?"

He seemed offended. "Why? Does the idea of living with them bother you? I thought you liked my family."

"That doesn't mean I want to live with them."

He was taken aback and opened his mouth to retort, but I cut him off.

"And what about my job? I don't have a car or even a driver's license. Do you expect me to take a bus and a train two hours to work every day? Or did you even think about that?" My face flushed with anger.

"I thought you hated your job. I'm sure you could get another job."

I'd tried to stay cool, to stay collected, but that was it. All of my anger about being out of control, about plans being made *for* me and not *with* me, about my independence going out the window, reached its boiling point. I stood, nearly yelling.

"That's not the point! You expect me to drop everything, my whole life, to live with your family in the suburbs? We didn't talk about this! Why can't you live with me, here, in Vancouver? They can look after themselves."

He stood, too. "You don't know much about Indian families, do you?" He asked, his tone contemptuous.

"Sometimes I forget you're Indian."

He glared. "My heritage is a huge part of who I am, Rebecca."

"I didn't mean it like that." "Then how did you mean it?"

"I just forget, sometimes, that our cultures are so different. Don't change the subject. Why can't we live in Vancouver?"

"I'm their only son. I can't leave them. The firstborn son stays with the family, and eventually leads the household. You'd know this if you cared to learn anything about my culture."

"Well *sorry,* I don't know the ins and outs of your complex family dynamics! I'm sure you wouldn't have to have this conversation with Sonja." I turned on my heel and stormed into the bedroom, shutting the door behind me. I hugged myself and paced, trying to cool down.

Thoughts spiralled in my head, attempting to organize themselves with zero luck. Between the getting married in a few months thing, to not being able to plan and organize it myself, to joining a culture I had zero knowledge of, to being part of a family that didn't seem to like me, to one day having to live in the same house with them...

It was a lot... A lot I hadn't considered earlier, when we were out in the forest with the trees and the breeze, and he was down on one knee, and nothing else seemed to matter.

Now the logistics of what it meant to marry Dev and be part of his family was fully visible.

And I wasn't sure I could do it.

I couldn't imagine being in that big house, with so many people around all the time. The thought made my chest tighten, and my breath come out in short gasps.

A quiet knock sounded at the door, followed by Dev's muffled voice. "Rebecca? We need to talk about this. Let me in. Please?"

"I need some space!" The walls were closing in.

He sighed through the door. "I'll wait out here. But we need to work through this together. Hiding from me? From whatever you're feeling? It's not going to help."

The sound of his voice soothed my nerves. I took a few minutes to breathe deeply, calm myself down, and then I opened the door.

Dev stood opposite the doorway, waiting patiently. His brow was furrowed with worry, but the second the door was open he bridged the gap between us and hugged me tight.

"Sorry," he whispered in my ear.

I hugged him back. "I'm sorry, too. I don't want to fight. Not on the day of our engagement."

"I should have spoken to you about all of this first before I proposed. It's all I've been thinking about all week. I've gone over it again and again in my mind. I want us to be together, but I also want to respect my family and everything they've done for me. This is the only way I can see it happening."

I closed my eyes and held him tight, breathing him in. "I'm sorry for bringing up your ex. And for panicking. I want to be with you, but I want you all to myself. I've never had a roommate before... I don't like living with strangers. You know that."

Dev rocked me lightly back and forth, kissing my hair. "I don't graduate for another two years. Two years of you and me, all by ourselves. And by then, they won't be strangers. They'll be family."

I wiped away my tears and exhaled, releasing some of the stress and tension in my shoulders.

Dev pulled away and kissed my forehead before looking deep into my eyes. "We love each other. That's all that matters. Together, we can overcome anything, right?"

I looked up into his eyes, and my heart thudded in my chest. I nodded. Tears slide down my cheeks, but he nuzzled them away with his nose before pressing his lips against mine. My lips joined his fervently. My body ached for his touch; my soul needed him closer.

Unwilling to separate even for an instant, we stumbled to the bed and collapsed onto one another. His weight on top of me, his lips on mine, our eyes searching one another, the sense of wishing our bodies would become one instead of two separate entities, that's what it was all about. At the end of the day, all the concerns, the problems, the lists, the plans, they all faded away.

It was just us.

~

"You are *what*!" Miranda screeched.

If we'd been in public, I would have been embarrassed,

but we were sitting in her spacious North Vancouver home. It was a craftsman with high, peaked ceilings and exposed beams. It felt like you could walk out of her backyard and right onto a ski lift in the winter. Now, in the early summer, the yard was lush and green with hummingbirds and Steller's Jays.

Miranda snatched at my hand and pulled it, nearly knocking our coffees off the table to ogle my ring. I don't know how she hadn't noticed it immediately. It kind of stood out.

"Rebecca! This thing is *huge*!"

"I know. It's too much, isn't it? It's so big. I'm constantly whacking it into things," I pulled my hand away and eyed the diamond with uncertainty. "But I thought you two were breaking things off."

"I tried to, but he proposed and he said he loved me and, you know, I love him, too, so I said yes..." "Obviously, I mean, look at that thing. I'd have said yes, too!"

The serious tone of her remark caught me off guard, and a touch of anger rose at her insinuation, but I took a calming breath and brushed it off.

"Okay, so, how did it happen?"

I told her about the suspension bridge, how he'd gotten down on one knee out in the trees, and how romantic it all was.

"But then, when we got home, he kind of laid a lot of information on me. I don't really know what to think, you know? When we're together, everything feels so perfect, and then when he's gone all I can think about is how *not* perfect it is and all of the problems."

"Problems? Like what?"

I took a deep breath. "Miranda. We're getting married in three months."

She screeched again. "You're pregnant! Our kids are going

to be the same age! This is how we always planned it, remember?"

"Miranda, listen to me. I'm not pregnant."

"You're not?" She was visibly disappointed. "Then why the rush?"

"We want to live together, but his family doesn't want us to unless we're married. He starts his master's program this fall, and we want to move in together before then. Otherwise, he'll have a ridiculous commute, and we'll never see each other, and it would put off moving our relationship forward for at least two years until his program is over."

"I see. Okay. Well, that's not too bad. Weird about his family, but I guess they are more traditional. Are you doing a destination wedding? We have to book flights! Oh, shit, we have to have a bachelorette party. Damnit, I'm pregnant. This is going to be a lame-ass party. I'll DD, I guess."

"It's not a destination wedding. It's going to be a traditional Sikh Indian wedding."

Miranda stared at me blankly for a moment. "But you're not Sikh."

"I know, but Dev and his family are."

"Yeah, but it's *your* wedding, not theirs."

I sighed. "It's their way of bringing me into the family or something."

"So? They've already had their weddings. You only get to have one in your life! Well, I mean, ideally. Do you really want your first one to be in a religion you don't even know anything about?"

I clenched my jaw. Really? Why did it matter if it was Sikh, or Catholic, or otherwise? And mentioning divorces and multiple weddings brought up the very day after I'd become engaged? She was really getting on my nerves, which was even more aggravating since I'd taken the long commute up to her house instead of meeting somewhere halfway like we normally did. Miranda had always spoken her mind, it was one of the reasons we got along so well together, but for fuck's sake, I wish she could just be happy for me.

"It's important to them," I pressed. "And it's not a big deal to me. I mean, it's just a wedding."

Miranda raised her eyebrow. "*Just* a wedding? Who are you and what have you done with my best friend? We planned our weddings together when we were teenagers! And now you're throwing away everything you want because some guy's family is super clingy? Just wait, next, they'll be moving in with you."

I scrunched my nose.

"What? No! They're moving in with you?"

"Not exactly. After Dev's program is over... he wants us to move out to Surrey. Into his house. With his parents, and his grandparents, and everyone."

Miranda stared at me for nearly a full minute while I fidgeted under her scrutiny. Then, she reached over and took my hand in hers.

"Rebecca. You can't even live with roommates. You moved out when you were eighteen to get away from your *own* parents. How are you going to live with someone else's? Not to mention the obvious cultural and language differences. What about your kids? Will they be raised Sikh? You're an atheist, for Christ's sake!"

My heart was sinking, knowing all of this to be true, but wishing it wasn't. All I wanted was my happily ever after, to be with Dev, to raise a family with him, to grow old and drink tea next to each other on the couch while watching the evening news. I didn't think there would be so many concessions.

I was having trouble meeting Miranda's eye. "What are my

options, then? To be alone and miserable for the rest of my life, watching everyone else get married and have babies?"

"Aw, sweetie. You won't be alone! Trust me, you're way too amazing for that. It's not a race. If you love Dev, if you're happy, then do what you need to do. But I don't want to see you throwing away what you want out of life to meet someone else's standards, you know? It seems like you're giving up a lot. What's Dev giving up? He's got to meet you halfway."

Eighteen

THE PHONE CALL with my parents was similar but more encouraging. They'd known in advance, of course, and had been awaiting my call. What they didn't know, however, was the strict timeline we'd set. My mom had asked if I was pregnant, too. She sounded disappointed I wasn't. Then, like Miranda, she'd begun rambling about everything that still needed to be done. Then, just like with Miranda, I'd told her about our plans for a traditional Sikh wedding.

"*Oh!*" she'd said, followed by a long, uncomfortable pause. "Well, dear, what exactly does that mean?"

"I'm not too sure, to be quite honest, but Dev's told me he has everything arranged already. I still need to go with him to pick out the venue. I guess there are only a few places left with time slots available."

There was an even longer pause. There was so much going on that I wasn't aware of, that I wasn't in control of, and it was all I could do not to panic about it. The last thing I wanted was for my mom to bring any of it up. I had to keep telling myself everything would work out. It would be... it would be fine.

"Is this what you want, Rebecca?" Again, with that question!

"Yes," I said without explanation. Did I want a traditional, religious ceremony for my (hopefully) one and only wedding? No. Did I want to be married to Dev and have his family love and accept me? Yes. One thousand times yes.

"Then that's all that matters. You let me know what I can do to help. I've been looking forward to dress shopping for *years!*"

I didn't have it in my heart to tell her there would be no dress shopping. "I'll keep you in the loop once we have times and dates sorted for everything. Okay? Love you. Talk to you later. Love you, too, Dad."

I hung up the phone and stared at it. My apartment was cool. Quiet. Empty. Without really intending to, I opened my text messages and re-read my brief conversation with Graham prior to our coffee date. I mean, *rendezvous*. He hadn't tried to get in touch since. I wasn't sure if I wanted him to.

I'd received two propositions for marriage within a week— one from an ex who had cheated on me and lied about it for months and then left me once I found out.

My mind had a will of its own, and without my consent, it imagined me standing next to Graham, getting married out in the woods with the giant trees and the hanging moss, the sound of a waterfall in the distant background; my white dress, elegant yet simple, the train dragging lightly across the ground; our small reception, with only close family and friends, followed by a honeymoon in Harrison Hot Springs.

It would be beautiful.

But then, when I tried to imagine Graham's face there, standing next to me, I couldn't do it. His soft, rounded features. His sandy-coloured hair, thinning on top. I couldn't see myself sitting next to him on the couch, drinking tea and watching the evening news. Any time his phone would ding with a message, would I be wondering who it was? I remembered so vividly him looking down at his phone, an amused smile touching his face, before turning it over so I couldn't see.

A friend from work was all he'd said. A funny meme. A joke.

It was sickening even imagining that scenario. My phone vibrated with a call. Seeing Dev's name and picture pop up brought with it a wave of serenity and a smile to my face. "Hello fiancée," he cooed.

I grinned. "Is there a reason why we aren't FaceTiming?" A second later, an invitation popped up, and I was looking at him.

"Hello, fiancé," I echoed back.

"I miss you, beautiful. Did you speak to everyone?"

"Most everyone, yes. I still have to tell my brother. I haven't talked to him in ages, though. I don't know if he'll even make it with such short notice."

"I'm sorry."

"It's probably for the best, to be honest."

"So, I have some bad news and some good news."

My heart sank. "Bad news first."

"The places I'd looked at for the reception are all full."

"Well. Fuck."

"But, the good news is, my parents have offered up their house."

Panic rose in my chest again, realizing I had met his family exactly one time before agreeing to become one of them. I swallowed hard. "That's good."

"Yeah. Oh! And they want to have an engagement party.

One month from now. Does that work? They're taking care of the food and whatnot."

"Remember the last time I ate Indian food?"

He laughed, which made me smile. "I'll get you some Pepto."

"I'm being serious!" I pressed. "And my mom didn't eat anything at that restaurant we went to. Can we have some food there that's, you know, western?"

"You want some burgers and fries?"

"Ha. Ha. You know what I mean. This wedding is about both of us, remember?" Saying it aloud did nothing to stop the feeling of being swept up into a tidal wave of things that weren't for me, into a place where I didn't belong.

"I'll make sure there's other food there, don't worry."

"Oh. Um. My mom has to be there for wedding dress shopping. It's kind of a big deal for her. Do you know when that is? Do I book a place at a dress shop? I don't even think they can have a dress ready in three months."

"All the dresses will be rented. Priya's very excited; she said she's going to show you everything you need to know. I'm worried, but I'm trying not to be, you know? She has good intentions."

I tried again, this time being very clear. "It is important to my family, to *my* culture, to wear a white dress and have my mom and friends help me pick it out."

He rubbed his beard some more, thoughtful. "The lehenga is kind of a big deal, Rebecca."

"So is a white wedding dress."

"Can you wear the white dress, too? We can get pictures of both if you want. I'll wear a tux. If you want your girls to wear dresses, then they can, too. We can do both, can't we?"

"That's a lot to have going on the same day."

"You're right. It can't be at the wedding." He paused, looking away from the camera to think. "What about at the engagement party? We could get pictures in the backyard with the mountains and the fields."

My face must have lit up at the idea because he was smiling.

"Great," he said. "Let's do that, then. It's your special day, too. Just because we're getting married in three months doesn't mean it can't be everything you wanted it to be. I want this all to be perfect, for you to look back on our wedding and only think good things."

I blushed at his phrasing, imagining us at eighty reminiscing about our wedding together.

He continued. "If there's anything else bothering you, anything at all, please tell me."

Where would I begin? The giant rock on my finger was too heavy and too flashy. The one time I'd met his family, his mother had basically scorned me, and I'd spent the rest of the night in the bathroom with a fiery butthole. I was destined to live in a giant mansion surrounded by his entire family. My wedding was coming up in two months, most of which I had zero control over, in a ceremony completely foreign to me and unlike how I'd ever imagined. How we were going to raise our children, or even name them, was still up in the air. And the panic rising in my chest any time I thought about any of this was enough to make me sweat profusely.

"Everything's fine." I smiled.

"Good. Oh. I have an engagement present for you. I'm going to drop it off as soon as I can sort out the details."

"Details? What details?"

He grinned. "It's a surprise, but you will love it."

I couldn't imagine what he had in store.

We exchanged "I love yous" and "goodbyes" and then hung

up, Dev needing to make more calls to ensure everything was going to be on track for the upcoming events.

His call disappeared and left me on the screen with my messages from Graham I was once again called back to my imagination, to the wedding I'd envisioned, to who was going to be standing next to me.

Then, I imagined Dev. Tall, dark, handsome Dev, with his stunning features and classic smile, with the eyes that still took my breath away. The way he looked at me as if I were priceless artwork, was what I loved. He touched me the same way, his caress intentional but gentle, always balancing his needs with my own. When I imagined my future, the rest of my life, Dev was there. Without question.

The wedding was a means to that destination, to happily ever after. It was one day. It meant the world to him and his family and less to me, and so was it really that much of a compromise?

WITH THE ENGAGEMENT party coming up, I had a lot to plan for. I was extremely excited to pick out a white dress and have my mom there along with my best friends. There weren't many places in town available on such short notice, and they were quick to tell me alterations at this point would be impossible, so whatever I bought was going to have to fit just good enough.

Along with my mother, I'd invited Miranda (of course), Angelina, Shawan, and Priya. It would be the first time my mom met his mom, and I hoped it would go off without a hitch.

With her fake-blonde pixie cut, often overdone makeup,

and visible tattoos, my mom was pretty much the opposite of Dev's demure, proper mother. I hoped mine would keep it to one or two drinks at lunch and not complain about anything. Was that too much to ask?

I arrived early at the dress shop and waited for everyone else, steeling myself with a glass of champagne (which I hoped was included). They arrived a moment later, all smiles and energetic chatter—except for Dev's mother. She stood next to my mom and nodded politely as mine prattled on and on about something I couldn't quite hear. Priya was in there like a dirty shirt, immediately engaging in conversation with Angelina, who was conveniently about her age.

Miranda stood next to me. "Geez, girl. You have to get some more friends. My sister as a bridesmaid? Seriously?"

"I work in a male-dominated industry, Miranda. Who else am I going to invite? My yoga instructor?"

She sipped her sparkling apple juice. "Anyone but my sister. At least she has Dev's sister to hang out with. Maybe she will get into less trouble."

"Don't be jealous that your little sister is cooler than you." I smirked and then was led away by our sales lady, all elegance and hairspray, to find my first dress.

I don't know why I thought trying on wedding dresses would be fun. I hate shopping in general, hence my attire from Winners that's all at least a year old. Shopping for wedding dresses was pure torture. You're practically naked in front of a stranger as she pulls on an extremely expensive dress that fits weird and wasn't designed for comfort, then you parade in front of your posse and watch their faces respond with either smiles or frowns. And, of course, no one can agree on anything.

Four dresses in, and I was done.

"Are you sure you've tried on enough?" my mother asked, already on her third glass of champagne.

"Yeah, I'll just pick one of those," I said, hurrying all of us out the door and down the street to a pub. I was in desperate need of something a little stronger than the watered-down champagne they handed out.

At the pub, I ordered a pitcher of margaritas to be shared amongst me, my mother, and Angelina, while Miranda had a virgin Caesar while pouting. Priya, still only eighteen, was not legally allowed to drink until the following year. Even still, I doubt her mother would have encouraged such behaviour, seeing as she'd ordered hot water with lemon. I'd almost reneged on my order once the server had gone around the table, ending with Shawan and her simple, free beverage.

Once the margarita was in my hand and, more importantly, in my belly, I felt better.

"So, what are we doing about the bachelorette party?" Priya asked.

Shawan tutted. "You will not be attending. You are too young! They will want to go out."

Priya thrust her hands to her hips. "That's not fair!"

Angelina chimed in. "We don't *have* to go out. Why don't we rent an Airbnb in Whistler or someplace cool and have a house party? Old school girls' slumber party!"

Priya squealed. "Ohmygod, YES!"

"Great! I'll get planning it." Angelina grinned.

"Wait," Miranda interrupted. "I'm the Maid of Honor. I plan the party. Remember? And I definitely don't think underage drinking should be part of it."

"Oh, lighten up. You really think Priya hasn't been partying since she was fourteen like the rest of us?" Angelina said.

Priya tensed as Shawan glared at her daughter. "Better not be!"

My mother perked up. "Well, I can always be there as a chaperone! Shawan, would you feel more comfortable knowing a responsible adult is present?"

Shawan glanced from my mother's half-empty margarita glass, which she'd already refilled once since the pitcher arrived, to her innocent teenaged daughter. You didn't have to be a mind reader to know what she was thinking.

"Do we even need a bachelorette party?" I asked. Imagining a scenario where I'm stuck in a house with my inebriated mother, two wild teenagers, and my sober, pregnant best friend did not sound like a good time. I'd rather skip the whole thing. With the clock ticking on my upcoming wedding, we didn't really have time for it, anyway.

"Um, yes! You definitely do! Don't be ridiculous. We'll take care of the planning,"

Angelina said, gripping her sister's arm.

Miranda rolled her eyes and shot me a look that said, *kill me now.*

The rest of lunch was fine. Priya and Angelina had their own, very loud conversation. My mother was quite engaged with Miranda, talking about all things pregnancy-related, asking questions I'd never thought to ask her, which made me feel like a shitty best friend. I'd had no idea how exhausted she was, how she spent most mornings wrapped around a toilet. It made me feel guilty roping her into helping me with my spur-of-the-moment wedding when she had a child to plan for.

Shawan and I sat in silence. I kept thinking of things to say but then couldn't bring myself to say them. Small talk was never my forte. Wherever Dev got his ability to make any situation feel comfortable and not awkward, it wasn't from his mother. I kept imagining myself sitting across from her at the dinner table at her huge house, her quiet, penetrating gaze silently judging me as I worked my way around the extremely spicy food they'd all been eating since they were toddlers. I couldn't stop thinking about the look on her face when she walked in on Dev and me together, the horrified expression she'd worn as if I were defiling her baby boy.

By the time I got home, I was exhausted—emotionally and physically drained. I hadn't really had time to digest everything that was happening. Between the wedding coming up so fast to moving in with Dev's family in two to three years, I was done.

I popped open a bottle of the good wine I usually saved for special occasions and turned on some junk TV to unwind. Then, I opened my beaten-up old MacBook, minimized the drawings and plans and data for my turbine, and navigated to YouTube.

Search: *Sikh Indian Wedding*

I should have done this ages ago.

Turns out, Sikh weddings were gorgeous. The dresses, the jewelry, the henna; it was all so beautiful. It was an honour to be taking part in something like that. As a Canadian of muddled ancestry and an atheist, I didn't really have any traditions to take part in and often felt unmoored.

I wondered what colour my lehenga would be, but hoped red. It looked like Dev would be dressed traditionally, with a turban, and I imagined how he'd look. Dashing, probably. How could he look anything but?

I began Googling Sikhism and the history of Punjabi immigration to Vancouver to get a sense of my soon-to-be new family's culture.

Halfway through an article on the differences between Sikhism and Hinduism, my phone lit up with a text.

Graham.

I took a deep gulp of wine and opened it.

hey.

Seriously, what the fuck! How had I ever put up with this guy?

I texted back. *What do you want?'*

Three dots emerged and disappeared multiple times. Not having the patience for that, I pressed on.

Look, Graham. No amount of apologizing can make me forget what happened. I don't trust you. I never will. I'm with someone else, and I'm getting married in a few months. So, kindly, fuck off.

u pregnant?

I gripped my phone so hard I thought the screen would crack. *No I'm not fucking pregnant you asshole!!! and it's none of your business if I was*

then why the rush?

I owed him nothing, least of all an explanation. Then, why did my face feel so hot? Why was my pulse racing?

He texted again. *it's less than a year from when we broke up and ur getting married already. Becky I know you want to get married but you can't replace me with someone else. u know we were on that path til I fucked it all up and I will always regret that but u know in ur heart ur supposed to be with me*

Angry tears began forming. *I don't have time for this. Don't contact me again.*

I blocked him like I should have done months ago. Miranda had been right. Of course, she was. Talking to Graham didn't give me closure. All it did was reopen an old wound I'd been trying so hard to heal and move past.

I looked back at my computer screen with its images of sarees and henna and wasn't in the mood anymore.

Closing it, I stared into my wine glass. Graham was an asshole. But... maybe he had a point. Maybe Miranda had had a point, too.

On his own, Dev was everything I could have ever dreamed of. But he didn't come on his own. He came with traditions and cultural expectations, and a family who

hadn't expected a white, atheist daughter-in- law to move into their house and raise their grandchildren.

I looked down at my ring. The type of ring someone would expect any woman to vie for. The type of ring that would have suited almost any woman.

Except me.

Maybe Dev didn't know me as well as I thought he did.

Nineteen

THE ENGAGEMENT present Dev had promised me? It was a 3D printer. He had someone truck it to my apartment, and then, when it didn't fit in my already crowded living room, we brought it back to the kitchen, where my tiny Ikea table was shoved to the side.

Dev, hands on his hips, a proud look on his face, clearly thought he was a genius.

"Now you can build your prototype!"

Great. I was thrilled.

"Thank you. This is really thoughtful. I mean it. But my place isn't quite big enough for it. And I'm not sure if I'm ready to be building prototypes," I tried to explain, hoping there was a way to turn his gift down without causing offence.

Dev's shoulders sagged. "You showed me what you had so far, and it looked really promising. My dad's been asking about it. His business partners are intrigued and were hoping you could pitch them the idea in a few weeks. I thought a working, scaled-down model would entice them. So, you can print it on this and show them exactly what their money's going towards."

My stomach did a flip.

"Besides," he continued, "I could have brought the printer to my place and put it in the garage for you, but I wanted it here to remind you to work on it in your spare time."

"Spare time? I have a wedding to plan."

"No, you don't. It's all planned. Relax!" He closed the space between us, which wasn't much now that half my kitchen was taken up by that ridiculous machine. "Rebecca. You know how you told me to follow my dreams? To forge my own path? This is me returning the favour. Knowing you go to work every day at a job you don't love but need to pay the bills... it doesn't feel right. I really believe you're on to something special here. All you need is a little push to make it happen."

He kissed my forehead, and I melted, as usual. He could get away with anything, kissing me like that.

I looked up at him and, very genuinely, thanked him for his gift.

Then we celebrated—in bed.

AT MIRANDA'S REQUEST, we were doing things a little backwards. Usually, the bachelorette party is right before the wedding, but Miranda was worried none of her sexy dresses would fit her if we waited any longer. I didn't see a difference in her body, but I also hadn't seen her naked since college, and my memories of that drunken skinny-dipping event were hazy at best.

From what I could gather, Miranda and Angelina had been fighting over what to do about my bachelorette party and had come up with a happy middle ground to which I was not privy. All I knew was we were staying overnight in Whistler.

I took the Skytrain as far as it would go and bussed the rest of the way up to North Vancouver, where Miranda picked me up with Angelina in the back seat.

"I didn't tell you this before," Miranda began, "because I didn't want you to freak out on me, but we have one more person to pick up before we go." She put her silver Porsche Cayenne into gear.

"Who else is there?" I asked, clicking my seatbelt.

"Nicole."

"Nicole?! Why the hell is Nicole coming to *my* party?"

Angelina piped up from the back seat. "I told you it was a bad idea."

Miranda had the audacity to be miffed. "You told me you'd be willing to try and be friends with her, for my sake, remember?"

"For your baby shower, yeah! Tonight's supposed to be about me! I only want *my* friends at *my* party." I crossed my arms and pouted.

"Oh, I'm sorry, who was the one who let you bring the stranger you were banging in Mexico to her wedding? Hmm? Oh, right, that was me! So, I guess you could say you owe me one."

"That's hardly fair. It's a completely different scenario, and you know it. I was all alone, and you were busy the whole time. I was really looking forward to this just being us!"

"Fine," she huffed. "I'll call her and tell her you changed your mind."

I put my face in my hands. "It's too late now. She'll know I told you she couldn't come and it will make everything worse. Let's go get her, I guess."

"You know," Miranda said, "I read in a book once that the things we dislike most about other people are the very things we dislike most about ourselves."

I glared at her, unable to see any similarities between Nicole and me. "You know, three psych classes in nursing school doesn't exactly make you Sigmund Freud."

Miranda chuckled but said nothing. A few minutes later, we pulled up to a private gate. Miranda rolled down her window and beeped the intercom.

"Nic! Babe, it's us! You ready?"

A buzzer sounded, and the gates opened, revealing a gorgeous estate with a gabled, stone house. Between Chaz's hockey money and Nicole's big-shot marketing cash, they were clearly doing well. To make matters worse, Nicole only lived ten minutes away from Miranda. The two probably hung out all the time. Meanwhile, I was an hour train ride away.

"One second," Miranda said, hopping out of the car.

Angelina tapped my shoulder. I looked back to see her offering a flask. This kid, I tell ya. Golden. I took it gratefully and chugged back three mouthfuls, realizing mid-way through that it was Jägermeister, coughing on the last swallow. Angelina took it back, had a sip, and then tucked it into her bag.

Miranda and Nicole appeared a few minutes later. I wasn't surprised to see Nicole with a giant Louis Vuitton bag, way over the top for a single night's stay. All I had was my carry-on, which matched my suitcase: bright pink with lime palm fronds. Of course, it reminded me of Dev.

"Congratulations!" Nicole said, her tone lacking the usual insincerity as she climbed into the back seat next to Angelina. "And thanks for the invite! This will be so much fun! I really need a girl's night."

"Yeah. No problem," I replied, keeping my eyes straight ahead.

Miranda turned on some music, and off we went along the Sea to Sky highway. I kept my gaze out the passenger window, watching all the little waterfalls pass by as I fingered my giant ring.

"Oh my *god*, your ring is beautiful!" Nicole squealed. "It's almost as big as mine!" She shoved her hand up between Miranda and me, showing off the absolutely ridiculous-sized diamond, framed with about a thousand other diamonds. So now she and Chaz were engaged, too, apparently. I would have known this already if I had followed Nicole on social media. I didn't, of course. The last thing I needed popping up on my feed was pictures of her over-the-top perfect *everything*.

"Oh, congratulations to you, too," I said, trying to sound earnest. "When did that happen?"

"A few months ago. We're just starting to plan now for next year. These things take so long if you want to do them properly. I mean, not that you aren't doing things properly. It's different, I guess when you have a guest list of over three hundred and need to decide on which golf course is best suited to the event. You know?"

I glanced at Miranda, who gave me an apologetic smile. Three hundred people! I snorted at the absurdity of a wedding of that size.

The trip to Whistler seemed to take forever, with Miranda and Nicole singing karaoke to old Britney Spears classics, Angelina in the back texting, and me staring out the window hoping the night would pass quickly. At least the Jägermeister was kicking in.

We pulled up to a building near the ski resort, the mountainous hillside all green meadow and sunshine in the summer. As we were making our way to the main entrance, a white sedan pulled up. Out came Priya along with Shawan and Jag.

Priya ran up and hugged me hard as if we'd always been sisters. Then, she turned to Angelina and hugged her the same way, which made me feel a little less special.

I approached Shawan and Jag with a bit of trepidation. "Hey, you two! I didn't know you'd be up here."

Jag smiled, his calm demeanour putting me at ease. "Well, Priya really wanted to come, and we felt much better being close by. We're going to be staying in the area, just in case."

Miranda appeared beside me, and I took a moment to introduce everyone.

"Don't worry," Miranda said. "I'm not drinking and will make sure she won't be, either."

"Perhaps we can all meet for brunch tomorrow?" I suggested, then immediately regretted it, remembering my plans for tomorrow involved being very hungover.

"That sounds like a tremendous idea!" Jag said.

Shawan smiled and nodded.

We said our goodbyes and headed into the building where we'd rented a three-bedroom condo on the top floor. Between Priya and Angelina being best buddies and Miranda and Nicole being best buddies, I started to feel like the odd woman out at my own bachelorette party.

As soon as we got in, Angelina popped a bottle of champagne and poured a glass for everyone except Miranda.

"Hey, Priya's not old enough to drink," Miranda said, filling her glass with sparkling cider.

Angelina rolled her eyes. "Relax. It's one glass of champagne. Let the girl have some fun, will ya?" Priya grinned and clinked glasses with Angelina.

"Actually," Priya announced, "I have something important for us to do. Give me a minute to set up."

We watched with slight confusion as Priya gathered a laptop and some cords from her bag and began plugging them all into the TV. A few moments later, a PowerPoint presentation was visible, and she was motioning for us all to take a seat. Angelina topped up all of our glasses, including Priya's.

Standing out in front of us like she was introducing the newest iPhone, Priya squared her shoulders, cleared her throat, and began. "Seeing as you all are super white, there are some things you need to know about Sikh weddings. Allow me to educate you." She clicked through the slides. "Before the wedding even happens, there are some traditions that will take place. There's the Sikh holy book, called the *Guru Granth Sahib*, and it has to be read from front to back with no breaks."

"Wait," I said, interrupting already. "I have to read this giant book?"

Priya laughed. "Hell no! First of all, it's not in English. Secondly, you don't even have to be in the room. Our family will make a donation to the temple, and the priests take turns reading it. You and Dev can pop in and out. He'll probably take a few turns. Don't worry about it."

I sighed with relief.

"Then, you present Dev with *shagan*. It's just like, gifts that are traditionally given." She pointed at some of the images on screen. "Saffron paste, a coconut broken in half, almonds, sugar, and some dried fruits."

This was all very technical. Miranda leaned in and whispered, "What the hell is saffron paste?"

Should I be taking notes? I raised my hand.

"Will this presentation be available afterwards?"

"Yes. I can email it to you all."

"I'm okay thanks," Nicole said then chuckled under her breath.

I glared at Nicole. Priya looked a little uncertain, so I gave her a smile.

Priya continued. "A few days before the wedding, usually the groom goes by the bride's house to drop off the wedding dresses and what-not, but you'll be getting ready at our house, so no need to worry about that."

"When does the henna happen?" Miranda asked.

"A day or two before the wedding. It's my next slide." She clicked. "It's called the mehndi ceremony, and all of the important female relatives and friends are invited to join, and you'll all give gifts to the bride. Wear as much colour and jewelry as you can. It's like, really fun."

"We all get henna?" Angelina asked.

"Yes."

"Sweet."

Priya continued. "There's one other ceremony called *choora*. These red and white bangles are like a big fat 'just married' sign, and they symbolize fertility and stuff. Your uncle will put those on for you."

I interrupted. "I haven't seen my uncle since I was a kid, and I don't expect to see him at the wedding. He lives in Nova Scotia."

Priya thought for a moment. "Your brother, then."

Miranda chuckled. "I highly doubt Kyle would be interested in taking part in a ceremony like that."

I nodded in agreement. I hoped to keep him far away from everything wedding-related, as he would only add to my stress.

Priya shrugged. "We'll figure it out. There's also the *Doli* ceremony which happens after the wedding, where Dev and all the guys would go to your parents' house to take you away and bring you back to our house. It usually gets pretty emotional and dramatic, you know, because it is symbolic of when the bride would have to leave her family and sometimes travel a long way away. I don't think we will do the *Doli,* though. Everything is going to be a little different. You know, because you're white."

My mouth twitched.

"Okay, so, the morning of the wedding. We have to get up at the buttcrack of dawn, so don't drink too much at mehndi. Rebecca, you will be wearing a lehenga. It's going to be red, which is symbolic for prosperity. It's usually pretty bedazzled. The dupatta is this head covering part here. You're also going to be decked out in a massive amount of jewelry."

I looked at the image of the lehenga, feeling uncertain. Yes, the outfit was gorgeous, but it also sported a bare midriff. I hadn't shown off my midriff since college. I made a mental note to add some extra core work to my fitness routine.

"You guys may all be familiar with this image. It's called a tikka, and it hangs down from your head to cover where your third eye would be. Rebecca, you get this, but everyone else gets a bindi. This dangly bit here around your wrists is called the kaleere. This super elaborate nose ring part is called the nath."

I interrupted. "Um, my nose isn't pierced."

She squinted, inspecting my nostrils. "Oh. I thought it was. Don't worry, we'll take care of that."

What did that mean? Were they going to pierce my nose? I swallowed, wondering what other permanent bodily alterations I'd have to make.

"Okay, so. The main event. The Anand Karaj. The bride and groom, that's you, Rebecca, will bow in front of the Holy Scripture, the *Guru Granth Sahib.* There will be some singing and prayers and what-not. You'll say your vows and then walk around the holy book four times. Okay?"

I nodded. "Do I make up my own vows?"

Priya shrugged. "Up to you and Dev on that one. Before this happens, the male heads of the family will exchange Milni, which is like a flowery necklace."

I interrupted. "Does my dad have to bring his own, or will this be provided?"

"He should bring his own."

"Gotcha. I'll look into this."

"Good."

Miranda raised her hand. "What's the dress code for guests?"

"You can wear a saree, or a salwar kameez, or you can dress conservatively. But in the temple, you'll need to cover your head. We'll have scarves for you, or you can bring your own. Oh, and take off your shoes when you come into the temple."

"Noted."

"When you get to the temple walk up to the Guru Granth Sahib and bow before you sit down on the floor near the front of the room. Whatever you do, don't point your feet at the book. Got it?"

We all nodded. My head was spinning with all the information.

"At the end, there's dessert. It's called Parshad, and it's like pudding. After that, there are pictures, and then we party. Sikh weddings usually involve the whole community, but this is being kind of

rushed together, so there will only be about five hundred people."

I sprayed my drink across the room. "Five... *hundred* people?"

Priya shrugged. "Like I said. It's rushed. I've been to weddings three times that size. Trust me, this will be chill by comparison."

"I don't even know five hundred people!"

She nodded. "Which is why it's so small. It's just our family, friends, people from the community, our temple, Papa's work friends, my grandparent's friends, and my school friends —and your friends, too, of course. Obviously."

My head was ringing.

Angelina raised her hand. "Um, will there be alcohol at this reception, or do I have to bring my own?"

Priya laughed. "There will be lots to drink, don't worry. Oh, but it's kind of frowned upon for women to drink openly... so, yeah. Be mindful of that. Some of the old people might give you a hairy eye. Usually, we ask one of the guys to go to the bar for us, it's no big deal."

The presentation ended, and the four of us on the couch stared at the blank screen.

"Any other questions? Concerns?" Priya asked, looking like the future CEO of a Fortune 500 company.

Of course, I had questions and concerns. I had many other feelings, too. But I wasn't going to lay them all on Priya. My little wedding in the woods had suddenly exploded into a giant, extremely intricate, and lavish party of over five hundred people.

Angelina filled up my glass.

The night went on from there. We all dressed up and went out for dinner at a rooftop patio with panoramic views of the mountains. Angelina kept sneaking Priya sips of her martinis. Miranda kept chastising her younger sister. Miranda and Nicole's conversations fluttered from pregnancy to weddings. I drowned my worries and the overwhelming amount of information Priya had so casually laid upon me with a pitcher of sangria and various girlie shots that came my way.

After dinner, Priya and Angelina went back to the condo, as Priya was too young to get into any of the clubs. We'd suggested joining them, but they insisted they'd be fine without us and encouraged us to have fun.

And you know what? We did. Nicole was actually a blast to hang out with. At one point, we found ourselves in a karaoke bar, and they even attempted to show me the choreographed dance moves they had for *Barbie Girl*. The night ended with a traditional trip to McDonald's, and we carried our bags of greasy food back up to the condo.

The door opened, and smoke billowed out. I coughed in the haze. "What the hell?"

The girls had hot-boxed the condo. There was giggling, a door slamming shut, more giggling.

Miranda coughed and ran to open a window. "Angelina Veronica Meyers! I'm pregnant, for fuck's sake!"

Nicole and I laughed, apparently already high from the contact fumes, and got to work opening windows to air out the joint. Ha. Joint. Damn, I really was high.

And extra hungry.

We sat out on the balcony and ate our spoils, all of us reeking of cannabis.

Angelina and Priya joined us several minutes later, unable to avoid the smell of delicious, deep-fried goodness. Miranda glared at her sister, then laughed, and before we knew it, we were all laughing.

I sighed, sides aching. "Thanks for this, guys. I mean it. I'm really lucky to have you all in my life." Smiles, group hugs, and happy chatter filled the balcony until we'd all eaten our fill.

Afterwards, Miranda announced she was going to bed. I smooched her cheek, and she got up to leave.

"Me, too," Angelina said.

"Samesies," Priya agreed, both of them standing.

I glanced over to Nicole, who was staring out at the night sky dreamily. We sat in silence, alone on the balcony, a weight palpable between us. I had to say *something*. I let out a steadying exhale.

"You know, Nicole. I'm glad you came tonight. I know we've never really gotten along in the past, but it was fun being out with you."

She looked at me, and tears welled in her eyes. Honest to God, tears. "I'm so glad you invited me!" Then she hugged me, her expensive perfume mixing with the weed and McDonald's to produce a somewhat noxious combination. I patted her back.

She pulled away and wiped at her eyes. "Sorry, it's been a rough few weeks. I don't have a lot of friends. My one work friend I thought I could trust betrayed me a while back, and I came close to losing my job. So now I'm like a pariah there. It's probably only a matter of time before I get fired. And... and Chaz. He's gone all the time for games. I'm alone in that big house. Thank god I have Miranda, you know? She's always there when I need someone to talk to."

I rubbed her back. I wanted to say something along the lines of 'if you weren't such a bitch maybe you'd have more friends,' but I realized the comment applied to me, as well, and held my tongue.

Nicole sniffed. "I'm pretty sure Chaz is cheating on me."

"What? What makes you think that?"

She chuckled. "Just look at him. He's gone more than he's home, and when he is home, he doesn't really seem interested.

We only have sex like twice a week now, which is basically nothing. And he won't let me look at his phone."

I didn't really think twice a week was a shortness of sex, but okay. "Doesn't seem like anything to me..."

"He's done it before. I found underwear in his car. Some fucking fan girl, probably. Ugh. Damn puck bunnies."

"Nic, if he's cheating on you... why do you put up with it? I mean, look at you. You're drop-dead gorgeous and smart, and you're a self-made person. If you can't trust him, why marry him?"

She smiled at me through her tears. "Because I love him."

I couldn't help but nod, feeling her pain.

"And his career won't last forever. He'll be home soon. His fame will fade. I'll have him all to myself. I just can't stand the idea of him being with anyone else, you know?"

"Love is one thing, but you shouldn't wait around for someone to love you back. Take it from me." I had already walked a mile in that particular brand of shoes and had the blisters to prove it. Even if I had something more to say, some advice to give her, she wouldn't listen. Love was blinding her, just as it had me.

There was a brief silence. I began formulating my excuse to go to bed when she said, "You know, I've always kind of envied you."

I snorted a laugh. "What?"

"Yeah. You're so confident. So capable. You don't try to pretend to be anyone but yourself, even if yourself is kind of awkward and strange."

"Um. Okay."

"Plus, you and Miranda are like sisters. I've always wanted a sister." She sniffed, tears rolling down her cheek.

I squeezed her arm. "Well if it makes you feel any better, the feeling is mutual."

"I'm so glad we're friends now!" She laughed and hugged me, snorting and sniffing right in my ear.

"Yeah. Me, too..."

She pulled away and touched the corners of her eyes to stop her mascara from running. "Anyways, I'm drunk. I need to go to bed. Good night."

For a while, I sat outside in the chilly night air, enjoying the stillness. Miranda's words came back to me, about disliking traits in others we didn't like about ourselves. I could see a shadow of truth in that. This whole time, Nicole had been envious of my bond with Miranda, and I'd felt the same way. We'd been so intimidated by the other, so wrapped up in our insecurities, that we'd let it get in the way of getting to know each other. On top of it all, she was in a relationship rife with infidelity she didn't want to leave, exactly as I had been.

I hoped Nicole would find the same good fortune I had.

Twenty

BRUNCH WITH PRIYA'S parents the next day could have gone better.

Priya was obviously hungover. Jag and Shawan were not impressed. Shawan kept looking at me as if I was responsible for their daughter's state which, to be frank, I kind of was. I'd dropped the ball, letting her and Angelina party alone in the condo, getting higher than kites and drinking an unknown amount of booze, while all three of the actual adults stayed out until two in the morning.

Jag graciously paid the bill and then offered to drive me home since they'd be passing through Vancouver on their way to Surrey. I accepted their offer gratefully, not eager to spend an hour on public transit.

The Sea to Sky highway is a windy one, and about ten minutes into the drive Priya was barfing. It was all I could do to keep myself together, helping her as much as I could—like brother, like sister.

Honestly, I was glad for the distraction. Otherwise, the awkward silence penetrating the car would have really gotten to me. There was so much to say, but also nothing. Where could I even begin?

Once I was home, showered, and recovering with a home-made Caesar, I FaceTimed Dev.

"Hey, gorgeous! How was your girl's night out? I heard Priya had a fun time."

I grimaced. "Well, I think it's safe to say your low alcohol tolerance is genetic."

He laughed. "Priya told me she was going to tell you all about Sikh weddings, how to prepare for them."

Once again, I had so many questions that I didn't know where to begin, not having had enough time to process all of the information Priya had laid on me.

Dev's forehead furrowed. "Hope she didn't overwhelm you. It's really not that much that goes on. The ceremony itself doesn't last more than a few hours. And getting ready, I'd imagine it would take a while no matter what type of wedding it is."

"Five hundred people?"

"Ah."

"When were you going to tell me there would be five hundred people?"

"Is that a lot?"

"Don't play dumb. You know I always imagined a small ceremony. Now I'm going to be at a wedding with five hundred guests and know about ten of them."

He nodded. "Well, they won't be at the wedding, only at the reception. The wedding itself will only be close family and friends. If it makes you feel any better, I don't know a lot of them, either. It's kind of a thing; we invite pretty much everyone we know. My grandparents have been part of this community from the beginning, so they know a lot of people."

"I can't afford anything close to this. You know that. Between my rent and my student loans, I barely have enough to cover my monthly expenses. My parents are retired, and I sure as hell am not going to ask my brother for money."

"Don't worry about it," he said with a shake of his head. "My family has had money set aside for a wedding since the day I was born. And it's going to be comparatively small and tame compared to other weddings I've gone to. Don't worry, I'm making sure they don't go overboard."

I rubbed my eyes. "Okay. I trust you."

"Is there anything else troubling you?"

I sighed. "Just the fact you're not here right now."

His eyes twinkled. "Only another month or so till I'm there all the time."

I didn't tell him it was exactly forty-two days.

"Have you gotten a dress for the engagement party?"

I groaned. "No. Dress shopping is the worst. I hate trying on clothes and being judged by everyone. And no one can agree on anything."

"Why don't you go by yourself? Get something that makes you feel good. I'll e-transfer you however much it costs. I want you to feel as beautiful as you look to me."

AS DEV HAD SUGGESTED, I decided to bite the bullet and go by myself. Instead of going to those fancy-pants dress stores with their overwhelming variety of options, I'd found a few vintage shops downtown that carried second-hand dresses.

The first place I walked into was small, cramped, and dingy. It had a smell somewhere between mothballs and an old bookstore. The lady who worked there was tiny, hunched, and had glasses so thick it made her pupils look like she was high on ecstasy. Thankfully, she was very sweet and knowledgeable.

"Oh goodness, a dress for *this* weekend? Why so last minute?" she'd asked, perusing the racks for something close to my size.

I began trying to formulate a response, but she interrupted me with a tut.

"None of my business, love. We will find something to make you feel like a princess, for sure! What style do you like?"

Breathing a sigh of relief, I moved between the hangers and tried to imagine what I wanted. "Maybe something with lace? Something kind of vintage-looking, but not too old-fashioned. You know?"

"Vintage, my dear, is what we do. Ah, this one." She pulled it out, the dress a little crumpled and deflated as it hung, but it showed promise. Lace along the arms and neck descended down the bodice in a floral pattern, the bottom trailing the ground. "This one here belonged to a lady named Margaret. Her husband passed, God rest his soul, and she decided to donate her dress. They'd lived happily together for over forty years before his passing, and she hoped their good luck would pass on through the dress. She'd not had any daughters of her own, you see."

My fingers felt the lace, a glowing sensation rising in my chest at the story. "Do you remember every dress you take in?"

She winked through her thick glasses. "Only the special ones."

Behind a dusty velvet curtain, I stripped down and pulled on the dress as best I could. The lady appeared several moments later and helped me do up the back, the length of satin buttons and loops beginning above my bum and rising up to my neck. I ran my hands down the material, smoothing it out. It fit. I didn't even have to look in the mirror. I just knew. It was as if I could feel the lifetime of happiness the dress symbolized, the years of sipping tea on the couch, watching children race down the hall naked after a bath, of cozy nights tucked up in bed together with soft, slow lovemaking that only came with years of commitment and comfort in one another.

I bought the dress on the spot and walked out into the rare Vancouver sunshine. I couldn't wait for Dev to see me in it! I wasn't even going to show my mom or Miranda or anyone. They'd all have to be surprised.

The dress made me feel as if it was all meant to be. I'd been in the right place, at the right time, and with the right person to help me. It was going to be fine. And tomorrow, when I put it on and Dev saw me, and I saw him in his suit, and we had pictures with the blueberry fields and mountains in the background, it would be perfect. We could both have exactly what we wanted and live happily ever after.

The next day, I was less confident.

I'd gotten ready all by myself in my apartment, the ritual comforting. The only thing I hadn't been able to do was all the buttons up the back, but I'd get someone to help me once I got there. My hair and makeup were done to the best of my ability; agonized over, yet somehow still looking like it did pretty much every other day. I wished I'd hired a professional to get me ready instead of trying to be a DIY bride. Even Nicole would have been a better option.

It didn't matter, though. This was only the engagement party, not a real wedding. The pictures would just be for me. This event was really about our families meeting and getting to know one another.

Mom and Dad were picking me up on their way to Dev's place and texted their arrival. Despite the gorgeous summer weather, I wrapped myself up in my tan trench coat to cover my dress. I got downstairs, stepped outside, and stopped dead in my tracks. Standing beside the car was not only my mom and dad, but my brother.

"Kyle!" I shouted, startled, nearly dropping my things.

He swept me up in a hug. "Baby sis! Surprise!" Kyle was the type of guy you'd expect to see in most college fraternity houses. He had blond hair styled with far too much gel. His skin, what wasn't covered in intricate Irezumi tattoos and various calligraphy in languages he didn't understand, was tanned red-brown from living in Australia. Though he was dressed in a suit today, his clothes could usually be described as playboy surfer guy. Because, to be honest, that's exactly what he was. He was the type of guy who never settled down, who always dated multiple women, and somehow thought the women were the problem in all his relationships, despite his inability to keep his dick in his pants.

The only thing that made it worse was that he was smart. Whip-smart. So smart, it made him kind of a jerk. He was a know-it-all, and he could back it up with data. While I'd worked my ass off to study and get into my engineering program, he partied through his and still graduated in a more prestigious program with a much higher GPA. Now he lived in Australia in a penthouse condo as a petroleum engineer making two hundred thousand dollars a year and spending pretty much all of it partying while I struggled to pay off my loans and rent in my tiny Vancouver shoebox.

Would he help me out if I asked him to? Definitely.

Would I let him? Absolutely fucking not.

"So, Mom tells me you're marrying an Indian," he said once we'd set out on the road. He then proceeded to say something racist.

I gasped. "Kyle!"

He laughed. "Joking! Obviously."

My jaw tightened, and eyes narrowed. "Please, for fuck's sake, do not say anything even remotely like that tonight. Or ever. Okay?"

He shrugged. "I don't see what's so offensive, but whatever, Snowflake. He's brown. I bet he drives a white Beemer."

I reddened at the accuracy of this one particular stereotype that happened to be true in Dev's case. "Please, Kyle. Don't embarrass me. Don't say racist shit."

He acted mock-offended. "I'm not racist! I have lots of Black and Asian friends in Australia. One guy is even part-Aboriginal!"

I ground my teeth and glared at him. "Please. I'm asking nicely."

It was hard to believe we were biological siblings. He'd always been an asshole, yes, but this was the first time I'd ever heard him say something racist. Had my response been enough? I should have said more. I'd always imagined standing up to racism with gusto and bravery but never thought I'd be dealing with it in my own family.

I lowered my head, swallowing hard. How could I be an ally to people of colour if I couldn't even properly stand up to my brother?

I mean, my future babies were going to be people of colour. They were likely to face obstacles I never had to and couldn't even imagine because of my white privilege.

We drove in silence for a while before he spoke again.

"Hey, how's your job? Still making dildos?"

I sighed, exasperated. "I don't make dildos and never have, Kyle. I used to help design the packaging they come in. We've moved on to other projects since then. And it's great, actually. I love my job." I hoped he couldn't tell I was lying.

He laughed and shook his head, muttering, "Dildos."

"Stop being such a dick!"

Mom piped up from the front seat. "Becky! Your brother came a long way to be here and surprise you! Be nice."

And just like that, I was a child again, their genius golden boy unable to do wrong, and me sulking in the back seat wishing I was anywhere else. I couldn't believe they were going to throw my brother, a live grenade of assholeness, into one of the most important days of my life without even consulting me.

I texted Dev. *My brother's here.*

Great! I've been looking forward to meeting him.

You will regret having met him once you do. Fair warning.

When we finally did arrive at the mansion, our car slowed, and all four of our mouths dropped open. Lined up outside had to be about thirty cars. People milled about dodging children running into and out of the house. Several large white tents were set up in their backyard.

Dad parked the old domestic among Mercedes, Porsches, BMWs, and Audis.

Kyle whistled. "Now I know why you're marrying the guy."

I punched him in the arm, and he rubbed it in mock pain. If only I could hurt him for real. Priya appeared outside as we were getting out of our vehicle and gave me a giant hug. After I introduced her to my family, she ran back inside to tell everyone we'd arrived.

"That's your boyfriend's sister?" Kyle asked.

"My *fiancé's* little sister. And don't even think about it. She's basically a child, you perv."

"Doesn't look like a child to me."

I glared daggers at him.

Shawan and Jag appeared a moment later and were extraordinarily welcoming. Shawan greeted me with the typical two kisses, Jag with a bear hug, and then proceeded to hug everyone else as if he'd known them his whole life. I couldn't have picked a better father-in-law. I could tell Dev got a lot of his personality from his father, and looks, too. I tried to imagine him without the turban and beard, to see what I'd be looking at thirty years in the future, but it all was such a part of him I couldn't imagine him any other way.

Shawan wore an orange saree with an ornamental jewelled bindi on her forehead. I sensed a bit of sadness in the way she looked at me, though she was doing her best to hide it. Then we were overrun with people, all introducing themselves with hugs and two-cheek kisses, with smiles both genuine and guarded.

We made our way slowly into the house, and I did my best to retain as many names and faces as possible, though with everything going on I could barely even remember my own name. Inside wasn't any better.

Crowds of people gathered, eating, drinking, and laughing, and all of them turned to look at me, the main attraction.

I hugged my trench coat tighter around my body, instantly regretting the white dress underneath. I wanted to disappear. I wanted a margarita. I wanted to be back at home in my sweatpants. I wanted Dev.

Then, granting my wish, he appeared. The crowd, the noise, and the chaos, all dimmed to a dull roar in the background. Angels began singing, and light descended upon him from the heavens. He was an oasis in the middle of the Sahara desert, and I was a parched and weary traveller.

And damn, he looked sexy as fuck.

His hair was styled perfectly. The black suit he wore was expertly tailored, worshipping his body, accentuating his broad shoulders, and tapering down to his narrow waist.

He floated towards me, and I found myself lost in his eyes and the playful grin flitting across his face. The gentle aroma of his citrus and clove cologne wafted ahead of him—no hint of tequila.

He stopped in front of me and took one of my hands, lifting it to his lips; a gesture I now knew to be risqué, especially in front of his entire family. Even so, I wanted more. I wanted his mouth on mine, his hands on my body, to be enveloped in his embrace.

Then I blinked, and the world came back to life around us, a crowd of people gathered to lay eyes upon me for the first time. I blushed, suddenly self-conscious and a little embarrassed by the thoughts that had just permeated my mind. I hoped none of his family were mind readers.

Dev reached to help me remove my trench coat, but that was the last thing I wanted. Not only because the buttons weren't done up in the back, but because the coat had become a security blanket. It was the only thing separating me from this huge group of strangers. The white, somewhat prudish dress I'd so carefully selected felt more like lingerie. Maybe Priya had something that would fit me.

I looked up at him, wide-eyed, pleading for him to understand. He looked back at me with concern, and then recognition came alight on his face. He nodded subtly and then began leading me through the crowd, hopefully to find somewhere quiet where I could have a panic attack in peace.

Dev introduced me to people as we went. Auntie so-and-so. Uncle so-and-so. So many aunties and uncles!

There was no way Shawan and Jag had this many brothers and sisters. I tried my best to remember everyone, but the effort proved futile. I'd have to get flashcards made.

Just when things couldn't get any more overwhelming, there she was. I recognized her from the photo in the hall, from the expertly curated images on her Instagram, from her flawless *everything*.

Sonja.

And holy hell, she was fucking perfect.

Her giant, gorgeous eyes were framed with long lashes and thick brows. Full lips turned up in a quirky smile as if the person next to her had made a witty comment. Her long, dark hair hung in waves down to her mid-back. The red dress she wore hugged her body, much more voluptuous and sensual than my own, but the dress still managed to be conservative and tasteful for the event. And the shoes. Real Louboutins.

I remembered the images from Priya's presentation, the cultural implication of the colour red. She may as well have been wearing white.

Instead of walking past her, Dev took us up the stairs. Once we were safely in his room with the door closed behind us, I found my breath and tried to calm myself.

"Is something wrong?" he asked, reaching out to touch my shoulder.

I pulled away. "I thought this was supposed to be just family. So my parents could meet yours."

"It is just family."

Unsure if he was playing dumb or what his schtick was, I glared at him. "Oh, is Sonja, your ex, actually your cousin or something?"

A note of anger touched his face. "Her family and my family go way back. Our mothers were best friends growing up, and Sonja is only a few months younger than me. We grew up together. They're practically family."

His explanation only made me feel worse. "What you're saying, is that your ex-girlfriend was your childhood best friend, your high school sweetheart, the girl who took your virginity, *and* your mothers pretty much planned your wedding as soon as they found out your complimentary genders? And she's here, right now, at our engagement party?"

Dev tucked his hands into his pockets and shrugged. "I guess so, yeah."

I turned away from him and walked toward the window, watching as even more cars pulled up, boxing my dad's sedan in. Now there was no escape.

"Are you mad at me?" He touched my arm again, but this time I didn't pull away.

Anger was only one of my emotions, but the main one was overwhelmed. It was all too much. Our rushed, giant wedding. Joining a foreign culture. Dev's massive family. His perfect ex. His mom's clear preference for her. Far too much.

"I'm fine," I whispered.

Feeling safe in our relative solitude, his arms found their way around me and pulled me close to his chest. I allowed my eyes to close, my body to relax against him, as his lips made their way down the side of my face.

"You look beautiful," he whispered in my ear. His warm breath on my neck sent a tingle up my spine.

Then his fingers found their way to my trench coat. Gently, as if unwrapping a gift and trying to save the paper, he peeled the jacket from me and took a step back.

I closed my eyes, cheeks burning, wondering if he'd expected something else. Something grander. Something befitting his family's class and wealth. Something that had at least cost more than a hundred dollars from a vintage store.

I forced my eyes back open and glanced over my shoulder at him, my naked back exposed.

His mouth hung open slightly, his huge eyes wide, pupils dilated. "Wow," was all he managed to say.

"Do you like it?" I smiled.

He closed the distance between us, and our lips met. His were eager, insistent, as if he could bear no more time apart from them. His hands trailed up the bodice of my dress carefully, not wanting to disturb the aged lace, and then found their way to the bare skin on my back. My hands found his beard, fingers trailing their familiar routes along his jawline and down to his chin. When our lips finally parted, he was slightly out of breath and rested his forehead against mine for a moment, swallowing.

"I love you," he whispered.

My throat was thick. "I love you, too."

"I can't wait to spend the rest of my life with you."

I fought back the tears welling in my eyes. And, just like that, nothing else mattered.

After buttoning up my dress, he kissed the tip of my nose, took my hand, and led me out of the room, the smile on his face the same as the day he'd proposed.

Twenty-One

༺⚬❀⚬༻

THE PHOTOGRAPHS TAKEN outside with the blue summer skies and mountains in the background were everything I wished they would be. Dev looked incredible in his suit, and I loved my unique vintage dress. I hoped the pictures would turn out beautifully, though I likely wouldn't see the end results until after our real wedding, which of course, was coming up way too fast.

After getting lots of photos of Dev and me on our own, our parents joined us. My dad cried. It was pretty cute. Dev's mother even looked halfway happy about everything.

Miranda, Angelina, Priya, and I posed for pictures together, too. We did the awkward fake-laugh thing, as is tradition. They loved my dress and said it looked stunning on me. Miranda remarked that it was too bad I wouldn't be wearing it at my actual wedding, which got a side-eye from Priya. We toasted the four of us and then had to separate as more relatives made their way out for photos.

The process took a lot longer than expected. When it was

finally over, Dev and I were famished and made our way to the outdoor tents where a buffet had been set up.

I took a plate and eyed the food, seeing only Indian varieties available.

"Dev?"

"Yes, gorgeous?"

"You said there would be western food here for my family."

He looked down the row of dishes. "There's salad."

I frowned. "All my parents get to eat is salad?"

"And rice? I asked the caterers to have something for everyone. It was the best they could do on such short notice," he said, dishing up his plate and moving along.

As much as I wanted to complain, I couldn't. It wasn't my family paying for all of this, it was Dev's, and the last thing I wanted to do was seem ungrateful.

As we moved along the table, Dev pointed to various dishes and put some on my plate he thought I'd like. He guessed right —delicious deep-fried goodness. There was samosa, masala chaat, dal, and roti. My favourite was gol guppa, a deep-fried crunchy hollow ball with liquid inside. If attending parties like this was going to be a frequent occurrence in my life, I'd have to size up my yoga pants. With each bite, I was more confident even my picky-eating mom would find enough to satisfy her.

Boisterous laughter rang out. Kyle was chatting it up with Dev's cousins while was making them all cocktails—Monster energy drinks and vodka, heavy on the vodka.

How much had he drunk, already? We'd left my brother unsupervised during the photos. Bad idea.

"I should tell him not to drink so much," I said, moving towards him.

Dev stopped me. "He's fine! My cousins are party animals. Trust me, he's in good company. Relax. Look around. Everyone's having a good time. Your mom is even eating some Indian food. See?"

I glanced around. He was right. My mom was sitting at a table with Shawan with a half-eaten plate of food, showing off her collection of essential oils. Oh god, Mom, please don't be giving her the sales pitch. Jag and my dad were talking about cars, eyeing up Jag's Mercedes. Miranda and Derek had found another couple who were expecting, discussing all things baby-related. I had no idea where Priya and Angelina were, but they were two peas in a pod. I didn't have to worry about them.

Then, why did I have this feeling of dread in the pit of my stomach, as if I was waiting for something to go wrong?

I tried to brush it off—pre-wedding jitters.

The next hour or so was spent with Dev continuing to introduce me to people, me explaining my job over and over again, them joking about me taking their Dev away to the Big City, which ceased to feel like a joke after the tenth time it was brought up.

Then, it finally happened: Sonja found her way to us.

Her dazzling smile lit up the room, completely disarming me. The way she strolled up, the sway of her hips, everything; she was like a movie star. I could sense her natural charisma, her charm. She had that *je ne sais quoi,* which floated ahead of her like her tasteful vanilla musk perfume.

Suddenly self-conscious, I looked down at my messy plate of half-eaten food and set it down quickly, spilling some sauce on the white tablecloth.

"You must be the Rebecca Dev is always talking about," she said, reaching her hand out to shake mine, her fingernails perfectly manicured. It hadn't even occurred to me to get my nails done for the party, and they looked rather boyish in Sonja's elegant grip. Her handshake betrayed her, being oddly firm. I'd expected the limp wrist of a proper lady. But no, Sonja wasn't fucking around. She wanted me to know she was there. Challenging me. On another note, Dev was talking to Sonja about me? What was this "always?" How often were these two conversing?

I managed to plaster on my best smile and took Dev's arm, but couldn't for the life of me figure out anything to say to this woman. Really, there was a lot I wanted to say to her, but nothing polite.

Even Dev, the king of making awkward situations less so, struggled as he looked between Sonja, me, and the glass in his hand.

Sonja plowed through. "I hear you're an engineer. That sounds like interesting work!"

"Well, no, not technically." I was about to explain why but decided not to expand on my lack of degree any further. I refused to make myself out to seem lesser in front of Sonja.

"Oh?" She gave a bemused smile.

Dev sensed my discomfort and chimed in. "Rebecca's working on a prototype for an eavestrough turbine to take houses off-grid."

Sonja's brows shot up. "Really!"

"She's using the 3D printer I got for her. It's really fascinating! Here, I'll show you some pictures—" He proceeded to whip out his phone to show off the tiny prototype pieces I'd built so far.

Sonja leaned in close to him, clearly interested, though if it was in the pictures on his phone or just getting a better whiff of his sexy cologne, I couldn't be sure.

I eyed the two of them. Their proximity was making me uneasy. "Dev, didn't you say your dad was getting some investors together?"

Jag sidled up. "I did, indeed! Is it ready?"

It was so far from ready. But with Sonja here, I couldn't back down. "Um. Yes. Close, I mean."

Dev stepped away from Sonja and pocketed his phone but continued to brag. "Didn't you apply for some government grant?"

Now I had Jag's undivided attention.

I doubled down. "Yep. I applied for the Green Energy R&D Grant and filed my patent. If I get the grant, I'd be about halfway to my goal of scaling up and installing models on buildings."

Jag grinned. "That is great news! I'll arrange a meeting with some business partners, see if we can get you the rest of that funding. I'll get everything sorted for next week."

Though the smile stayed on my face, internally, I was screaming. A meeting? With his business partners? Next week?! I wasn't even sure if the thing would work in real life yet! I fought back the anxious ball of stress in my stomach and changed the subject.

"What do you do for work, Sonja?"

"I work with Dev in the shops. Jag and my dad went into business together a long time ago, and they're co-owners. I have my accounting degree and help run them. We'd still be working together, except he decided to go back to school. But, you never know how things go, what the future holds."

"And a great accountant you are, Sonja!" Jag complimented. It felt like someone was stabbing me in the chest, the way Jag looked at her. He obviously liked her. *I* was going to be his daughter-in-law. *I* was supposed to be his favourite.

Sonja smiled at him and then glanced at Dev.

The way she looked at him tied my stomach in knots.

These two had been working together this whole time? Why didn't Dev ever mention it?

Painful memories resurfaced. Graham's late nights at work. Me, walking into his office, pitiful glances in my direction as I ignorantly walked past the guy he was having an affair with day after day. The lying. The embarrassment. The heartache. The shame...

Fool me once.

"Yes, the future sure is a mystery," I agreed, trying to smile, but managing only to produce a wane grimace.

The boisterous laugher from the tables next to us turned to yelling, drawing our attention. Kyle was face-to-face with Moe. Of all the people for Kyle to interact with, it had to be Moe. Together they were a powder keg, the drinks in their hands a lit match. There was finger-pointing, more yelling, and then it happened.

Moe launched himself at Kyle, tackling him into a table. The table collapsed under their weight, glassware crashing as their drinks hit the ground.

A lady screamed. Shawan. Jag scrambled to her side, pushed her back, out of the way.

Dev had his arms out, one in front of me and the other in front of Sonja, protecting us both.

Kyle made his way to his feet, touching his nose. His fingers came away bright red with blood. Two others pulled Moe up and dragged him away as he continued to point and yell Punjabi in Kyle's direction.

My brother pushed past me, through the crowd, and into the house. Mom, Dad, and I trailed.

In an angry burst, Kyle bellowed and punched the wall, leaving a hole.

"Kyle!" I cried, eyes wide in shock at the damage he'd inflicted on Jag and Shawan's home.

He turned and glared at me, but before he could say anything, my parents were at his side, escorting him down the hall and out the front door.

I followed close behind.

"What the fuck happened?" I yelled as we stalked along the lawn back to my dad's car.

"I made a joke! It was a fucking joke. Jesus Christ, those people have no sense of humour," he said, wiping his nose on the back of his hand.

I stopped and watched as my mom herded my brother into the car. "Sorry, Becky! We'll take him to the hotel. He's had a bit much to drink. Love you, sweetie. We'll talk tomorrow. Please tell Jag and Sharon thank you and sorry, and we'll pay for the damages." Mom and Dad climbed in, shutting the doors with apologetic half-smiles.

"Her name is Shawan," I mumbled, hugging myself as a chilly wind made its way across the blueberry fields.

Dev appeared behind me. "You okay?" He touched my shoulder, but I withdrew.

"I'm fine." I turned to walk back towards the house. I needed a drink. Or several. My brother causing a scene hadn't distracted me from the fact that he and Sonja were rubbing elbows at work every day of the week while I only got the occasional text or FaceTime call.

Dev was close behind. "Don't worry about the fight, Rebecca. Trust me. It happens all the time at events like this. Moe has a big mouth. I'll call your mom and dad tomorrow and apologize to them on his behalf."

I shook my head but didn't look back at him. "Trust me,

my brother got what was coming to him. He's the one who should be apologizing."

In the kitchen, I poured myself a big glass of wine as Sonja walked in through the back door.

"Hey, is your brother okay?" she asked.

I grimaced. "He's fine, thank you. Want some wine?" I offered, having filled my glass up.

She held up her hand. "No thanks, I don't drink."

Of course, you don't.

Miranda and Derek came in from outside. "What happened? I heard Kyle got in a fight?"

"You didn't see it?" I asked and then gulped down half of my glass of shiraz. "He punched a hole in their wall, too."

Miranda's eyebrows shot up. "Again? He always does that. No, I was looking for Angelina. Have you seen her?"

I shook my head. Shawan and Jag came in then.

"Sorry," I said sheepishly. "I'm so embarrassed. I'll pay for your wall."

Jag shrugged. "These things happen. Don't worry about it. We have a cousin who's a contractor. Is your brother okay?"

I nodded. "He'll be fine, thank you. Is Moe...?"

"Fine, yes."

"Have you seen Priya?" Shawan asked, mouth downturned in concern.

"Can't find Angelina, either," Miranda said.

Shawan pushed past us and went up the stairs in search of her daughter.

Miranda seemed to notice Sonja for the first time and introduced herself. To my utter despair, the two of them really hit it off. Miranda brought up how we'd accidentally 'liked' one of her old pictures when she was doing the requisite best friend snooping, and Sonja thought it was hilarious. I wished

Miranda hadn't brought it up. From there, they dove into an effortless conversation as if they'd known each other for years. Jealousy piqued inside me, and my skin felt hot.

She's my *goddamned best friend, not yours*! First, it had happened with Nicole, and now it was happening with Sonja. I wanted to hurl what was left of my wine at her annoyingly perfect face but lifted it to my lips instead.

A scream echoed through the house. Startled, Dev bumped into me, which made me bump into my wine, which caused it to slop all over my dress.

Miranda, Sonja, and I stared at the red stain, mouths agape.

"Mom! Get out of my room!" Priya yelled.

Our group made their way to the bottom of the stairs in time to see Shawan dragging Priya down by her wrist, a flurry of angry Punjabi escaping her lips. Shawan pulled Priya past us, an intense aroma of marijuana accompanying them.

At the top of the stairs stood Angelina, having followed behind the two of them.

"Angelina! What the hell!" Miranda chastised. Angelina descended the stairs, righting her dress and wiping a bit of lipstick off her mouth. It didn't take a genius to figure out the lipstick wasn't hers and hadn't been applied the traditional way.

"Yeah, we should probably go," she said, nonchalant as ever. "Shawan walked in on us doing... things."

"Hot boxing her room?"

She smirked. "That, among others."

Miranda groaned. "Sorry, Becky," she said as she walked past. Derek offered me a smile and nodded to Dev. Angelina winked at me. *Winked*! Then the three of them trailed out.

Which left me with Sonja and Dev. And a huge, red stain on my dress.

I sighed. "I'm going to go try and get some of this out."

"Need some help?" Sonja called as I walked away.

I ignored her and made my way to the hall bathroom, locking the door behind me. Closing my eyes, I rested my back against the door and counted to ten. It didn't help. Still unsettled and irritated, I gave up and looked into the mirror to assess the damage.

My dress was ruined. My perfect dress, with the buttons up the back and the lace and the everything... it was done. Sorry, Margaret. Your good luck wasn't enough to help me.

A quiet knock interrupted me before my thoughts could begin to spiral.

"Hey, it's me," said Dev through the door. "Can I get you anything?"

I sniffed. "Yeah. Um. Can you find me something to wear, please?"

"Of course. I'll be back in a minute."

I listened for his retreating footsteps to disappear and then made my escape. I walked down the empty hall, everyone apparently outside, and found my way to the side door next to the garage. I needed fresh air. A minute alone. A minute to think, to process.

It was beginning to get dark outside, but the moon was up and full. I walked along the side of the house until I found a rock to sit on, nestled amongst some professionally maintained flowers and shrubs.

Then, and only then, in the near-darkness and the stillness and the silence, did I allow myself to cry. Not loudly; there would be time for that later. Silent tears slid down my face, likely messing up my makeup, which would go well with my ruined dress. It had all gone to shit. My family was gone. My friends were gone. I was alone here, with these strangers—these strangers who were supposed to become my family in a few short weeks. A deep sense of not belonging filled my chest, of being in the wrong place at the wrong time.

My pity party was interrupted by the sound of two men approaching, talking to one another. They walked right past me as I was hidden in the dark tucked away behind a corner of the house. The smell of weed accompanied them as they passed a joint back and forth. One of the guys was Moe.

It was impossible not to eavesdrop, and I certainly wasn't going to make my presence known. The last thing I wanted was for them to see me in this state, sitting in the dark and crying like a weirdo.

"Seriously though, I remember that Angelina girl from Mexico. Don't you?" Moe stated, exhaling a cloud of smoke.

"The slutty blonde? Shit, yeah. I remember Becky, too, only barely. Didn't she turn you down?"

"That gori bitch? Hell no, she isn't my type."

The other guy laughed. "Anything with legs is your type, bro."

Moe spat on the ground. "She's too white for me."

"You don't have a white girl fetish? Oh yeah, I forgot, you're into that lemon party shit."

"Hey, fuck you!" Moe shoved him playfully. "Seriously though, I'm shocked this is happening. Banging a white girl on the side is one thing, but bringing one home to mama?"

The other guy agreed, muttering something about Dev being some kind of nut before the pair disappeared around the corner of the house.

It took me a moment to remind myself to breathe.

A white-girl fetish? That's a thing? Is that what everyone thought about my and Dev's relationship?

I was done with this party.

Once inside the house, I walked down the hall and back to the kitchen, hoping I'd find Dev along the way. Maybe talking to him would make me feel better. He had a way of making things make sense.

Not seeing him in the kitchen, I went upstairs to go get my trench coat from his room, remembering I'd left my phone in my pocket. As I turned the corner to his suite, I looked up to see he was already in there.

"Oh, there you are," he said, his eyes wide.

"Yeah. Coming to get my coat and call myself a cab."

"What? You're leaving?"

I shrugged. "No point in staying."

"Let me drive you, at least," he said.

Before I could agree, the door to Dev's ensuite opened, and Sonja walked out. She paused, looking between the two of us, a deer caught in headlights.

I glared from her to Dev, a sick feeling in my stomach making its way up my throat. Then, before they could protest, I grabbed my jacket and ran out the door.

"Wait!" he called, chasing after me as I descended the stairs.

"Stop!" he yelled as I ran through the house. Tears blurring my vision, I burst out the front door and slammed it behind me.

"It isn't what you think!" he continued to call after me, pushing the door open. People turned to stare as we ran past.

A taxi was already parked outside, the only luck I'd had all night. I ran up to the open passenger window and relayed my address as Dev caught up to me, pushing against the door so it couldn't open.

"Rebecca, let me explain! The other bathrooms had a line-up, and Priya's room was a mess, and she was—"

"Save it, Dev," I said, wiping an angry tear with the back of my hand. "This isn't just about Sonja."

"Then talk to me! What's wrong?"

"Everything!" I shouted. I tried again, a little quieter. "Everything. The rushed, huge wedding. The moving in with your parents. The fact that you should be with Sonja like you were meant to be. *Everything*."

"What do you mean?"

I opened the cab door but hesitated to get in. "We're too different. It will never work."

Shaking, I removed the giant ring from my finger and pushed it towards him. He held out his hand, and I dropped the jewel into it. I couldn't look him in the eye.

I watched in the rear-view mirror as he got smaller and smaller behind me, looking down at the ring I'd left behind.

Twenty-Two

I THOUGHT ENDING things on my terms would lessen the blow. Reduce the pain.

I was wrong.

The hardest part was telling everyone the wedding was off. I'd ignored the calls that had started lighting up my phone after sending the texts, unwilling to even try to find the words to explain what had happened or why. Soon after, the texts had become too much, as well. I silenced my phone.

Sunday passed in a haze of tears and self-medicating with ice cream. Monday morning came, and I still couldn't bring myself to leave the house, despite the absence of junk food and liquor.

I called in sick to work. I never called in sick. Another week of staring at a computer screen doing mindless tasks was beyond the current state of my mental health.

To make matters worse, I'd told Jag the meeting he had planned with his investors was off. The last thing I wanted to do was stand up in front of him and a bunch of other people who had probably been invited to the wedding, I'd cancelled.

Besides, going into business with my ex-boyfriend's dad sounded like a bad idea. That level of awkwardness made me want to bury myself under a pile of blankets and never emerge.

But without the additional funding, I was only halfway to my goal of making a scale model of the turbine. Now it would never happen. I was stuck, exactly where I had been six months ago before I'd even met Dev.

Only now I knew what I was missing out on.

I took a shuddering breath.

It had all come crashing down. *Everything.*

My mind kept replaying our romance over and over, and over. I should have known earlier it wasn't going to work between us—I wasn't right for him, and he wasn't right for me.

If the two of us could live in a bubble, unaffected by anything else in the world, we would die happily together at the ripe old ages of one hundred and one hundred and five. Holding hands, like in some Nicholas Sparks novel.

In reality, it couldn't be so. There were things he wanted from me, needed from me that I was unable to provide. I loved him enough to let him go, to let him find it elsewhere while he was still young.

Not that he needed to look far, with Sonja waiting in the wings, eager to remind him of their predestined nuptials.

As much as it hurt, I hoped he and Sonja would be happy together.

I imagined the two of them as children, playing together in the blueberry fields, and then growing into teenagers, exploring their own sexualities and one another's bodies for the first time. I imagined their wedding, the wedding Priya had described in such detail in her presentation. I imagined their families mingling together and becoming one, as they'd planned since Dev and Sonja had been babies. I imagined her in the red lehenga. Red suited her, as I'd witnessed at the engagement party. The jewels, the bracelets, the nose ring... I bet her nose was pierced.

They'd have beautiful children with tan skin and dark brown eyes and thick eyelashes and gorgeous smiles. They'd live together in his house with his family, raise their children, and take care of all their aging parents when the time came. They would cook the type of food they'd both grown up eating. Shawan and Jag would smile at their son and daughter-in-law, glad everything had worked out as they'd always planned. They would all talk and joke and laugh together in Punjabi.

At least Dev would be happy. Knowing that made me feel better. If I had to live my entire life being miserable, at least I'd know the man I loved was happy.

For myself, almost thirty, the dating pool had evaporated to a scummy pond, littered with garbage and used diapers.

I stared down at my muted phone as unanswered calls and texts piled up and reinstalled Tinder. Then, I ordered a cheap pizza and a box of wine to be delivered. If I was going to go through the hell of Tinder I could at least be drunk and full of carbs.

There was no time to waste. Best to jump back in, to find someone who would erase the memory of Dev's body on mine, the feel of his beard on my cheeks as he kissed me, the touch of his hands on my body. His smell. God, his smell. The way he breathed on my neck, the sounds he made when he was close, the sounds he made when he knew I was close, the satisfied look in his eye when he brought me pleasure—

Those memories had to be overwritten. I had to move on. I had to stop thinking about him with me, about him with Sonja, about him altogether.

I began swiping. I swiped right on everything. Guy holding

a fish? Right. Guy flexing in the gym? Right. Guy making a duck face in the mirror? Right.

Guy complaining about his baby momma? Fuck it. Right.

Then, a familiar face popped up, and I nearly choked on my saliva.

Graham.

He was on Tinder. No doubt doing the same thing I was, trying to move on. Trying to find someone so he wouldn't die alone. Looking at him like this, with only a picture and a short caption outlining his job and height, it made him look so innocent. If I hadn't already known him, I would have swiped right in an instant. He was good-looking. He seemed responsible. He looked like the type of guy I wouldn't mind dating, wouldn't mind looking at forever, wouldn't mind the eventual boring repetition of a long-term marriage. He looked like he might make a good dad, help with the diapers and the homework, and teach the kids to ride their bikes.

But I did know him. I knew the sex would quickly devolve from decent to dull. I knew his cooking repertoire rotated between chicken with rice and spaghetti.

I knew he was a good liar.

Grouped amongst these other Tinderers, were all those traits that bad? The qualities of all the other men unknown, yet to be discovered, could be much worse. Drugs, possibly. Gambling habits. Abusive tendencies. My mind circled back to the same idea; with Graham, at least I knew what I was getting into.

And here he was, on Tinder, staring back at me. He'd found a way to reach me, despite being blocked on my phone.

Was it a sign?

I didn't believe in signs.

... Maybe I should start.

My thumb hovered between the swipe buttons.

Right or left. Right or left.

What would my parents think? They'd liked Graham well enough, didn't they? If I forgave him, they could, too.

What would Miranda think? I shook my head. Who cares what Miranda thought? She was already married, pregnant, and living her happily ever after. I could settle for slightly less. Even a fraction of what she had would be better than my current situation. As a feminist, I knew I didn't need a man to complete me, but dammit, I didn't want to end up alone, either.

His explanation from our *rendezvous* swirled within my mind. I understood why he did it. It made sense. He wasn't ready to let go of other possibilities, of closing a door to a side of his sexuality he hadn't had a chance to explore yet.

My stomach soured, recalling our last fight. I'd found out about Victor, how they'd been sleeping together behind my back for months, how Graham had been lying about it the whole time, and how everyone seemed to know except me. If he'd just told me, instead of lying, instead of hiding, things could have been different.

If he'd chosen me, when I'd given him the ultimatum, instead of Victor...

Things would be different.

But he'd lied to me. And he'd chosen someone else.

And I never wanted to be someone's second choice.

My thumb hovered over the icon. I'd told myself I would swipe right on everyone, as Miranda had instructed when Graham and I had broken up months ago. But this wasn't right. It wasn't what I needed. Not being with Dev didn't mean I had to reduce myself to going back to someone who held so little respect for me. If it meant being alone for a while, to eventually taking a risk and opening up to someone else, then it was what I would do. If it meant waiting for my happily ever after, perhaps indefinitely, then that's what I'd do.

My plans of getting married by thirty, and having babies alongside my best friend, were just plans. They were arbitrary. Real life was different, and it didn't care about my plans or the ridiculous timeline I'd set for myself.

Life existed after thirty.

Love existed after thirty. And even if it took me my whole life to find it, I wouldn't give up.

I swiped left, and Graham's face disappeared. The oxymoronic sensation of relief and anxiety washed over me as a stranger's face took his place. I inhaled a steadying breath, feeling that sense of closure I'd been looking for.

After all this time, it wasn't Graham who needed to give me closure.

Only I could give me closure.

As I settled in to continue swiping, the buzzer sounded at my door.

Grunting, I got up from the couch and pressed the button to let the delivery person up before shrugging on my robe to hide my exposed nipples under my threadbare and heavily stained tank top. A moment later, there was a knock at the door. I opened it, expecting pizza and wine, to see my dad instead.

"Dad! What are you doing here?" I pulled my robe a little tighter. I'd completely forgotten they were still in town. He'd probably tried to text and call me. I dropped my gaze, feeling guilty for ignoring him.

He looked at me with doe eyes, his mouth pressed into a firm line. "On our way back to the ferry. You weren't answering your phone. Thought I'd drop this off."

In his hand was a package wrapped in silver and black paper with a red bow.

"What is it?" I asked, taking it from him.

"An engagement present."

I tried to push it back to him, but he held up his hands. "You don't need to open it if you don't want to. I wanted you to have it. But I have to go, sweetie. Your mom and brother are in the car, and it was all I could do to make them wait down there. They won't wait forever, though."

"Thank you." The last thing I wanted was to deal with my mom and brother.

"I know you need your space right now, sweetheart. You're like your dad in that way. Don't be afraid to call me, okay? I'm a good listener."

"I know." I sniffed, lip trembling.

He took me in a big bear hug and squeezed me tight. When he pulled away we were both crying. Clearly embarrassed by his tears, the Boomer that he is, he turned and left quickly. I closed the door, eyeing the package through my blurred vision.

I flipped it over, a small smile quirking up the corner of my lips at the overabundance of tape used—typical Mom.

Unsure if I should open it, I turned the package over in my hands, weighing it. Before I could make a decision, the buzzer sounded again, startling me.

I pressed the button to let the person up and set the package down on my 3D printer, deciding to wait until I had the accompanying wine. I eyed the bulky machine and little pieces of a half-built turbine littering my table and counter space, a permanent reminder of Dev. As soon as I was done getting drunk, I'd drag that thing out into the hallway and push it down the stairs.

There was a knock at the door. I opened it and nearly jumped out of my skin.

"Shawan!" I shouted. Then, more quietly, "What are you doing here?"

She looked from me to the car keys she fidgeted with and back up. "I'm sorry for barging in on you like this, Rebecca. I just wanted to talk to you."

I frowned, unsure of what to do or say. We looked at one another, silence building. The buzzer sounded again, startling us both. I pressed the button and asked who it was, unable to take any more surprises today. This time it was, in fact, my delivery.

"I'm sorry, I would have called, but I didn't think you would have answered," she continued to explain.

She was right. I wouldn't have.

The delivery person was there a moment later. I paid for it and then gestured down at the bags in my hands.

"You like pizza and cheap wine?"

Having Shawan in my apartment under normal circumstances would have been stressful. This woman was used to living in a mansion that was immaculately clean and smelled like Indian home cooking and fresh chai. My apartment, currently, was a bit of a gongshow. I didn't care, though. She was no longer my future mother-in-law. She no longer had the capacity to have any bearing on my life. So those dirty clothes on the floor? Whatever. Dishes in the sink? Who cares. Trash on TV? Judge me for my poor taste all you want, lady.

Seeing as how all my wine glasses were dirty and stacked up in the sink, I grabbed two coffee mugs from the cupboard and then plopped down on the couch.

"Sorry, I forgot. You don't drink. Tea?" I offered, filling my mug with cheap cabernet.

Shawan slipped off her jacket, set down her purse, and sat on the couch next to me. "I drink when the time calls for it. Pour me a glass."

I handed her the mug I'd made for myself and poured a new one. "Sorry, I got pepperoni pizza." "Wine's fine for me." As she leaned against the back of the couch, mug of wine in hand, I couldn't help but smile. Seeing her in a relaxed state humanized her. It was nice getting to see her from the perspective of an equal. She wasn't so scary this way.

I leaned back, too, and turned my attention to the TV. For several minutes we sat in silence, other than the sound of the TV and me chewing, acclimatizing to one another's presence.

"Is this *Real Housewives?*" she asked.

"Yeah, Beverly Hills edition," I said, lowering the volume.

"Ah. I prefer the Orange County one. Those girls are crazy."

I smirked. "Didn't know you watched reality TV."

"Oh, beta. Being a stay-at-home wife can be awfully boring. I used to work in the shops, but since I retired, I have to do something to fill my time. Especially now that the kids are all grown."

Mentioning her kids made me stiffen. A palpable silence grew between us until I got the nerve to say his name out loud. I swallowed hard, staring down into my cup.

"Did Dev send you?"

She sipped her wine. "He would kill me if he found out I was here."

Huh. "So... what *are* you doing here? I'm sorry I called off the engagement. I mean, if I owe you for the party and the deposits and stuff, we can set up some sort of payment plan."

She waved her cup in the air. "Rubbish. No, I didn't come to say that. But I did come to say something." Shawan took a long sip of wine. Then, she turned in her seat to look me in the eye. "Rebecca. Why did you break off the engagement with Jagdev?"

What a loaded question, one I didn't know how to begin answering. Nor did I particularly want to.

"Is it because you don't love him?" she asked. I set down my half-eaten slice of pizza.

"No."

"You broke up with him... *because* you love him?"

How did she know? I managed to nod, fighting back a fresh wave of tears.

"How does that make any sense, Rebecca?" Her voice was soft, soothing.

She waited as I found my words, as I granted myself permission to be vulnerable around her. I didn't owe her an explanation, but it didn't feel like that was why she was here. It didn't feel like she was here to judge me or convince me to do something outside of my own interests. It felt like she was here to support me, too. To make sure I was okay. It was the first time she really felt like a mother to me, and I had to admit, it felt good. It felt really good.

"It's just... everything he wants, everything that would make him happy, it's not me who can do that for him. We're too different. We come from different worlds. It would never work."

Shawan tutted. "Being from the same culture, of the same religion, these things are important, but they don't guarantee happiness. They don't guarantee a good marriage. You know what does?"

"Hmm?"

"Love. And that is what you two have, in spades."

"Why are you telling me this? I thought you didn't want me to marry Dev. I thought you wanted him to marry Sonja."

Shawan nodded, weighing her words. "I'd imagined my children's lives to be one way, and it takes some getting used to watching them forge their paths. You will understand someday when you are a mother. You can do everything to help your child, to do what you think is best for them, but in the end, they are their own person. They know what is in their own best interest. Do I worry about Dev? Yes. And about Priya? Heavens, yes!" She smiled. "But I also trust them. I trust that I raised good, smart people who are capable of making their own decisions. And in the end, what I want more than anything is for my children to be happy. And Rebecca?"

She reached out and took my hand. "You make Dev happy."

I smiled and sniffled.

"You make him happier than I've ever seen him. His whole life, he's tried to be the good son, the responsible son, to do what he's told. It made me proud, yes, but it also made me sad. There was something missing. The spark. The light in his eyes. Then he met you. I could tell right from the first date something had changed in him. It was like a rainbow followed him around everywhere he went. He didn't even need to talk about you, I could simply look across the table and see the smile on his face and know he had you on his mind. You encouraged him to do what he loved, to follow his heart, even if it meant changing things in his life, taking risks. He knew you'd support him if it made him happy. That is what I want for my son. Someone to see the most in him, to encourage his happiness. Everything else? It's just background noise."

By now, tears were running down my cheeks. Shawan shuffled closer and hugged me, both of us holding our mugs of wine out to the side so they didn't spill.

She pulled back, her own eyes shimmering, a smile on her perfectly lipsticked lips. "I can't tell you what to do, beta. But do not end things because you think it is what Dev needs. He needs someone to love him. That is all."

I nodded and wiped at my tears with the palm of my hand. "I thought you didn't like me and that you didn't approve of me... That you didn't think I was good enough for him."

She laughed. "No woman would ever be good enough for my baby boy. That's another one of those things you will understand when you become a mother. As for liking you? I just needed to get to know you a bit. And what I've gotten to know so far? I like very much."

With that, Shawan gulped down the last of her wine and stood.

"I don't want to take up any more of your time. But you know how to reach me if you should need anything," she said with a kind smile.

I stood as well and gave her another hug at the door, closing it behind her, my heart heavy. Her absence was like snuffing out a candle as if all light and warmth suddenly vacated the room. I didn't want her to go. I didn't want her to walk out of my life, to close the door on the possibility of having her as my family, to call her mom.

Then, on the 3D printer, I eyed the black and silver package, half-opened. I ripped through the rest of the paper.

It was a framed picture; the one Dad had taken of Dev and me down at the dock, the fog rolling in off the forests and across the water, the setting sun glowing upon our faces. Dev held me in his arms, and we gazed at one another in complete and utter rapture.

That was the day we'd first exchanged "I Love Yous," even though we'd both felt it much sooner. I stared at the two of us, two people so completely lost in one another that the world could go up in flames around them and they'd hardly notice.

Before I could change my mind, I opened the door and ran down the hall.

"Shawan! Wait!"

She was still waiting for the elevator. "What is it?"

I grinned, hopeful. "Can you give me a ride?"

Twenty-Three

WITH SHAWAN'S SUGGESTION, I took a few minutes to clean up. It had been a while since I'd done the bare minimum of personal hygiene, after all. From the time it took me to shower, brush my teeth, apply deodorant, and change my clothes, Shawan had tidied my apartment. She couldn't turn off her motherly ways, and I have to say, I didn't mind that her instincts applied to my space, as well. It was her love language.

Besides, my apartment needed a bit of attention.

Shawan, I was surprised to see, didn't drive a basic old Corolla as I'd expected, but a Mini Cooper. A fancy one!

"You drive stick, too?" I commented, climbing in and clicking my seatbelt.

"Who do you think taught Jagdev to drive?" She threw the little hatchback into gear and launched us out into traffic.

The car ride was a bit tense on my end. Shawan seemed perfectly at ease, dodging in and out of traffic a little more aggressive than I thought was necessary, but far be it for me to tell someone how to drive. My internal stress wasn't only about her speeding, but about what I was about to do.

We pulled up to the mansion, which looked empty compared to how it was the last time I'd seen it. The tents, the lines of cars, the hordes of people, and the decorations were all gone as if the engagement party had never happened.

Shawan led me into the silent house, the huge door closing behind us and echoing throughout the empty corridors. I eyed the wall where Kyle had punched, but it was already patched and waiting for paint.

She gestured for me to follow and led me up the stairs, each increase in elevation transferring directly to my heart rate. I hesitated in the hall as she knocked gently on the door to her son's room.

"Jagdev? Are you decent? May I come in?" she cooed before cracking the door open a hair. Then, she nodded and held the door open for me to enter. It felt awfully intrusive. I wasn't exactly sure what I was walking in to, or what I was going to say when I got in there, but I certainly couldn't back out now. Shawan's encouraging smile beckoned me forward. I peeked into the doorway, the room darkened by heavy curtains and smelling slightly of booze, which was strange considering Dev didn't drink.

A wave of nausea rose in my throat, wondering if Sonja had stayed in here, and I sniffed the air for a hint of her vanilla perfume.

Apparently losing her patience, Shawan pushed me through the doorway and clicked it shut behind me. A few weeks ago, this woman had been aghast finding Dev I alone in his room together, and now she was encouraging it.

"Rebecca?" a groggy voice mumbled from his bed.

I inched forward. "Dev?"

He sat up slowly, his thick hair mussed and curled from sleep. My heart ached seeing him, wanting to both curl up next to him and run in the other direction. I held on tight to what Shawan had told me, hoping she was right.

"Hang on, let me put on some pants," he said as he stood, his tight black boxer briefs not leaving anything to the imagination. He pulled on some loose grey sweatpants, which only made him sexier. Dark hair trailed from his chest down past his belly button, framed on either side by the suggestive V shape his abdominal muscles—

Focus, Rebecca.

"Can I sit?" I asked.

Dev patted the bed beside him. I sat on the edge of his mattress, inches away from him.

I took a steadying breath and began. "I'm sorry for how I left things the other day. And for not answering your calls. Or your texts. I needed to think about some things."

He leaned forward, resting his elbows on his knees, and clasped his hands.

I continued. "There are so many things about us being together that scare me. I'm scared we're rushing into a marriage without knowing each other well enough, or taking the time to live together first. I mean, what if we hate living together? What if you can't stand the way I leave my clothes lying around. What if the sound of you eating cereal in the morning drives me crazy after two weeks?"

Dev smiled and looked up at me but didn't say anything.

"I'm scared about a wedding ceremony I still don't completely understand, held in a language I don't speak, and being surrounded by people I've never met or only did a few days ago. It's so far from how I imagined my wedding, my life, but I was willing to look past that— for you. I'm scared of living with your family. I really don't want to. I've been on my own for so long, in my own space, the thought of living with a big group of people scares the shit out of me. I mean, I was just getting used to the idea of living with *you*. As much as I love you, as much as I love us, I don't know if I can be happy like that."

Dev was about to interject, but I kept going.

"But mostly, I'm scared I'm not the right person for you. Sonja, she's so perfect. Everything about her. She is everything you want. She can fit perfectly into the mould for the life you'd envisioned. I'm scared you're trying to fit me into a place where she was meant to be. I'm scared you're supposed to be with her, and I'm supposed to be alone. And... I'm scared of being hurt again. You didn't tell me you worked with Sonja, that you saw her every day. You know what Graham did to me, how he cheated on me with someone he worked with. How am I supposed to trust you if you don't talk to me?"

"It didn't seem important at the time," he mumbled. "But that's a poor excuse. I should have told you. I can see why you're upset."

"I haven't been completely honest with you, either," I said, swallowing. "I lied to you. A few weeks ago, I told you I was going to work out with Miranda. I met with Graham for coffee."

Dev got up from his place beside me and walked across the room, his hands on his hips. I stayed seated; shoulders slumped.

"He had messaged me. I don't know what I was thinking."

"Was it just coffee?" he asked, turning, pain in his eyes.

I nodded emphatically. "I promise, it was just coffee. Honestly, I didn't even drink it."

"Why?"

His question wasn't one why, but multiple, and it was the same question I had asked myself at the time and every time I remembered my coffee *rendezvous* with Graham since.

I swallowed, my voice thick. "I was having second thoughts about us. About our future together. I thought seeing him would bring me some peace about what he did to me. Some closure. I thought it would make me feel better."

"Did it?"

I choked on a sob. "No."

Dev walked back over and sat next to me again, his body tense as his mind worked through what I'd told him.

I kept talking. "Even if you decide to be with Sonja, I won't go back to Graham. I'd rather be alone the rest of my life than be with him, after knowing how good it was to be with you. But I want you to be with her, with Sonja, to be with whoever makes you happiest. Because I love you."

I sniffled. Dev reached across and set his hand in mine, threading our fingers together.

"Can I say something now?" he asked.

I nodded.

"Sonja... she's a nice girl. She's a good friend. And you know what? If I married her, I'd probably find some happiness there, in time. We tried to be a couple, remember? Our families kept pushing us together, so, you know, why not try it? It just... didn't feel right. I don't see her that way. She's always been a friend. It was the same with her. We didn't connect. There was no spark, no fireworks. We separated amicably after trying to date for a few months. But if we were to get married? We would have made it work. We'd eventually find our way of love, of companionship. But that's not what I want. Not after being with you, of feeling what it means to truly, completely love someone, and be loved back in the same way."

Dev inched closer until our thighs were touching.

"Rebecca. Our marriage wasn't meant to be all about me. I'm sorry I made it feel that way. If you want to elope, I'll do it.

If you want to live in a one-bedroom apartment for the rest of our lives, I'll do it. Being with you is the only thing that makes sense to me anymore. Without you, my whole world falls apart. I love you. I want to be with you. But I need to know, what is it *you* want? Because I'm only happy when you're happy."

I looked up at him, into those incredibly sweet brown eyes, wet with tears. "Does mean you still want to marry me?"

"I'll get on a plane with you today and fly down to Vegas and get married by Elvis if it would make you happy."

I laughed.

"We can elope in the redwood forests of California, the way you pictured it if it means I get to spend the rest of my life with you."

He kissed my forehead, and I rested against his lips, my soul warming at his touch, aching to never part from him again.

"I don't want that, Dev. But can we meet halfway on a few other things?"

Dev inched away to look into my eyes, listening with his whole body.

I exhaled. "I still don't want to live with your family. Maybe when your parents are old and need the help. But while they're young? I just want it to be us, in our space, with our kids. We don't have to live in Vancouver, but I just need it to be us."

"Part of being in the family is *being with* the family. While I'm in school, we will have two years of us alone in Vancouver, but after that... they need me here. In my culture, a son always stays with the family to take care of them and continue the legacy. I'm their only son. If I'm not with them, I don't know how my family will be able to move forward. If I leave, it will cause a rift, and... I don't think we'll be able to move past it." His voice was strained, wrestling with reality.

I mulled it over. I could tell he'd put a lot of thought into it already, that he'd considered every other option.

He thought for a moment. "What if we moved into the basement suite? After I've gotten my MBA, I mean. It's self-contained. And by then, who knows? Maybe we'll have a baby on the way, and you will want the extra help."

I considered that. Their basement suite was four times the size of my current apartment, and it walked out to the blueberry fields. We wouldn't be completely alone, no, but close to it. It was a compromise. But that's what this was about—finding a middle ground, finding a way to make both of us happy.

"Okay," I said finally. "If it's important to you and your family, then I'm in."

He grinned. "Thank you. I can't live without you, but I don't want to give up my family in the process."

"And I don't want you to, either. I never meant for you to choose between me and your family." I gripped his hand tight.

"Is there anything else?"

"Well. Since we're on the subject of babies. Our kids' names."

Dev sucked air in through his teeth. "I've given it a lot of thought and was wondering if you'd be okay with western middle names. A Punjabi first name is very important to my family. Then the kids can decide whatever they want to go by when they grow up."

I thought about it for a moment. I remembered seeing a Punjabi baby-naming website I'd stumbled upon while researching Indian weddings (because of course my mind went there), and recalled several names that I thought would be perfect. This one wasn't even a compromise. I nodded. "Yes. Deal."

"What else?"

I scrunched up my face. "Working with Sonja...?"

"I'll be in school for the next two years. Afterwards, I can work from a separate office. And that's *if* I go back to work with my dad's businesses. A lot can change in two years. Honestly, we never even saw each other that often. She was in accounting, and I was in the shop. Our jobs crossed over maybe twice a week. And trust me, there's nothing there between us. We're just friends. But I completely understand why you feel that way, given our history."

I shook my head. "No. If you tell me there's nothing there, then I trust you. I don't want to go into a marriage telling you who you can and can't see."

"Well, I'd prefer if you never saw Graham again."

I chuckled. "I'd prefer that, too."

We looked at one another. The twinkle was back in his eye, the light shining from within, and in that instant, I understood. I was the twinkle this whole time.

"So... does this mean I can have my ring back?"

He kissed my forehead again, his lips light, lingering. Then, taking my face in his hands, he kissed my closed eyelids, my nose, and then finally my lips. His touch was so gentle, so light. It was as if he was worried I was a mirage this whole time and might vanish in an instant.

I ran a hand up his forearm, along those muscles and tendons I'd coveted from the moment I met him, to his bicep, and then to his chest, where I could feel his heart beating beneath his ribs. My other hand trailed his jawline, teasing his beard, and then my fingers found their way to his hair, where I gripped him and pulled him closer.

Our lips met, our kiss quickly becoming more fervent. We were starving, aching for one another. Our tongues reunited,

eliciting a deep moan from the back of his throat, which triggered an insatiable heat within my body.

Suddenly the distance was too great; we needed to be as
close as possible. Our inhales and exhales were quick gasps as
our lips fought to stay together while we pulled our clothes off
and tangled up with one another on his bed.

A moment later, we were together, and I could no longer
focus on our kissing. I tucked my face into his neck, wrapped
my arms and legs around his body, and embraced the sensation
of being with him, of it being just us, the way it was supposed
to be, the way it would be for the rest of our lives.

Twenty-Four

THE FOLLOWING WEEKS WERE A BLUR. A blur in a good way, at least.

The morning of my wedding, I sat in a chair in Jag and Shawan's spacious main bedroom as two women bustled about doing my hair and makeup. I sipped a mimosa and listened to the girls chat excitedly with one another. Music reminiscent of my college years played in the background. A photographer fluttered from here to there, the sound of her camera shutter click-clicking as she went, capturing every moment.

Miranda was starting to show now, but with the saree she wore you couldn't tell. She said she was feeling fine, better since her first trimester ended. Priya and Angelina, now dating openly, sat close to one another. Angelina absentmindedly trailed her fingers up and down Priya's back as they talked. Shawan had recovered from the initial surprise quite well. She was even letting Priya drink a mimosa with the rest of the group. My mom sat next to Miranda, glancing over to me every now and then, a proud look upon her face, probably wondering how long it was until I graced her with her first grandchild.

As I watched these important women in my life, I recalled the events of the past few weeks. Everything had happened so quickly, and for that, I was thankful. I was excited to move on to the next chapter.

When Dev and I had experienced our momentary break-up, he had put his mother in charge of cancelling the wedding. The smart woman that she is, she'd waited to do so until she spoke to me herself. I was so glad she did.

Since then, she and I had become thick as thieves. She seemed all proper and what-not on the outside, but in secret, she was kind of a badass. I could tell Priya got her personality from her mom, which was why they butted heads. She was even trying to teach me how to drive her Mini Cooper, though I argued it was probably best to start with an automatic and then work my way towards a manual transmission. She laughed so hard every time I stalled the damned thing, which was constant. I didn't mind her laughter, though; it was contagious.

During the week, Dev would pick me up after work and drive me home where we would spend the evening with his family, eating meals and getting to know one another better. Even his grandparents began opening up. Punjabi was still their main language of communication, but now they were trying to teach me some words and phrases. My pronunciation was horrid, but they appreciated the effort I was making. Shawan took it upon herself to teach me some of Dev's favourite recipes, and I made a point of including Dev on the instruction — because like hell I was going to be doing all the cooking.

As for the food, my digestive system was slowly acclimatizing to all the different spices. They were sure to stock up on milk (and Pepto), so I could remain seated through the meal. Dev was growing accustomed to my gastrointestinal struggles, the poor guy.

After dinner, my evenings were either fully engulfed in the final stages of wedding planning or soaking up time with my fiancé. He still hadn't given me my ring back, saying he was going to wait to put it on my finger until we were exchanging vows. I didn't mind, to be honest. The giant thing was kind of a pain in the ass, anyway, and far too shiny for my monochromatic wardrobe.

Sitting there, I couldn't imagine things being different. I didn't want to imagine where I would be, what I would be doing instead of this if I hadn't let Shawan into my apartment that day. I would probably still be in my sweatpants, eating ice cream, and swiping right on the swamp of available men on Tinder.

The day before the wedding, I'd brought my shagan gift to present to Dev and his family. Miranda and I had scoured various markets and put together a decent little gift basket from ideas on Pinterest. They accepted it graciously, though I have no idea if I did any of it correctly. It's the thought that counts, right?

Then, it was the mehndi ceremony. Dev and the rest of the men retreated into the basement while the women took over the main floor of the house, which was decorated to the nines. There were red and gold draperies, strings of beads and bangles, and flowers galore. Many women were present that I didn't know, but they were all friendly and welcoming. I'd even invited Sonja and Nicole.

After our blunt drunk conversation in Whistler, I looked at Nicole differently. I was protective of her in a strange way. I knew in time I could be friends with Sonja, too, thanks to

Miranda's wise words and Dev's indication that he and Sonja were more like cousins than ex-lovers.

I'd expected the mehndi ceremony to be a very serious matter, but it was more like a bachelorette party. We lounged on the furniture with one another, drinking champagne and having gorgeous henna tattoos inscribed upon our hands, arms, and feet. The precision of the application was incredible to watch. I joked with Priya that she could still be a tattoo artist by doing henna instead. Shawan agreed, but Priya didn't seem convinced. I kept looking down at my hands, the designs catching me off- guard; it was a visual reminder it would be my last day as an unmarried woman.

I'd slept over at Dev's house to make getting ready easier, though we didn't share a bed. Shawan and Jag had been very welcoming to me, but after the one time together in his room, we had been respectful and kept the sexy stuff to my apartment in the city. Dev slept downstairs on the couch that night. It was everything I could do to keep myself away. Lying in his bed, enveloped by his scent, was almost too much. I wished I'd packed my purple rabbit.

After our makeup and hair were done, they helped me into my gorgeous red lehenga. It fit perfectly and was much more comfortable than Margaret's old vintage dress—though it still had a place in my heart, hanging red-stained and sad in my closet for now. I didn't even mind that my midriff was bare. My golden maang tikka hung down to mid-forehead. Above it, the phulkari, the veil part, covered my hair. Everything was adorned with sparkly decorations. The intricate designs had surely taken hours to sew on. I didn't want to know how much it cost and didn't have to, since they'd rented all the dresses for the occasion. Thankfully, the nath and earrings were all clip-on. Priya had been joking when she insinuated I needed to get my nose pierced. Dev was right; she did have an odd sense of humour, and I loved her for it.

Pretty much everything was ready, or so I thought. Priya approached with a sly look on her face and a red box in her hand, a card taped to the side. It read:

Hey sis!

Sorry I couldn't be there for your big day. Priya told me you needed these fancy bracelets, so I bought them for you. Pretend I put them on, ok? Have a fun wedding! You and Dev should come visit me in Aus sometime. Priya can come, too ;)

PS: Sorry for what happened at the engagement party. And for what I said in the car. Mom bought me this book about being an anti- racist... I realize now what I said was wrong. I'll do better.

Love ya Kyle

Mom bought Kyle a book to educate him on racism? And he read it? *And* apologized? Tears glistened in the corner of my eyes. His apology meant more to me than he could ever know.

I opened the box, revealing a multitude of glittering red and white bangles. The choora bracelets! It was his way of showing all of us how much he cared about my new family's culture. *Our* new family's culture.

Shawan and Priya knelt beside me, and each slid the bracelets up my arms. Tears misted my eyes, my throat constricting. It was such a simple act, but it meant the world to me. I wasn't of their culture, but they had every intention of including me and teaching me to be part of it.

Finally, I was ready.

I took a deep breath and stepped towards the mirror. I hardly recognized the person staring back at me.

I was a princess.

The elegant eye makeup, the sparkling jewels, the vibrant

red dress, the henna... it was better than anything I could have dreamed. It looked like I belonged. I belonged in the dress, belonged to this incredible family, belonged to this beautiful culture I was just beginning to dip my toes into. I lifted my chin, the amount of pride swelling in my chest alarming, considering weeks ago I was having a panic attack thinking about doing exactly this.

"I changed my mind," Miranda said.

I looked to her, confused and a little worried. "About what?"

She joined me at the mirror and looked me up and down. "This was always meant to be your wedding dress. You look gorgeous."

My mom smiled and nodded, patting at her eyes so her tears wouldn't smear her makeup.

Looking at each one of the women present, all dressed in their traditional Indian clothing, I couldn't help but smile and agree. They were ready.

I was ready.

We descended the stairs and piled into various vehicles to head to the temple. The Gurdwara was massive. I had been there before; Shawan had made a point of bringing me once to introduce me to some of their traditions and customs, and also to meet the person marrying us.

Our cars pulled up beside the front doors, and we all climbed out, energy buzzing between everyone else while I remained the calm, cool, center of it all. I'd always imagined being nervous for this part. But I wasn't.

"Are you ready?" Shawan asked, smoothing my clothing from the ride.

I nodded, not sure if I could find words. My mother joined us, and the two matriarchs shared a look at each other before turning their attention back to me, glowing with pride. It was enough to make me blush. Time to get out of there.

One by one, my bridesmaids entered the building, followed by the mothers, which left me last, the doors held open. I took a moment to breathe, to feel the sun on my face, to relish the last few seconds I'd have alone that day. Then I walked inside.

I'd hoped to see Dev before the ceremony, to share a moment with him, but it was tradition to not see him until we were up at the altar. Shawan and I had gone over the intricacies of everything the day she'd brought me to the temple.

My father stood by the door to the main room, a proud look on his face. Smiling, I slipped off my white lace flats and took his arm. He patted my hand and looked down at me, eyes twinkling, and my chest swelled with elation that we were finally here at this moment.

I realized then, as long I'd been dreaming of my wedding, he had been, too. Had he been imagining this moment since I was just a baby? Was it okay that it was happening in a different culture, a different religion than he'd imagined? The proud look on his face removed any doubts in my mind.

We entered the room and people kneeling on the floor turned to look. I scanned past a sea of bright colours, faces both familiar and not, eyes quickly finding their way down the path to where Dev knelt. He was facing away from me. All I could see was the cream colour of his top, contrasted with the bright red of his turban and sash draped around his neck.

All I wanted was for him to turn, to look at me, to see me in the beautiful clothing that meant so much to him and his culture. All good things come to those who wait, I tried to remind myself, adhering to the ceremonial customs.

Dad left me with a kiss on my hands, and I knelt next to Dev. Close, but not close enough. There was nothing more I wanted than to reach out and touch him, to feel his skin on mine. The electricity buzzing between us, I was sure, could be felt by everyone in the room.

Dev glanced at me; his mouth pursed as if fighting a grin. Our eyes met briefly before flicking forward, trying to remain stoic and solemn as the officiant began the ceremony. Prayers were read, songs were sung, and then Dev and I made our way to our feet. A red cloth hung from Dev and trailed behind him to me, wrapped around my hands. He proceeded to walk slowly around the altar that held their holy book, me one step behind. It was all I could do to keep my gaze low and not look up to the crowd to catch Miranda's or my parents' eyes. After that, there was more kneeling, more singing, and all of it in Punjabi. Right around when I was beginning to get antsy, the parshad was served. More weddings should have breaks for snacks.

Though the event was supposed to be solemn, inside, I was giddy. We were one step, one song, one minute closer to our forever after. When the documents were brought to us, I couldn't contain the excitement rising in my chest as I signed my new name for the first time. It all felt surreal.

Finally, it was time to exchange rings. Dev and I turned to face each other. He looked at me fully for the first time since the ceremony had begun, and I did the same. From his red turban to his gorgeous brown eyes, his impeccably maintained beard framing those full lips I knew so well, down to the cream tunic with intricate designs along it... he looked incredible; like royalty. Judging by how his pupils dilated and his mouth parted when he saw me, he felt the same way. I blushed, remembering suddenly how many eyes were upon us.

Jag approached and handed Dev and me both a tiny box. We'd decided to say our vows in Punjabi, me repeating the words as best I could manage as I slipped Dev's ring over his finger. I'd designed the ring myself using the 3D printer and had it custom-made. It looked like it had been beaten together the old-fashioned way, with a hammer and anvil. It was a little understated but incredibly masculine and suited him perfectly.

Afterwards, Dev opened the box for my ring and removed it. He held it up, ready to slip on as he repeated after the officiant. But the ring in his hand wasn't mine. Gone was the giant, gaudy jewel. In its place was a gorgeously intricate band of woven white gold, tendrils wrapping around themselves until they joined at the centre to hold a perfectly reasonable one-carat diamond, with tiny diamonds studded throughout the band. It looked vintage, like he could have gotten it from Margaret herself, but it shone as if it were new.

Perfect.

I looked up at him, tears welling in my eyes. He winked at me and slid it onto my finger. It fit as if it had always been there.

One by one, our parents approached and adorned us with garlands of flowers around our necks. My dad was crying, something I was becoming accustomed to.

We stood and turned to face the assembled group. Everyone from Dev's parents to my own, to my friends old and new, to the various strangers who were now family, they all looked at us with so much promise and hope, so much joy and elation. My chest swelled with pride, gratitude, and with the sense that this moment could not have been more perfect.

Dev and I exited the temple, but he kept going all the way out the front doors.

We stepped into the perfect, clear day, the sun nearly overhead and reflecting brightly on the white walls of the temple. I turned to Dev, confused, unsure if this was part of the ceremony or what was going on.

He looked down at me with those giant brown eyes, the smile that played upon his lips full of promises and future delights.

"You may now kiss the bride," he whispered, just for the two of us.

Resting one hand on his chest, my other found its way to his beard, my fingers trailing along the jawline I'd memorized by now. He pulled me closer, his hands wrapping their way around my lower back.

As he bent down towards me, I lifted onto my tiptoes to meet him halfway.

Epilogue

I ALWAYS HAD A PLAN. *Always.* One year ago, I sat down on a plane, salty about the empty seat next to me. If that seat hadn't been empty, if my life had gone according to plan, I never would have met Dev.

Now, the empty seat next to me brought no anxiety. I'd boarded early, as always, though I'd forgone the airport beer. It was no longer a necessity of travel.

People shoved past me, maneuvering their luggage as best as they could down the narrow aisles. There was an old couple struggling to read their tickets, followed by a big buff guy who would easily take up two seats with his muscles, and then a young family, the woman with her newborn babe wrapped tight to her chest.

Right when I was beginning to wonder where he was, he appeared. Tall, dark, handsome. All of the clichés.

My heart skipped a beat, and I momentarily forgot how to breathe. I thought I'd be immune to his charm by now, but I wasn't. His V-neck shirt hugged his torso, stretching around his biceps ever so slightly. His sleeves were rolled up, and I eyed those sexy forearms, gaze lingering, but only for an instant.

I looked up to see his dark eyes twinkling, the smile on his lips one of amusement.

"Is this seat taken?" He smirked. I shook my head but made no move to get up, forcing him to slide past me, that great ass of his only inches away from my face before he found his seat.

"Did you get what you were looking for?" "Yep," he said, showing me the bottle of Gravol he'd retrieved from his overhead luggage. I laughed at the memory of how we'd met.

Time had gone by very fast, and we hadn't been able to escape for a honeymoon until the first semester of his master's program was over. He was loving school and didn't regret continuing his education.

His additional time getting his Master of Business Administration is proving most useful. With his expertise, he helped me orchestrate a pitch meeting with Jag and several investors. The pitch had gone swimmingly, and they'd all been very enthusiastic, as well as generous. That, paired with the Green Research & Development funding I received from the Canadian government (woo!) I was able to purchase the next contract at work, which starts in just a few short months. No more monotony for me, baby!

My first official patent had been approved and was displayed proudly on the wall of my and Dev's new apartment.

We'd moved out of my old space and into a two-bedroom condo, close to both my work and his school. My 3D printer, desk, and a new computer took up the spare room. The walls were covered in diagrams and drawings, and shelves lined the walls with little printed turbines. A half-sized model sat leaning against the wall, the original proudly displayed in a prominent location—Dev's idea, not mine.

With Dev busy in school, I'd devoted all my spare time to the project. Jag had volunteered one of his shops to be the first to have my prototypes installed, paying for them to be built and hiring an electrical engineer and electrician to tie them into a giant battery and inverter they'd installed next to the building's electrical panel. He said it was an investment. Jag was very optimistic and wouldn't talk about anything else during our dinners.

Jag was still able to take a step back from work, thanks to Sonja. Since her family was also involved in the businesses, they decided she'd be put on the advancement track to be the next CEO of their conglomerate when Jag retired. I could totally see it; she has a good head on her shoulders.

Shawan said it was good fortune that Dev was getting his master's degree, seeing as we would need an expert in the field to help spur the business and bring it to the mass market. Though Dev hadn't approached continuing his education in the best way, his family was incredibly supportive of his dream, and they admitted later it was the best thing, not only for him but for the future of the entire family. Shawan was also adamant that once Dev was finished school, I go back to finish what I'd started.

The thought of going through the final exam again didn't scare me as much as it used to. Maybe it was Dev rubbing off on me, but I was much less anxious and neurotic than I used to be. I hadn't scheduled myself to take it, yet, but the date was saved into my calendar so I could begin mentally preparing. Third time's the charm, right?

But for the present, I was content.

No... Beyond content.

Joyous.

Just Dev and I, sitting on a plane, about to celebrate our one year of being together and our wedding at the same time.

Dev rested his hand on my leg, and I took his hand in mine, the ring I'd made him in its rightful place. I glanced down at my own and thought of how perfect they were together. Not matching, exactly, but complementing one another so well they may as well have.

As we taxied down the runway, he gave my hand a squeeze.

There was so much to look forward to, and not only the ocean view suite we'd booked, or the couples massage, or the room service in bed we had planned.

I looked forward to the next few years of him in school, pursuing his dream, listening to him talk excitedly about his projects and future, watching his eyes light up, and his face become animated. He could talk about anything like that, and I'd be rapt. I looked forward to starting our family. We'd decided to wait until Dev's program was over before adding a new little addition. The spare room, so full of engineering things, wouldn't be the ideal space for a nursery. The basement suite back in Dev's family home would be perfect.

Having spent so much time with Dev's family, I now looked forward to moving in with them. We'd already arranged with his grandparents to trade the upstairs for the basement suite, which was better for them since they were getting older and needed more assistance. Priya had been accepted into an arts program for graphic design. She would live in the basement with us for the time being, which was totally fine. Priya was an awesome little sister to have, plus it would include regular visits from Angelina.

But what I looked forward to most?

The regular days. Him crunching through his morning

cereal before racing off for the day. Me, trying to remember to pick my clothes up off the floor, drinking chai on the couch, watching the evening news.

Everyday life, for the rest of my life, with him by my side.

The End

Acknowledgments

As mentioned in the beginning, there were many people who were immensely helpful for ensuring cultural accuracy and sensitivity with this novel. Thank you, again, for all your help!

A huge thank you to Alex and Tina at Rising Action Publishing Co. for taking a chance on me, for seeing something special in this story, and for helping me turn it into the beautiful novel it is today. I am beyond lucky to have met you both and to be given this fantastic opportunity.

Thank you to #pitmad on Twitter, where I received so much support for this story, made many friends in the writing community, and first connected with Alex at Rising Action.

Thank you to Ashley Santoro for designing and illustrating such a beautiful cover; I am beyond proud to have this book displayed on my shelf, and I know it will stand out in any bookstore! Thank you to Chris at Crafty Cocktails Canada for helping make my pre-order launch a smashing success!

I was very lucky to have MANY people read this book in its early forms, so buckle up. Thank you to my mother Stephanie for being my rock through life, for cheering me on, and for reading every first draft of everything I've ever written. Thank you to my mom's work friends/sisters Carrie and Ashley for reading my book and being my cheerleaders. Thank you to my best friends Brittany, Amber, Lyndsay, and Ariane for constantly listening to me talk about writing stuff, answering questions about your careers for character backgrounds, reading early drafts for me, and generally being an inspiration for all the shenanigans I write about. Thank you to Kayla for being my earliest critique partner; I'm so excited that we will have our books on each other's shelves. Thank you to all my other writing friends on Twitter for your constant support through the ups and downs of writing, querying, and publishing; you all truly mean the world to me— especially my writing family "The Screaming Peens" (don't ask). Special shout-out and enormous thanks to Jackie, Liz, Grace, and Shelley; your help beta reading made me a stronger writer and I can't wait to have a library full of your books.

Thank you isn't enough for my husband, Tom. You always believed in me. Thank you for being my muse, the love of my life, and the inspiration for every sexy male character in every book I'll ever write.

And, finally, thanks to me, for never giving up.

About the Author

Lindsay Maple is a Canadian Author residing in British Columbia with her husband, two little boys, and giant tortoise named Doug. A certified yoga instructor, Lindsay manages a local yoga studio while teaching several classes per week, including goat yoga. When not inundated with laundry, she can be found hiking in the old-growth forests, drinking wine with Doug in the backyard, or baking her famous chocolate-chip banana muffins.